PRAISE FOR ARAN JANE

THE WATER COLUMN

"Enthralling. A smart, offbeat detective story with an entertaining ... sinuous plot turn."

— *KIRKUS REVIEWS*

"An imaginative thriller ... Aran Jane's *The Water Column* plunges into a mystery from the get-go [and] suggests more rousing adventures to come."

— *FOREWORD CLARION REVIEWS*

"Engaging. Crisply written with skilled dialogue and description. Readers will find the portrait of Lila Piper authentic and refreshing. Aran Jane has penned a thought-provoking character who deserves her own series."

— *BLUE INK REVIEW*

* * *

MONDRAGON

"Fans of immersive sci-fi, like the work of Philip K. Dick, should take a look; an auspicious start for Jane."

— *KIRKUS REVIEWS*

"An inventive, ambitious sci-fi adventure ... incredibly expansive and well-drawn."

— *KIRKUS REVIEWS*

"Heavy in theoretical science, but lighthearted in its approach to such complexity, Mondragon is intelligent, multifaceted, and engaging."

— *FOREWORD CLARION REVIEWS*

"Entertaining characters and an intricate plot that culminates in a compelling and satisfying conclusion."

— *BLUE INK REVIEW*

ALSO BY ARAN JANE

MONDRAGON

"An inventive, ambitious sci-fi adventure ... incredibly expansive and well-drawn."

— *KIRKUS REVIEWS*

THE WATER COLUMN

ARAN JANE

ROQUEBRUNE BOOKS—CARLSBAD, CA

PB ISBN: 978-0-578-62289-7

EB ISBN: 978-0-578-62290-3

Library of Congress Control Number: 2019919693

For Sheri

We must assume our existence as broadly as we in any way can; everything, even the unheard-of, must be possible in it. This is at bottom the only courage that is demanded of us: to have courage for the most strange, the most singular and the most inexplicable that we may encounter.

— RAINER MARIA RILKE

PROLOGUE

June 15, 1990

The Piper Family Home
Northbrook, Illinois

WHILE IT WAS THE SUMMER HEAT THAT KEPT LILA'S SIX-YEAR-OLD brother, Ulli, busy in the kidney-shaped family pool, happily diving again and again to retrieve his leaded toy submarine, it was the maddening buzz of thousands of cicadas bouncing around the lush, forested backyard that kept Lila—ten years old and wearing her new powder-blue Speedo one-piece—feeling like she was caught in a vortex of rotating speakers hidden in the surrounding trees.

Her father had told her that she needn't worry about the cicadas; that they didn't bite, and that their freaky cyclic bloom only happened once every seventeen years. *The next time they show up,* he'd told her, *you'll be twenty-seven—a grown woman. And believe me, dear, twenty-seven is a lifetime away from ten. Bugs will be the last thing on your mind.* But *right now* was all Lila was worried about, and right now those creepy little monsters—like gigantic flies the size of her palm—were making her life miserable.

From the foot of her poolside chaise longue, Lila watched her mother spill her drink for the second time. The woman cursed, standing and wobbling off toward the house. Lila swallowed and looked away, feeling suddenly very small.

On the surface of the water, a couple of dead cicadas floated legs-up. Lila shuddered inwardly and pressed her ear tight against the phone, straining to hear what her friend was saying.

But she couldn't concentrate. Something was wrong—a shadow hung at the back of her mind, a concern that her little brother had been quiet for far too long. Smokey went on in her ear about the new horror flick she'd seen, *Arachnophobia*. Lila was deathly afraid of spiders— wasn't keen on cicadas, either—so Smokey's take on the modestly successful film was about as close as she ever intended to get to that picture.

Her eyes drifted over to the unperturbed expanse of clear blue water dotted here and there with dead insects, the roar of cicada-song intensifying. Slowly, her brother's absence began to creep its way to the top of her head, which was otherwise frozen in space, listening and thoughtlessly observing.

"I watched it all the way through," Smokey was boasting, "I thought it was cool. More funny than scary, really. But you wouldn't like it, Lila. I mean, even the boys screamed."

Screamed. Lila jerked as if struck. The pool was eerily still, and Ulli had been gone for far too long. The scene seemed to crystallize, a frieze of tension snaking outward.

Lila dropped the phone, shot up, and dove into the water. With her eyes open wide, she spotted the blurry outline of Ulli's small figure at the bottom of the deep end; he was lying face-down, as if he was stuck to the drain.

When she finally reached him, Lila frantically grabbed him under the arms—alarmed as her hands seemed to pass through him. A trickle of bubbles rose from her nose as she placed one foot flat on either side of him and tried again; but, once more, her grasping hands appeared to phase through his flesh.

Her lungs were burning. Neon-colored zig-zag patterns arced across her vision, and that's when she saw it—there, glowing like a magic lamp, shimmering with color and spherical in shape, casting a faint light on her brother's motionless body. For a fleeting moment, it looked like a writhing dandelion, with legs like a spider's, only too many to count.

Instantly, she reached across her brother and wedged her hands between the drain and his body. She began to roll, slowly peeling him off the drain the way she used a spatula to peel burning pancakes from the frying pan. Once she had him on his side, she pulled him towards her as hard as she could until he finally broke away. She swam with one arm hooked around his small shoulders and, lungs burning, eyes red with chlorine, burst above the surface.

She gasped, sucking in a desperate breath of air, then dragged him over to the steps and out of the pool. As soon as he hit the hot, dry pavement, he lurched, vomiting water and gasping for air.

"Are you okay Ulli?" she said, shaking him, tears streaming down her cheeks.

He coughed and sputtered, his eyes filled with terror.

"You almost drowned!" she panted, trying to calm her breathing, her pounding heart.

He looked up in bewilderment at his big sister, his lower lip curled downward, his mouth forming an odd shape. And then he began to wail. Lila scooched in close and wrapped her arms around him, holding him tight to her chest. She looked back at the house over the top of his head. There was no surge of movement, no desperate shrieks—only Lila and her little brother, just the two of them ... and the roar of the flies.

Later that night, sitting at the dinner table in numb silence, Lila watched her father rise and return to the sideboard. Once again, he picked up his large Erlenmeyer flask from where it sat in a silver bucket filled with crushed ice, poured a measure of clear liquor, and then used his long

3

"*pipette*," as he called it, to reach deep into a dark green bottle and draw out a few precious drops, which he then judiciously added. He stirred gently, regarding his handiwork with silent satisfaction.

"How was your day, dear?" Lila's mother droned as she reached for her highball glass.

Her father gave the answer he always gave. "The usual." He poured his concoction from the flask into a glass beaker containing exactly three large cubes of ice. "A couple of brain transplants, a heart massage, and a few spinal reconstructions." He turned to Lila and gave her a meaningless frown. Then, lifting his beaker, he gave it a little bell-like rattle as if calling the family to order and took an invigorating sip, which elicited a loud "Ahhh!"

Sinking into his chair at the head of the table, he turned to stare at his son. "All this for a toy? For a submarine, you could've drowned." He shook his head. "You know what they say in the submarine fleet? Their ... er, motto?"

Ulli sat there, sullenly hunched over in his chair, staring blankly at the untouched food on his plate.

Her father took another sip and thrust his beaker forth as if in salute. "*Profundis cogitate.*"

Lila darted an uncertain look at her mother then back at her father, her brow furrowed.

"*Profundis cogitate,*" Dr. Piper said again. "*Think of the depths.*"

* * *

October 29, 2017

1100 North Dearborn Apartments
Chicago, Illinois

Marina Resnick's first year at the University of Chicago's Pritzker School of Medicine and she's pulling another all-nighter, hunched over the dining room table under a wan cone of forty-watt light, cramming for the two toughest exams she'll face this quarter: Biochemistry and Gross Anatomy.

The smoked glass tabletop reflects her exhausted face in the gaps between the stacks of open textbooks and dog-eared flashcards. She's got her hair up in a twist, spiked in place by two No. 2 pencils that look like chopstick antennae in the darkened glass. She reaches for the nearest stack of 3-by-5s and settles on the one entitled *Lumbar Radiculopathy.* Idly flipping it over, she mentally drones:

"Sciatica."

"My back!" she protests suddenly, reciting half from memory and half from the in-the-moment pain shooting down her leg. She winces—"I can't"—and then expels a loud breath—"feel my *bomzh!*" She removes her oversized red readers and drops them on the tabletop.

Shifting uncomfortably in her seat, she stifles a yawn and lets her head fall back for a moment, one hand massaging the small of her back. *"Without torture, there is no science,"* she's repeating to herself as she drifts off.

Several minutes on, she's jarred awake by her Hamilton clock's Westminster chimes. With sleepless eyes, she stares blankly at the clock hands, unable to blink, unable to focus. The clock's bells rise and fall in the key of E Major, and three demoralizing gongs somehow sap what little motivation she has remaining. It's three o'clock in the morning, she realizes, and it's way, *waaay* past her bedtime. She wonders whether she's finally got a lock on all this brutal memorization crap or whether she's just been surfing the text like some bleary-eyed freshman fish.

"Enough!" She drops her cards on the table.

Switching off the light, she squints into the unlit room beyond her desk to avoid tripping over the mess she knows is there: a scatter of unfolded laundry heaped on the sofa, piles of discarded clothes that dot the uneven parquet floor like so many sleeping dogs. The shadow of a large *Giordano's* pizza box lies open on the claw-footed ottoman that takes up a big chunk of the room. Like a scented candle, it fills her apartment with the pungent tang of oregano and garlic tomato sauce from the gnawed crusts left to petrify in the box, evidence of her painkilling snack habit.

She likes to tell her med school classmates that she doesn't see the mess, that, as she's Russian, she has "high tolerance for clutter." But that's BS and she knows it. She sees it when she's forced to climb over it all to get to the loo.

Halfway into the darkened room, the vague impression of something —some*one*—stops her. An icy shiver lifts the hair on the back of her neck.

She squints at a misted silhouette of something in the shadows of her living room—a man-shaped absence of light that her exhausted brain somehow transforms into a *chort*, an extradimensional Slavic fiend plucked from her childhood fairy tales. Her eyes open wider. "Impossible!" she mutters, cautiously inching forward. It's only when she realizes that she's *not* seeing things that she finally screams.

Instantly, her perception shifts; the image clarifies.

Outside!

Jolted from her stupor, Marina sees her muscular demon more clearly: it's not a demon at all, but a man—she can make out the dark ski mask, dark gloves, dark trousers, and the dark puffy jacket. And he's not inside; he's seemingly defying gravity outside, dangling in mid-air like some eldritch string-puppet, sixteen floors above the black, ice-slicked ground.

"*Oh shit!*" she exclaims. Deep in an adrenaline rush, a single word overtakes her thoughts—*Facebook*. Her last post: *Looking forward to making party for Halloween.* Instead, she decided to stay home and study. Did this man, whoever he was, see her post? Was he trying to break in?

When he lifts his gloved hand in a kind of awkward conciliatory gesture, saying, "Sorry, Ma'am, I've got the wrong apartment," she spots something at the boundary of her vision: a second line, perhaps, a trace of reflected light, or maybe ... *maybe* the wire holding him up is unraveling. Instinct draws her eyes upwards, but the window frame obstructs her view; she can only see so far.

Another shiver tingles Marina's skin. Why can she hear him so clearly through the high-tech, high-strength glass? Her heart pounding, she glances at the open space between the slider and the window sash. The chill flashes her back to the moment she cracked it open earlier this afternoon to counter the oppressive forced-air heat. All at once, she's aware of the unwanted intimacy between them; aware that she's completely vulnerable, all alone, standing there in her PJs. When his slushy black shoe soles slap flat against the glass, she sucks an icy breath between her teeth.

Thoughts of her imminent annihilation begin to overcrowd Marina's brain as the intruder's shoes slime the glass like a couple of giant black slugs.

Thud! Thud-thud-thud! Thud! Her eyes widen; she cannot look away. She watches the intruder jockey into position and settle into a deep crouch as if preparing to stomp through the glass. Suddenly, he jumps, pushing himself *away* from the building; not to shatter the glass, it seems, but to rappel down to some other, lower floor.

"*This guy!*" she says out loud, watching him leap. "This guy is ... *crazy!*"

He's no more than a few feet out when the line gives way. He drops so fast that her breath catches—and she lets out an anguished sigh of relief when he bounces back like some crazy bungee jumper at the end of his cord. Then, a moment's reprieve before the line abruptly snaps—definitively, this time—and he drops. The fear in his saucer-wide eyes, for a split second visible through the eyeholes in his ski mask, sears into her mind.

Marina rushes forward, pressing her hands to the glass, straining to see. She can't shake the horror; vivid pictures of what she can imagine but cannot see—his body slamming into the icy concrete sixteen floors down.

"*Oh my God!*" She rushes to grab the wall phone. "*Oh my God! Oh my God! Oh my God!*" She fumbles with the handset, frantically pounding 911.

THE HUNTING OF THE BEAST

1

January 26, 2018

Law Offices of Savage, Lutz, Finnegan & Foehl
Chicago, Illinois

Lila Piper leaned heavily on the sink, staring at her reflection in the mirror of the otherwise empty women's lounge. She pulled in a deep, stabilizing breath and let it out slowly through pursed lips. Closing her eyes, she tried to will the wispy remnants of her unnerving dream out of her head, out of her consciousness—a hundred long, spindly, segmented legs emanating from a small gelatinous body, strobing multicolored patterns playing over the spider's dandelion surface. The lurid recurring nightmare of this eerie, gossamer ball—flashing bright then faint, bright then faint—had tormented her like some kind of demonic emissary since she was a kid. She opened her eyes and clasped her hands together so tightly she could almost feel each bone individually. When she finally shook her hands loose and turned to go, she stopped, quickly returning to the sink. She shoved her hands under the faucet's sensor and let the stream of cold water soak her hands. She cupped them, brought the water to her face, and pressed her hands against her flesh. Just as quickly, she grabbed a paper towel, blotted her face, and hurried out and down the hall to the meeting where she knew they were waiting for her.

Once she'd recited an apology to her boss and their client, she began. She knew the drill—the punchy, professional kick-off, the compassionate outcomes-oriented soft pitch followed by the altruistic "appeal to heaven and justice" closer. This plaintiff was different, though; he wasn't there to talk about a personal injury lawsuit at all.

"I am well-acquainted with this firm *und* I am not the plaintiff," he snorted in his thick Austrian accent. "I am not here to enrich myself. I'm already rich."

For the past nine years, Lila had worked as the lead investigator for Chicago's premier personal injury lawyer, James Patrick Savage, frequently astounding him with what he considered her uncanny knack for digging up dirt long hidden from view. A *"bloodhound's gift,"* he liked to tell their prospective clients; the "special sauce" that had helped Savage, Lutz, Finnegan, & Foehl win dozens of eight-figure settlements. Such success had propelled Jim Savage to the pinnacle of his profession, abundantly compensated his clients, and made Lila comfortably well off. A lot had changed since their first meeting twelve years prior.

She had been one of the two prostitutes Savage had consorted with in his life. The first, he'd confessed to her, had been a raven-haired beauty he'd met in Vegas. That was 2004.

Lila met him closer to home, in 2006. She was sitting alone in a slinky backless sheath at the far end of the bar of the Chicago O'Hare Hilton, all dolled up with long bleached-blonde hair spilling beguilingly over one shoulder. She was sipping the last of a white wine spritzer when Savage sat down next to her and ordered a bottle of Kristal. Soon, they were chatting each other up, each with one eye on the flat-screen TV behind the bar, tracking the breaking news: a whale had been spotted swimming in the Thames, its unusual appearance apparently fitting the mysterious pattern of beaching deaths taking place the world over. "Pollution? Global warming?" Savage said disgustedly to the TV screen before turning to Lila. "You know," he said, "certain Native American people of the Pacific Coast actually worship whales."

"Did not know that," Lila replied, sipping her champagne. A bit forced, she thought. "Though I can't say I'm surprised."

Savage reached for his iPhone and keyed something in. "See what Google has to say." He looked down at the small screen, reading. "Okay … says they see them as teachers of compassion and solitude, of knowledge of both life and death." He took a sip from his drink. "Oh, and boundless creativity. They believe sudden exhalation—as through a whale's blow-hole—represents the freeing of one's creative energies." He raised an eyebrow.

"Well, let's hope *you* don't free too much creative energy through *your* blowhole," she shot back with a snarky grin.

"*Whoa ho!*" he said.

"I know someone who has a thing for whales," Lila put in. "Says they're her '*spirit animal*'—claims they're the keepers of the records of time, the holders of wisdom."

"Sounds like a lovely friend."

"She's my shrink, actually."

"You see a shrink?!"

Lila snorted. "Ha, are you kidding? My dad's a doctor, my family's fucked up, I'm a mess, so … yeah." She nodded a few times. "I see a shrink. Have since I was a kid. Doesn't everyone?"

Afterward, they got a room, ordered a second bottle of Kristal, and did a few lines of coke from the diamond-fold she had hidden away in the lining of her Louis Vuitton purse. When Savage asked her where she got her supply, she told him that, like a lot of white kids from the suburbs, she just drove down to the subsidized housing complex in Lawndale on the city's West Side. She told him how, whenever she was back from the University of Arizona, she'd slow to a crawl at the corner of 19th and Karlov, roll down her window, and hand over a hundred-dollar bill to the tall, lanky black guy she'd singled out as being the most non-threatening.

She'd gotten to where she liked the guy. "He's my G," she said, affecting a kind of gangsta-rap attitude. "'*Hold up, Snowflake! You seri-*

ous!' he says whenever he sees me." She gazed down into her champagne flute and shook her head. "*'Comin' up in here all alone in this crazy hood! Drivin' yo' daddy's whip! What! You think jus' cuz you good-lookin' you bulletproof?'*"

Savage laughed. "So, what made you choose the University of Arizona?"

"Main reason, I couldn't wait to get out of the snow. And, of course, get as far away from my family as possible. But, also, my shrink was a big influence. She was moving down there to get involved in some advanced research. You've heard of Sir Roger Penrose?"

Savage frowned. "The quantum physicist?"

"Precisely. He was working with this famous anesthesiologist, Dr. Stuart Hammeroff, on some arcane theory of quantum consciousness. Something about tiny cellular structures called microtubules underlying conscious thought."

"Wow!" Savage remarked, topping off each of their glasses. "Sounds ... *deep.*"

"She said I should come with because of the cutting-edge stuff they were doing down there involving psychedelics, hypnosis, research on something called Transcranial Magnetic Stimulation—TMS. She thought it might help me. Oh, and she was eager to be so close to what she called the 'Sedona Energy Vortex—'"

Savage put his drink down mid-sip. "Yeah," he said, "Sedona's famous for that. It's a whole touristy thing."

"Exactly." Lila smiled and turned in her chair just so. She caught his eyes as they wandered to the deep V of her low-cut sheath. She straightened her spine, stretching like a cat, the better for him to glimpse her flesh-colored G-string as her backless dress opened just a little, taunting him.

They took off their clothes and embraced without kissing.

While Savage's performance in bed was perfunctory, hers was single-minded and determined. She was not merely plying her trade, exchanging a zesty round of no-holds-barred sex for money; she was experimenting with exercising power over the men she allowed to get close to her. The attraction for her was the purity of the act, stripped of all societal pretense—it was the physical, mental, and ultimately glandular conquest that, for her, fueled an irresistible fascination. At least, that was what she told herself.

Of course, she also wanted to keep herself in blow without having to ask her financially, legally, and medically burdened father for money. The drug gave her a nice buzz and she relished the independence it gave her and, she thought with a smile, got to look rich to her high-school friends and her wealthier suburban posse who had no idea what she was up to.

But all this would prove a passing phase. She'd already followed Dr. Ross to Arizona, and it was thanks to the meds she received there—the experimental TMS therapy her father had recommended, the hypnosis therapy, and the cognitive-behavioral techniques—that she'd overcome her crippling depression and would soon finish school, get her law degree, and leave her reckless behaviors behind her.

Now, more than twelve years later, Lila was back in Chicago, the days of her dangerous liaisons long gone. Gail Ross too had followed her back here to fill an open position at the Stone Mental Health Center, which suited Lila just fine—she had grown rather accustomed to her little "maintenance" sessions.

As soon as Lila passed the Illinois State Bar Exam, she accepted the offer from Savage, Lutz, Finnegan & Foehl. Neither Lila nor Savage had spoken since of their one-time tryst.

Savage, too, had grown up since then. No more drugs, no more professional girls; these days, especially during their prospective client interviews, he was a study in composure. He would ask his young PI to list for their prospects the many reasons why SLFF's investigatory capabilities remained unparalleled in the industry, hitting the high points of their firm's deep-bench contacts and myriad capabilities with an emphasis on "the human factors." *Important to establish a good working relationship right upfront,* Savage had quietly nudged when he'd first offered her the job.

For their part, most clients listened intently. Anguished and despairing, most had suffered some severe harm or jeopardy. Others came on behalf of a beloved family member hurt or sometimes killed as a direct result of the negligence of some deep-pocketed individual or organization. For both groups, Jim promised to *"Whip the lousy bastards back into the light of compliance. Everybody wins: the bastards pay, the victims get their compensation, SLFF earns a reasonable fee for their efforts, and, perhaps most importantly, we avert further human tragedies down the line."*

All praiseworthy objectives, to Lila's mind.

Lila's role in all this was a little more complicated. She was there to offer their clients more than the plodding bloodhound services for which Savage praised her; she was paid to provide real comfort and support, lay the foundation for a good working "Relationship" with a capital "R," and deliver "the human touch" Savage so highly prized, all while laying the necessary groundwork to nail the bastards responsible. She took her job seriously.

Most clients were relieved when she told them she would be working diligently to quickly gather the evidence Mr. Savage needed to close the gap between the multi-million-dollar settlement he'd implied they were entitled to and some tossed-off take-it-or-leave-it deal that so many victims received when they placed their trust in less competent hands.

To reinforce her point, she grabbed her iPad off of Savage's desk and pulled up a copy of *The American Lawyer,* drawing attention to the 2018 *AM Law 100 Survey.*

"This is the definitive ranking of America's top one hundred revenue-grossing law firms," she explained. "We sit right at the top of the heap. And that's not based on billable hours," she added, speaking faster than usual, "that's cases won. We're a personal injury firm; we get paid when our clients get paid."

Savage smiled and slowly blinked both eyes shut—twice, their mutually agreed-upon signal that she needed to take her foot off the gas.

She dropped the iPad back onto Savage's desk and turned to their visitor. Hans Holzinger was different—she'd known him by reputation and seen him in and out of the office for years, but they'd never spoken.

She recognized his thick, wavy gray hair and long, narrow face creased with crow's feet around his sullen gray eyes. He was a tall, gaunt man, long-limbed, with big knuckles on his heavily calloused hands that seemed vaguely arachnid. It was a thought that had stuck in her mind since she'd first seen him, a stressor that triggered something in her; just the sight of his spidery hands seemed to reignite every one of her child-hood fears and revulsions.

He looked down at the discarded tablet in contempt. Her "mania"—that ceaseless and pleasurable flow of thoughts and energy that height-ened her senses—told her that he was a stern, sad, and distrustful man.

"Hans runs the biggest private dairy operation in Wisconsin," Savage reminded her. He turned to his friend. "Remember the Colusa rice fields, outside Sacramento? Just a couple of young Turks squatting in a muddy duck blind."

"Long time ago," Holzinger replied. He looked like he wanted to say something, but let the thought hang. He finally settled on "Old friends."

"Too old," Savage laughed. "Neither one of us could hit the broad side of a barn that day."

"*Und* there was a good reason for that," Holzinger grimaced. "We did hit the *pils* pretty good, as I recall."

"Pilsner," Savage clarified, nodding to Lila.

Lila smiled. "Jeez, I have been to Germany, Jim, and it may surprise you to know that I've had more than my fair share of *pils*."

She earned a tight, polite smile from her boss and one more cautionary double-blink.

She remembered how, when she had first signed with the firm, Savage had just gone in with Holzinger to purchase the vintage Convair CV-540 turboprop plane they still used for their annual hunting treks in Alaska. She was well acquainted with her boss's Alaskan back-country expeditions. Savage kept a solid pewter model of his beloved Convair on his desk as a reminder, proudly displayed on a polished mahogany stand. On its tail, *LPF* was written in slanted script. "*Le plus fort*," Savage had explained to her, "'The fittest,' as in, *La survie du plus fort*—'Survival of the fittest.'"

"Hans is a damn fine bush pilot," Savage insisted, dragging Lila back to the present. "He's"—he clapped Holzinger on the shoulder—"practically blood." They fell silent a moment before Savage seemed to shake the mood off and returned to his desk. "Now ... where to begin?" he asked, leaning back and crossing his legs at the ankles.

Lila lowered her gaze. Savage's polished brown wingtips and tailored blue pinstripe suit stood in stark contrast to Holzinger's more utilitarian work boots.

When she looked up again, she noted Holzinger's face had once again darkened.

Savage cleared his throat and looked her in the eye. "Hans has come to us, Lila, because he's distraught over the circumstances surrounding his son's recent, tragic death."

Holzinger's gaze snapped upward and fastened on Savage. "You should say 'justifiably distraught.'"

"Justifiably," Savage amended quickly.

Lila reached into her brown leather messenger bag, pushed aside her bottle of lithium, whipped out her well-worn quad-ruled composition memo pad, clicked her pen a few times, and began scribbling preliminary notes.

"Wolf Holzinger," Savage continued, "thirty-three years old, bright young man, full of promise. Twelve weeks ago, Wolf plummeted sixteen stories to his death while rappelling down the side of the 1100 North Dearborn Apartments. You know the building—corner of Dearborn and West Maple. Three o'clock in the morning. Climbing in freezing weather late Saturday night/early Sunday morning. Three nights before Halloween."

Lila's jaw dropped; abruptly she stopped scribbling and gaped at her boss. "I remember reading something about that!" The story had stuck in her head in a weird way, she recalled, because it had coincided with a particularly bad night's sleep.

"No doubt. Probably read this." Savage reached behind him and produced a neatly folded copy of *The Chicago Tribune* that had run the day after young Holzinger had hit the pavement. He handed it to her.

Man Dies in 16-Story Fall Climbing down Building

October 30, 2017

A Near North Side businessman fell 16 stories to his death on Saturday morning after tying himself to television cables on the roof of a North Side high-rise and attempting to rappel his way into the window of his girlfriend's 15th-floor apartment.

Wolf Holzinger, 33, was pronounced dead on arrival at Northwestern Memorial Hospital.

Police said the cable apparently snapped after Holzinger swung away from a 16th-floor apartment when a woman inside screamed.

"When the woman approached the window screaming, he (Holzinger) said 'Sorry, ma'am, I've got the wrong apartment,' or something to that effect, and headed for his girlfriend's apartment directly below," said Detective Robert Krzyskowski of the Belmont Area Violent Crimes Unit. "When the woman told the doorman what happened, he investigated the situation and found Holzinger lying directly below her window."

Holzinger had tried to reach his girlfriend at her apartment at 1100 North Dearborn Apartments several times on Friday evening and early Saturday morning, Krzyskowski said.

"When she did not answer his telephone calls, he must have gone to the building," Krzyskowski said.

Lila shook her head and handed it back. Savage jabbed her with a second identically creased paper. He jerked his chin toward the exposed headline. "*Times* ran this on Halloween," he said, waggling the article in front of her like a lure on a line.

She hesitated a beat before accepting the paper, thinking she'd spotted a subtle smirk at the corner of her boss's mouth.

Two Men, Two Women, and Two Deaths
CHICAGO, Oct. 30—Two men died within half an hour of one another on Saturday in separate accidents in which they fell from apartment buildings, one while trying to climb in to see his girl-friend, the other to see his wife, the police said today.

Skimming through the standard filler, Lila found the following passage:

Less than a half-hour later, Louis Breem, 25, fell from an eighth-story ledge while trying to get into his apartment after his wife locked him out during an argument, said Patrolman Oscar Levine.

Mr. Breem's wife, Angela Breem, had run him out of their apart-ment at a West Side housing complex run by the Chicago Housing Authority, Officer Levine said.

Mr. Breem went next door to a vacant apartment and climbed out on the window ledge. He fell while trying to get into his apartment, the officer said.

"Unbelievable! Two on the same night!" Lila said, unable to muzzle her dismay. She quickly jotted down a note to call her contact at PD to get the witnesses' names and numbers. "Any connection between your son and the, uh, the second man? Have you ever heard that name mentioned before?" She glanced up at their client, her mind racing, then quickly re-scoured the article. "Louis Breem. Recognize that name?"

"No," Holzinger replied curtly, flexing his jaw.

Lila shrugged. "We'll have to look at that, for sure." She and Savage exchanged wary glances.

"PD ruled it accidental," Savage explained. "Coroner recorded it as 'death by misadventure.'"

"*Bullshit!*" Holzinger protested. "Let me tell you something. When I got up to deliver the eulogy at my son's funeral, I bends down *und* kisses the funeral urn on the way up to the podium. They set it out on this small presentation table in front of the altar; covers it *mit* de white ossuary pall, er—cloth *mit* de single gold-embroidered Maltese cross."

"I remember that," Savage said, nodding, his voice subdued.

"When I straighten up again"—his left hand loosely curled into a fist, his thumb on top, as if he was driving a mule team—"this loud groan comes out of me from somewhere so deep, so entirely ... *unerklärlich* —*inexplicable*—it was almost as if this comes from somewhere else. Comes from someone else." His clouded eyes cleared and for a brief moment became fiery and inspired. He wagged a wary finger. "And that's when I knew. This was no death by misadventure, Ms. Piper. Not this. *Nein.* Somebody murdered my son. And knowing that they murdered him haunts me."

A chill crawled slowly over Lila. "So sorry for your loss," she said quietly. "You have my deepest sympathy."

Hans's begrudging nod only made him look frail and weary.

"And please, 'Lila's' fine." She gave a tight-lipped smile and turned back to her notebook, finishing the sentence. When she looked back up, the grim-jawed sixty-eight-year-old was still glaring at her with those stern, fierce-looking eyes. She could tell that they were reading her, that something wasn't adding up, so she tried to hide her consternation.

"Something on your mind?" Jim queried.

"Well," Lila started, trying to walk the fine line between diplomacy and confrontation, "if I may ..."

Savage nodded.

Lila turned to their guest. "Your son died two nights before Halloween. And it's now how many days later? Let's see, thirty-one days in October," she began slowly, "so there are three days there. Thirty days in November, so that's thirty-three days; thirty-one days in December, that's sixty-four days. And this is what—the twenty-sixth of

January? So, that's ... twenty-six plus sixty-four makes ninety days. Ninety, right?"

"*Richtig*," Holzinger replied, looking mildly confused. "Correct."

"I guess I'm wondering what took you so long to reach out to us? You said 'And that's when I knew.' So, in the days following your son's death, you have this sudden epiphany of almost spiritual clarity and yet you wait a full three months before reaching out to your old hunting buddy here. You obviously know he's preeminent in his field; your closest friend ready, willing, and able to help you at all costs—well, is my guess." She darted a quick glance Savage's way and was met with an accommodating nod. "Right. So, all you had to do is pick up the phone. But you didn't do that. I'm curious. *Why?*"

There was a lively, awkward stillness, like air before a storm. When Holzinger didn't answer, Lila sat forward in her seat. "Could it be that maybe you had your doubts about this not being a murder at all but rather some monstrous coincidence?" Seeing his irked expression, she added, "And I'm speaking here of the two identical deaths on the same night at roughly the same hour."

"This is starting to sound like an interrogation," Holzinger said. He stood and shot Savage an angry, defiant glance. "What's going on?" he demanded, his voice rising. "Am I on trial here?"

"Just doing her job, Hans," Savage said, fluttering his hand impatiently in the air before easing back into his characteristic coolness. "She's just being thorough; instead of pissing you off, that ought to give you some comfort. Think about it: if she's this thorough with you—and you're paying her—how much more comprehensive will she be during the next interview she has on her list? And the one after that?"

To Lila's ear, Savage's attempt to calm the waters was just another manifestation of his magnanimous attitude toward the members of his tight-knit SLFF family. Working for a boss who gave her a wide enough berth to do her work without interference—a boss who'd had her back since her very first day on the job and who never threw her sometimes dramatic mood swings (or their dodgy past) back in her face—well, it had been one of her life's great pleasures.

"Strains credulity," Holzinger said, stiffly indignant. "The idea that my son's death was due to some ... nightmarish coincidence!" He shook his head and held up the magazine he'd brought, the one he'd since rolled into a baton that had been going *tap tap tap* against the leg of his chocolate-brown corduroys.

Lila watched his creased face redden as he unrolled his magazine. Its title read,

CLIMBING

Two glossy climbers ascended a shadowy crack in an otherwise sheer rock face. The sun-bleached blond in the foreground was secured to a yellow harness drawn snug at his hips.

"Okay." Lila nodded slowly and shrugged, keen to be helpful, to connect the dots between Holzinger's conviction that his son's death was foul play, the three months it had taken him to seek help, and the sport-climbing rag he held aloft. "So ... your son was a climber, I take it," Lila observed.

"Wolf was an avid climber," Holzinger replied, his voice cracking. "A member of the American Alpine Club. Joined when he was sixteen years old."

"American Alpine Club," she repeated, glancing at Savage for help.

Savage shrugged back at her. It was clear to her that he had no better idea than she did.

"AAC's been around since 1902. They're dedicated to 'competent climbers *und* healthy climbing landscapes.'" He nodded an emphatic full stop.

"Ah! Okay, so the connection, in your mind, is that, since your son was a serious climber, he would ..." Again, Lila's gaze dithered doubtfully between her boss and their fiery old client. "He would what?" Surely Wolf wouldn't have been rappelling down the side of a Chicago high-rise at any time, let alone at three o'clock in the fucking morning. A litany of various explanations presented themselves: *sex, drugs, alcohol, mental instability ... uh, all of the above ...*

"One other item," Holzinger said. "When they find him, he was wearing ... *eine Schweizer Sitz*, er—a Swiss seat."

Again, the dithering look. "Sorry." Lila frowned.

"It's an emergency rappelling harness, Ms. Piper, like the one on the cover"—he held up the magazine to point it out—"here." He rested his dairyman's gnarled forefinger emphatically below the image. "These are typically tied from a twelve-foot section of the climber's rope."

"Okay ..." she said, squinting at the picture, searching for deeper meaning, feeling unsettled by his knuckles so close to her face.

"The police claim my son died when the 'TV cables'"—Holzinger seemed to have trouble pronouncing the words—"he was supposedly using to rappel down the side of this sixteen-story skyscraper—that's *television cables*, mind you—suddenly snapped." His face darkened. "One—why would Wolf use TV cables when he has his climbing rope? Hmm? Ah! So how do we know he has the rope, you ask? Right here! He ties the damned Swiss seat, does he not? *Ja!* He does; they find it on his body! It still has a carabiner clipped to it! No, he has to have an ample length of rope in his possession. *Und* two, being an expert, possessed—you must remember—of unrivaled climbing skills, my son would know better than to entrust his life to an unrated, untested line, especially one that's *chimmy*-rigged from cable made from cheap molded plastic *mit* a thin copper wire core inside. He knew better. The core of a climber's rope is critical; it bears eighty percent of his weight. To top that off, it was hellishly frigid that night. It's a tricky business, this climbing, *und* extremely dangerous if done improperly. Substituting cables for a climbing rope would be like a skydiver using his underwear in place of a parachute. In an emergency, when that's all you've got, maybe you take a hare-brained risk like that. But there was no emergency that night. Wolf wasn't fleeing a burning building. Hell, he could've taken the stairs! *Herrgottsakra!* His girlfriend lives one floor down! Wolf was in and out of that building all the time; doorkeepers knew him by name. They were friends. He has a key!"

"Forgive me, I don't mean to sound like I'm blaming the victim here," Lila said, shooting a quick glance back at Savage, "and I apologize in advance if that's what it sounds like, but I have to ask: Was your son ever known to be prone to—I don't know—any other incidences of similarly reckless behavior? Acting out? Maybe episodes of impulsiveness or depression in the past? Did he use drugs? Alcohol? Were there any"—a second quick glance back at Savage— "cognitive issues we should know about?"

"No. Absolutely not."

Holzinger's glare and terse reply struck Lila as odd—he seemed too dismissive by half; she wondered if he was having second thoughts. Again, the curled fist with the thumb on top. "Wolf does not have anything to do *mit* de ... drugs or *psychische probleme* or whatever the hell obscure point you're trying to make here." He shook his head. "Casting aspersions on a highly accomplished young man you know absolutely nothing about."

Emotional *and* overbearing, Lila concluded, weathering the not entirely unexpected gale.

"But something led your son to the top of that building that night," Lila replied. "If we can't figure out *why* he was up there on that roof that night, then we have no chance whatsoever of finding out *who* was there with him."

"Let me tell you something about my son."

He was changing gears, Lila noted, shifting from blunt confrontation to the protective paternal reflex.

Holzinger's jaw tightened. "Wolf graduated *mit* de BS in History from the University of Nebraska, Lincoln. He finishes Summa Cum Laude while competing in UNL's Men's NCAA Division I Gymnastics program, *nicht wahr?*"

"Not exactly the profile of someone clinically depressed," Savage muttered to himself, "or ... unable to bridle their impulses."

"*Ja, richtig!* After graduating, he continues competing *und* qualifies as one of the elite American athletes selected for 2008 US Olympic Team."

"In Beijing?" Lila's eyes widened. "That's cool."

"*Ja*, it was cool."

"How did he do?" Lila asked, scribbling a few more notes.

"Pulled a hammy," Savage muttered, shaking his head.

"He'd been immersed in gymnastics since he was five—this is twenty years of relentlessly grueling preparation. All his hopes, all his dreams—ruined by *diese* one pulled muscle."

"How did he take it?"

"Tough. Eventually, he gets over it. Wolf was smart as a whip. After his injury, he applies to Georgetown Law *und* he gets in *mit* de little help from his Uncle *Chimmy* over there."

Lila smirked at Savage. "Uncle *Chimmy*?"

"That's ... not entirely accurate," Savage said. "As I told you when Wolf got notice of his acceptance, your son got in under his own steam. Sure, I made a call; as I told you at the time, I know the president there. But it was very brief, and its only outcome was learning that there'd been no need to make that call. Woody told me they were 'damned lucky to have a young man of Mr. Holzinger's character, caliber, and accomplishments.' I remember like it was yesterday. I can still hear his damned adenoidal bean-town accent ringing in my ear."

"He gets in, *diese ist* the important thing," Holzinger said. He turned to Lila. "Georgetown, as you probably know, is one of the top law schools out there. No, he was not depressed. He was not impulsive. You ask about my son's flaws? He had no flaws. He did not do drugs. He was exceptionally bright; he was mature *und* he tackled life head-on *mit* discipline *und* enthusiasm. He was disappointed there for a while, pissed off—sure! *Absolut!* But this he puts behind him *und* he moves on. Like the man that he was."

Lila looked over to find Savage nodding.

"You said he was in and out of his girlfriend's building all the time. You two talked about that? His romantic life?"

"We did."

"You must have been pretty close, I take it."

"We were. Very close."

"Do you happen to know how they met?"

"His girlfriend?"

"Yes."

"He tells me they met at a gala in DC."

Lila jotted down a few more lines for follow up and then said, "One more thing—did they find any additional rope at the scene, other than the, uh ... the twelve-foot section you mentioned?" She glanced back at her notebook. "The Swiss seat?"

"No, they did not. And this is the most curious thing."

His eyes were pained; he'd lost his son, but he had his contempt, his fiery nature to cling to with both fists clenched, all to preserve his sense of normalcy, Lila suspected. His Teutonic sense of absolutes—his perfectly ordered world populated by winners and losers—had gone entirely off the rails.

"Think about that: if you're going to rappel down the side of a building, especially being an experienced climber *und* a world-class athlete, as was my son, are you telling me that you show up *mit* just enough rope to tie the Swiss seat *und* nothing else? What the hell are you going to use for your descent? Are you just going to rely on whatever you happen to find up there on the roof when you get there? Improvise? *Niemals!* Impossible! No one would do that!"

"No, I get it," Lila said, staring at the faded burgundy carpet below her boss's wing-tipped shoes while trying to puzzle out what she was hearing.

Savage pushed himself away from the desk and said, "Clear the decks, Lila. I want you to get into this; see what you can find out. Give it your full attention." Then, to his longtime friend, he added, extending his hand, "Lila's the best in the business. We *will* get to the bottom of this."

After the two men shook hands, Holzinger turned a baleful eye on Lila. "Coming from *Chimmy* Savage, this is high praise," he said without softening.

"He likes to see me blush, I'm afraid." Her gaze traveled out across the polished hardwood floor around the rug and she thought about her options, trying to push the arachnid imagery out of her mind. "I've got a buddy who might be able to help—Cornell Williams, Chicago PD Deputy Chief." She looked Holzinger in the eye. "I can talk to him, see if he'd be interested in re-opening the case."

"No," he shot back. "No police."

"You have reservations about taking this on?" Savage asked.

"It's just," she drew a deep breath and turned to Holzinger, "with all due respect, sir—"

"*Ja*, put it out there. We're all adults," he replied, steely-eyed.

Then, to Savage: "I've got a lot on my desk as it stands. Maybe we should talk about this in a sidebar."

Savage replied mildly, "I told you, Lila, we're all family here. Do what he said, just ... 'put it out there.'"

"There's the Coopersmith case. Rosenblatt is still open. Carney. Anwar. The thing with the city. And there's that mess with my brother."

"And?"

"And ..." Lila glanced over at Holzinger, her lips in a pursed grin. His hardened expression had not changed. "And ... what he's asking us to do isn't exactly in our wheelhouse—we're not a PI firm. As I said, I've got a good friend at PD that I can refer this to."

Savage grinned at Holzinger. "She's good. *And* she's by the book."

Holzinger cocked his head briefly to one side. Clearly, he just wanted results.

Savage turned back to Lila. "Look, this thing may be outside our purview, I'll grant you that, but sometimes, Lila, you don't go strictly by the book. The cases you mentioned are all in good shape for where we are on the docket. If that should change, I'll let you know. As for your brother's needs, the preliminary work we can hand off to Charlie O'Shanahan. Charlie-O's been after me for months for something to do. Loves to dig in and get the ball rolling. Don't worry; we're not going to let Ulli dangle."

Lila forced a smile. "Yeah, well, your name's on the door, not mine."

"Maybe it should be," Holzinger quipped.

"I'll need a chance to digest all this," she said, ignoring the remark, thumbing through her notebook. She looked at Holzinger and added, "Perhaps the two of us should meet again tomorrow, see if we can clear up at least some of the vagaries?"

"I fly back home this evening. Got an early appointment that I expect will run all day long. Make it the day after. I'll be in the office first thing in the morning." He shook Savage's hand and then headed for the door.

"What time?"

"Whenever you get there. Where I come from, we start very early. The cows cannot wait, *und* they have no patience for delay."

"Good," Lila said, trying to shake the weird images of Holzinger's spiderlike hands, his face telescoping forward and back. She looked at Savage and nodded with forced resolve. "Good."

"Oh"—Holzinger stopped at the door and turned back around— "*und* as for the ninety-day delay you ask me about—his *Mutter*, my wife, Sabine, she was devastated, as you can imagine."

"Of course," Lila said.

"Wolf's sudden death has become the bane of both our lives *und* is hanging over the two of us like the blackest curse imaginable."

"Completely understandable," Lila put in, soberly.

Savage nodded.

"*Und* so, I tell myself—Hans, you take your wife on this cruise around the world Sabine *und* Wolf were planning before his death. Sabine, she loves to travel; turns out it was cathartic for her to do something the three of us once did together. Enjoyed so much as a family when we were younger." His eyes brimmed briefly with a sad, nostalgic gleam. "I tell you, *Chimmy*," he frowned, "there were a few times when it was ... almost like he was there *mit* us. My boy. Wolf. My son." His voice cracked.

Lila looked at him with sympathy. "I understand," she murmured, watching the old dairyman weaken before her eyes.

"Indeed. It gives Sabine *und* I some time to think. I needed ... time to sort out what happens. When we set out from New York Harbor, the Statue of Liberty ... *und* the mist coming in, I wonder ... would the anger *und* outrage I was feeling be a passing thing or not. That troubled me."

"*Not*, I'm guessing," Lila quietly ventured.

He turned from Savage to fix his eyes directly on her. "Mine, it turns out," he started, drawing in a deep breath and exhaling slowly, his left hand once again clutched as if holding reins, "is an abiding anger. Und my *empörung*—er, outrage, Ms. Piper—Lila—at what was done to my beloved son, done to my beloved wife, done to my family, done to *me, Ja,* my outrage borders on the darkest, blackest form of madness. It preys on my mind. This is why I am here. You do what Chimmy asks you to do; you find out who is responsible. Money is not a problem. You find who's responsible *und* then I am going to rip the sonofabitch's heart out."

2

January 27, 2018

Stone Mental Health Center
Chicago, Illinois

MUNICIPAL SNOW PLOWS HAD CLEARED THE SIDE-STREETS BY THE time Lila pulled her black Toyota 4Runner up to the valet in front of the Northwestern Memorial Hospital parking garage on Huron Street, a block and a half back from Chicago's famed Magnificent Mile. She had just rolled to a stop when her cell phone rang.

"This is Lila," she said, dropping the SUV into park and waving off the young, fresh-faced parking attendant suddenly standing at her door. She gave him an apologetic shrug as he stood there in the gentle snowfall, his cap and shoulders dusted with white. She lifted a forefinger for him to give her a second.

"Hello, Ms. Piper," said the woman's voice on the phone, "this is Naomi, Chief Williams's assistant. The chief wanted me to pass along the name and number you were looking for."

"Okay," Lila replied, disappointed not to hear the news from the horse's mouth. "Go ahead," she said, and then, after taking down the information—*Marina Resnick* and a telephone number—hung up and forced an exhalation through pursed lips. She locked her elbows and pushed herself away from her steering wheel, her face turned toward the windshield. With her palms pressed tight against the wheel and her fingers spread wide, she watched the large snowflakes fall, so slow that they almost appeared not to be moving at all. Even robed in the splendor of a picture-perfect snowfall, the stillness still rankled. Inaction drove her crazy; it reminded her too much of the sickrooms and deathbeds of her conflict-stricken family. It made her feel isolated; the silence rang in her ears like electronic feedback.

Time to rate her mood. She reached for her bag and took out her notebook. Naught-to-ten scale, with naught being *"profoundly depressed,"* five being *"okay,"* and ten being *"the most awesome I've ever felt."* She damn sure wasn't that. *"Pissed off,"* just like the Almighty in the comic strip, was more like it. She clicked her pen a few times, scored herself a three, and stowed away her notebook. She was tired; it had already been a long day, and the visual distortions hadn't helped.

She had her head down—and was busy texting her psychiatrist, Dr. Gail Ross, telling her she was on her way in for an unscheduled "tune-up" session—when the valet tapped the window.

"Will you be long?" he asked. His voice was muffled through the glass; he sounded like he was underwater.

Lila stuffed her phone back in her pocket and let down the window. "An hour, maybe more," she said.

The man nodded and backed away. Recovering herself, Lila grabbed her bag, got out of the car, and headed for the Stone Mental Health Center across the street. Despite the recently cleared street's dark, glistening gash of asphalt, she was beginning to feel enveloped in thick, suffocating clouds; she felt snowed over utterly, bogged down.

"Nice to see you again, Ms. Piper," the receptionist said when Lila checked in. "Just have a seat. The nurse will call you when Dr. Ross is ready for you."

It seemed to take forever for the nurse to finally poke her head out and call Lila's name.

Lila followed her to Dr. Ross's office. "Doctor will join you in a minute," the nurse said, glancing at Lila only briefly, "she's just finishing up with another patient."

Lila nodded and sank into the seat in front of Dr. Ross's desk. Her gaze fell on the poster hanging on the wall beside her.

Has there ever been a period of time when you were not your usual self and thoughts raced through your head and you couldn't slow your mind down?

"Sorry, Lila, we're slammed today," Gail said, patting Lila's shoulder as she passed her. She wore a fitted winter-white pantsuit with a red knit turtleneck. A red silk pocket square hung from her breast pocket like a giant wilted flower.

Lila gave a weak grin to her back, checking out the water stains on the heels of her red leather pumps.

"Are you keeping up with your journaling?" Gail asked, sitting down and resting her elbows on her desk.

Lila cocked her head in an ambivalent nod.

"Okay, good. And at the moment, what would you say? How would you rate your mood?"

"Three," Lila replied. She shook her head, feeling suddenly exhausted by the whole process.

"Something got you upset? Maybe something you're dealing with at work, or on the personal front?"

"It's work. Jim's pulling me off my cases to deal with a friend of his. Not a personal injury case—a favor. Not exactly over the moon about that."

"How about sleep? Are you sleeping through the night?"

"Yes." Lila's gaze wandered over to the window, to the snow coming down at a slant.

"Any thoughts of self-harm? Killing yourself, wanting to die?"

"No. Thoughts of *'am I going to get a brain tumor from this machine of yours,'* maybe."

"Ha!" Gail shook her head. "We've been over this, Lila. It's perfectly safe and you've never had any side effects, so I'd say you're worrying over nothing."

Lila gave a soft snort, her gaze still fixed on the snow outside.

"Tell you what." Gail stood up and came out from behind her desk. "Let's take you back, get you situated." An understanding smile.

Lila got up and followed her down the hall, feeling no impulse at all for small talk.

Gail said a few words to the tech inside the treatment room and, to Lila, added, "I'll see you at your next scheduled appointment. We'll talk more then."

"Thanks, Gail," Lila said, handing over her coat to the tech waiting inside. She sat down in the TMS recliner, closed her eyes, and drew a deep, cleansing breath while the tech slid the TMS headgear onto her head like a 1950's-style salon hairdryer.

Soon she was listening to the soothing sounds of ocean waves washing over her. She was on a beach somewhere, sun beaming down on her, while the TMS machine delivered a powerful magnetic field to the left side of her skull, just behind her forehead—her *"dorsolateral prefrontal cortex,"* Gail had explained to her back in Tucson, "that area of your brain known to affect mood."

The magnetic field was delivered in a series of rapid pulses that sounded like antic woodpeckers hard at work. "One-and-a-half teslas," the TMS researchers had told her during her initial visit, "the equivalent of a magnet used in one of those big MRI imaging machines."

Across the cyan ocean, a reddish-gold sun sank slowly. Lila peered down at her feet, ankle-deep in the crystalline water. She felt an odd presence beside her.

Nothing.

Lowering her gaze back to the wavelets lapping at her feet, Lila felt her awareness expanding. She paused, straining—she could hear the popping and clicking sounds of sea critters beneath the water's surface.

Just then, the sky took on a magic-hour aspect as the uppermost rim of the sun finally slipped below the horizon. She waited for the customary green flash, but there was none.

Again, she looked around. There stood a giant gossamer ball reaching nearly waist-high, its dandelion silhouette the product of its hundred writhing legs. Flashes of red, green, blue, and yellow swirled across its surface like the colors of a soap bubble.

Abruptly, the TMS machine clicked off, and Lila woke up.

A full forty-five minutes had passed. After collecting her coat, Lila was smiling again, wishing everyone a nice day as she headed out to get ready for her upcoming meeting with Holzinger.

3

January 28, 2018

O'Brien's Restaurant & Bar
Chicago O'Hare International Airport

LILA CHECKED HER WATCH AS SHE REACHED TERMINAL THREE. Twenty minutes to spare before boarding began for her flight to Milwaukee, and then on to Holzinger's dairy farm in Kewaunee. She spotted O'Brien's directly across from her gate and headed straight for the bar. Once inside, she dropped her coat on the barstool, leaned her messenger bag against the brass foot rail, grabbed her notebook, and took out her phone.

The bartender rested both hands on the bar. "What can I get you?" he asked.

"Perrier," she said, dialing the number linked in her iPhone's notes app.

After three rings, she got voicemail. "Hi, this is Marina. Wait for beep."

Lila left her name and number for the second time in as many days, explaining that she wanted to talk to her about Wolf Holzinger and requesting would she kindly call back as soon as possible.

"Thanks," Lila said to the bartender as she stowed her phone away. She reached for the ice-filled collins glass and bottle of Perrier in front of her.

She looked around, sipping from her drink. A dark-haired naval officer to her immediate right stood chatting with a stunning blonde wearing a tailored black-and-white plaid suit and stiletto heels. He looked like the sharp end of the spear standing there in his dress blues. Graying just a little at the temples, she noticed. Lila glanced down at her lace-up boots, wiggling her toes inside the soft brown leather. She took another long sip.

Navy reached for his beer, and Lila counted the three stripes at his wrists, embroidered in gold thread and topped by a single gold star. From there, her eyes traveled leisurely up to the near side of his chest, itself adorned with several rows of multi-colored campaign ribbons and topped by a striking gold breastpin that showed two dolphins flanking the bow and conning tower of a submarine. All familiar; her father had served in the Navy during Vietnam. Dr. Frank Piper. Orthopedic Surgeon. Commander, US Naval Medical Corps.

She set her glass down on the bar, leaned forward, and casually craned her neck to listen in. Maybe get a better look at the guy—the woman, after all, was gorgeous. Lila's hand unconsciously fussed with the back of her wild spray of dark hair that looked like she'd gotten up late and hurriedly dragged an electric egg beater through it. She hadn't glammed herself up—grown her hair out or bleached it blonde—since law school. Those days were gone, as were the suicidal thoughts that had preceded them. No, Lila never regretted having been born. All things considered, she loved her life (such as it was) the way many women loved their difficult husbands and lovers—despite the rough and turbulent patches with which she had to contend.

"What? The fish?" she overheard Navy say. She watched his hand reach up, lightly touch his chest pin, and hover there for a moment. "Submarine warfare insignia."

"That's so *inter-estin'!*" the woman gushed in her thick Texas drawl, her dangling hammered gold earrings intermittently flashing out from beneath her blown-out blonde hair which just barely brushed her snug jacket's shoulders. She took a sip from her fruit-frilled drink and said, "So, how does that work exactly? I mean, how long do y'all—" She absently plucked the tiny pink parasol from her drink and twirled it between her thumb and forefinger.

Navy finished her sentence for her. "How long do we stay down?"

The woman gave a self-conscious chuckle and placed the tiny parasol down on the bar. "So, how long do y'all?" A coquettish grin.

"Depends. Typical deployment rotation on a fast attack boat like the one I was on runs anywhere from three to six months."

"Oh, my *gawd!*" She reached out and lightly touched his bicep and let her hand linger there.

He laughed, glanced down at her hand, and lifted his glass, "Hey, life below the waves."

"But six months! Whatever do y'all do down there?"

"What do I do? Sonar signal processing engineer." Responding to the woman's unblinking stare, he shrugged and added apologetically, "Advanced degree in applied mathematics."

Lila snorted so loudly that she almost choked on her drink.

Navy spun around to face her, catching her frantically wiping her nose and chin with her cocktail napkin. He shot her a bemused grin. "Are you laughing at me?" he asked, two deep creases appearing between his brows.

"Sorry," Lila apologized, still chuckling—rapidly blotting nose, lips, chin—noticing for the first time his truly compelling dark brown eyes. "Don't mind me." She shook her head, identifying herself with a roll of her eyes as a *dork!*

Navy repositioned himself to face her, casually leaning against the bar to give her his undivided attention.

Newly confronted with his back, the blonde in stilettos, evidently feeling upstaged, quietly set her cocktail down, snatched up her black Gucci handbag, and, offering Lila the one-sided pursed grin of the vanquished, slung her full-length coat over her arm and silently took her leave.

"So tell me, what's so funny?" Navy said, arching an eyebrow.

"Seriously?"

"Seriously. I'm all ears."

"Well, if you must know," she replied with a tentative smile, "I was thinking—is that your best line?"

"What line? I'm not aware I—"

"'*Advanced degree in applied mathematics?*'" She shook her head again, reached for her Perrier, and held it up to offer a toast, "Good luck with that one!" she said, laughing.

"She asked."

"Did she?" Lila shot him a skeptical look as her gaze traveled out into the hall, resting on the blonde's gracefully swaying hips as she disappeared into the dense crowd. "Yeah, I guess I missed that."

Tucking his chin to his chest, Navy appeared to sink into a moment of befuddled self-appraisal, muttering a few barely audible words to himself, including a pronounced *"Hmm!"* Then he chuckled and looked up at Lila. "You know, maybe she didn't." He set his beer down and extended his hand. "Hi, I'm Mark. And you are?"

Lila glanced down at his chest and read his name tag—black plastic engraved with his surname in white block letters: *Morgan*. She turned the name over in her mind: *Mark Morgan*.

"Lila," she replied, shaking his hand. Firm handshake. Not too eager, she cautioned herself. "So you're in sonar signal processing." She nodded, casually checking out his other hand, looking for a wedding ring or maybe a tan line. "You said 'submarine warfare,' but I'm guessing *anti*-submarine warfare." Her eyes narrowed. She was playing verbal battleship, curious to see if she'd struck her target.

"Ah! So, you're familiar with the Silent Service!" he said, brightening.

Lila found the sudden twinkle in those dark, expressive eyes surprisingly engaging.

"Wait, don't tell me," he brandished his palm and glanced down toward the floor, his gaze moving up slowly from her weathered boots to her tight-fitting jeans to her autumn-colored Pendleton shirt-jac to her free-spirit hairdo. She'd gone easy on the makeup—maybe that caught his attention. "You're a ... a sound engineer, working with a rock band." His eyebrows rose playfully. "Studied ... let's see ... acoustics engineering at some liberal East Coast college. Sarah Lawrence, maybe, or Swarthmore. But lemme guess—you couldn't resist the call of the road. Maybe you tour with one of those British rock bands. Don't tell me. Don't tell me, I got it —*Coldplay!*"

"Nope."

"No?" he practically whimpered, suggesting that her terse reply had crushed something young and playful inside of him. "Okay ..." He reached for his beer and took a rejuvenating slug. "That's it, kid. That's all I got. You got me stumped. Besides, *A Rush of Blood to the Head* is the only *Coldplay* album I know." He laughed and shrugged. Again came the hoisted glass in mock salute. After they clinked glasses, he said earnestly, "Seriously, what is it you do?"

"As one motley roadie to another—"

"Hey, wait a minute, I certainly did not mean to imply anything by that. You're—well, you are lovely. What's more, I think you know it." A devastating masculine smile appeared.

For the second time, she squinted at Commander Mark Morgan. "Lovely" was not a term she used to describe herself—it was a word she typically reserved for other women.

What the hell! As she looked at Morgan, she recalled the old photos of her father in his Navy uniform as a young man. But it was a scene involving her mother that sprang to mind:

> She is seven years old, listening to her mother's music playing on CD, twirling in her new dress with her arms stretched out, delighting in watching her skirt fill with air and lift waist-high around her like magic.
>
> "Mom, am I pretty?" Lila asks.
>
> Hanging on the walls and framed on side tables in their family home are various black-and-white glossies taken in the '50s by a young

unknown photographer, shot when her mother was a young, scantily clad chorus girl, a Rockette at Radio City Music Hall.

"Oy! Are you pretty?" her mother replies, attending to her "morning toilette," as she insists upon calling it. She smiles back at her daughter in the mirror as she applies mascara to her large and extravagantly shadowed blue eyes. "Is Daddy pretty?" She finishes with a light dusting of rose-scented powder that makes the little girl sneeze.

"Noooo!" Lila can't help but giggle at such a silly notion, wiping her nose. Though Dr. Frank Piper is an orthopedic surgeon, he looks more like an overfed bus driver—a few loose black curls the centerpiece of his dark, thinning hair, a kind face but puffy under the eyes.

"No, he is not," her mother quietly reassures her, speaking matter-of-factly. "But there are some things better than being pretty, are there not?" Dropping her powder puff back into its rhinestone casket, her mother turns her striking beauty-queen face to her daughter. Her unrivaled glamour warms the little girl's heart like a Hollywood arc light.

The child's lip curls downward as she nods. She looks up at her mother, crestfallen. Somehow, she no longer feels like twirling.

"But you are smart like your father, and you look just like him—you have the cutest little Frankie face!" she laughs, pinching her daughter's chubby cheeks with both hands. Her mother notices her little girl's growing distress. She lets go and tilts her head in a kind of alien curiosity, her elaborately arched and penciled brows cinching together. "What's this punim! Why so verklempt? Where's this coming from?"

"What I know is that I shouldn't be talking to the likes of you," Lila said with a devilish grin.

"What are you saying?" Commander Mark Morgan asked, "You mean you don't normally talk to the men you meet at bars?"

"Oh, all the time. I'm just not sure I want to talk to you," Lila teased.

"Ouch!"

She looked at him thoughtfully, then said, "I work for a local law firm."

"*Ah!* A lawyer!" he said, duly impressed.

"No. Oh, God no! No, I handle the firm's field research." She picked up her Perrier bottle, poured the remainder over her lime wedge, and watched it pool.

"Field research," he repeated. *"Ah!"* His mouth widened into an odd smirk. "You're a PI."

"I am." Her palm shot up to silence him. "Hold on!" She inclined her ear to hear the boarding announcement crackling over the airport's PA system. "That's me," she said. "Sorry." she frowned, reaching for her bag to settle her check.

"Hold on!" He snatched the check before she could grab it and dropped his American Express on the bar.

"What do I owe you?"

"Permission to call you."

"What? Are you asking for my number?"

"Yes, ma'am."

"You live in the city?"

"I do. Just bought a brownstone in Lincoln Park." He lifted his lapel. "Retiring in a couple of days."

"Sorry to be so direct, but ... married?"

"Nope."

"Divorced?"

"Nope."

"Serious relationship?"

"Just me and my dog, Bertrude."

"Bertrude!" She looked at him askance.

"Long story."

She let it go. "Lincoln Park brownstones aren't cheap."

"Spent twenty years underwater. Generous run of hazardous duty pay."

"Okay," she said begrudgingly. "So call me a sucker for guys in uniform."

"You're a sucker for guys in uniform," he dutifully replied.

She smiled and obligingly dug into her bag like she was going for her business card, but stopped midway. Her hand came out empty. "Yeah," she apologized slowly, avoiding his eyes. "I appreciate the drink, thank you, but ... I don't think so. I—I gotta go."

Mark's head rocked back slightly. "Wow," he muttered as he wavered. Drawing in a recovering breath, he said, "Okay, well"—he lifted his drink in salute—"it was lovely to meet you, Lila. Another time, perhaps. A *better* time."

4

January 28, 2018

Holzinger's Lakeview Dairy
Kewaunee, Wisconsin

LILA PARKED HER RENTED WHITE TOYOTA CAMRY SEDAN IN THE
space marked, *Welcome VIP Guest*, grabbed her bag, and headed for the
entrance to the wood, steel, and clinker-brick two-story building that
served as the business end of Holzinger's thriving Lakeview Dairy. She
waited for the dueling hand-push snowplows, piling up steep salt-and-
pepper-tinted snowbanks on both sides of the walkway, to clear the sidewalk. The resultant waist-high channel, speckled with soot, salt, and
mud, amplified the sound of her crunching boots.

Once inside the dairy's spacious lobby, she approached the reception
desk, gave her name, and took off her coat.

The silver-haired receptionist peered up at her over her half-moon
reading glasses and told her that Mr. Holzinger was expecting her and
would be a few more minutes. "Can I get you anything, dear?" she asked,
a warm, grandmotherly twinkle in her eye.

"Can I plug into an outlet?" Lila waggled her iPhone, "My cell's out of juice."

"Of course," the woman said, nodding toward the electrical outlet by the cream-colored leather sofa in the reception area.

Lila looked past the settee to the life-sized multi-colored fiberglass sculpture of a Jersey cow in front of the plate glass window that framed the mostly empty parking lot outside. The furniture and architecture struck a stark, minimalist contrast to the cow's bizarre paint-splash skin: the furnishings were all ivory and chrome—clean colors, clean lines. The cow, on the other hand, was a technicolor acid trip. Chaos and order, side by side.

She plugged in her cell phone and once again dialed Marina Resnick. Waiting for the elusive Ms. Resnick to pick up, Lila glanced around at all the promotional posters of Lakeview Dairy cattle hanging on the walls.

And again, three rings and Marina's voice message clicked on. For the third time, Lila left her name and number.

She clicked the phone off, laid it on the arm of the sofa, and reached for the magazine lying on the oval coffee table. *Hoard's Dairyman*, the cover read. A sudden roar from outside drew her attention—she looked up to watch an enormous yellow "John Deere" wheel loader groan loudly by, clearing the far end of the parking lot.

The receptionist emerged and, mouthing something over the noise, waved Lila toward a closed door at the end of the hall. Lila pushed it open and halted, dumbstruck by the bizarre décor. She had come expecting "family-farm utilitarian"—maybe an old two-cabinet desk with a couple of straight-back aluminum chairs out front. Maybe a *Hoard's Dairyman* 2018 wall calendar featuring "Hoard's Heifer of the Month" or a "Key to Kewaunee."

Clearly, Hans Holzinger was a complex man, and Lila was curious to find traces of the extraordinary leadership and civic spirit it must have taken to grow a small family-owned farm from thirty milk cows into the sustainable large-scale agri-business it had become. Savage had told her that Holzinger's operation produced over 32,000 gallons of milk a day. *That's four full tanker cars*, he'd remarked, *seven days a week. Non-stop.*

Day in, day out. He'd mentioned that Holzinger was an ambitious man, determined to grow his operation to ten-times its present size, how he was endlessly quoting J. Paul Getty: *"A sense of thrift is essential to success in business. The businessman must discipline himself to practice economy whenever possible, in his personal life as well as his business affairs."* Savage gave a telling example of Holzinger's so-called "thrift": after knocking down several old wooden outbuildings on his property, Holzinger'd had his son fill a collection of rusty coffee cans with the used nuts and bolts he'd gathered from the debris. "With Hans, it's more than thrift, it's 'control,'" Savage told her. "Austrian—it's in his blood."

That explained the gray-green wood-paneled trophy room she'd just entered—clearly, the man had big ambitions and equally big appetites. Rather than the quaint, no-frills office of "Hoard's Dairyman of the Year," she found herself in the trophy room of Herr Hans Holzinger—business leader, dairyman, and, evidently, great white hunter. Various animal heads hung on the wall above the credenza behind his desk. "Talk about control," Lila muttered. At the center of the room, a zebra skin rug covered the wide-plank aged-oak floor.

Behind the desk, hanging in an arched niche, was a landscape oil portrait: a solitary acacia tree set against an amber-colored Serengeti. The sun appeared to be rising behind it, casting golden beams through the tree's branches, lighting the surrounding grass like a numinous flame.

"How hard is it to keep your damned pictures straight?" she said to herself out loud, crossing the room to straighten it. Stepping back to check her work, she looked up at the head of the massive Cape buffalo mounted directly above it, black soulless eyes glaring down at her. "Pet peeve. Sorry," she said.

Turning her back on the ghoulish wall, she crossed the room to the ceiling-high bookcase, carefully perusing the photos and personal memorabilia scattered among the leather-bound books. While continuing to straighten the odd picture frame, she noticed, upon turning back to the desk, that there, front and center on the desk itself, sat the identical twin of her boss's solid-pewter model of the Convair CV-540 with the same "LPF" tail markings.

"Oh, God, there's two of them!"

Returning her attention to the credenza behind the desk, she picked up a framed family photograph of a much younger Hans Holzinger posing with his teenage son. Both had their dark polished Browning BAR rifles balanced on their hips, elaborately scoped muzzles pointed skyward. They looked transported, the two Holzingers—happier days, father and son with big broad grins, kneeling proudly over the dusty carcass of a dead male lion. The lion's mane, low on the animal's chest, was stained red.

Someone cleared their throat behind her.

Carefully returning the photo to its place, Lila turned to find Holzinger's gaunt-hidalgo figure framed by the doorway. She circled back to stand in front of the sofa while her host lingered at the threshold a moment, speaking in hushed tones to his receptionist.

"Agnes will bring us something to drink," he said, striding into the room. He reached out his hand in sober welcome.

"Thank you," Lila replied, waving him off, "but I'm working on a cold."

He shrugged slightly and, as he did, she couldn't help but stare at his huge knuckles as his hand dropped to his side, the large glinting Rolex loose on his wrist as if he'd recently lost some weight. She followed his open-palmed invitation, beckoning her to sit in the stuffed club chair nearest the bookcase.

"Quite a place you have here," she said, perching on the edge of her seat and giving a tight smile. Her eyes made one last circuit around the room before she adjusted the vintage German Reich gold eagle pillow at her back and delved into her messenger bag.

"Not the same now that Wolf is gone." He fell silent a moment until the rattle of clinking glass brought him around. "*Ah!* Here we are!"

His receptionist entered the room with two cut-crystal glasses and a fluted pitcher on a serving cart.

While the lemonade was being poured, Holzinger asked, "Did you fly out of Midway?"

"O'Hare," Lila replied. She accepted the glass and glanced up at the receptionist, "Thanks."

After the woman had retreated, Holzinger leaned back on the scroll arm sofa with his drink in hand and said, "Shall we get on *mit* de work you have come to do?"

Lila peered into his eyes as he came forward and rested his elbows on his knees. Easy to see the grim determination there, the forced mask of civility. Taking a sip and then setting her drink aside on the coffee table, she opened her notebook, reached for her pen, clicked it a few times, and began.

"I'd like to talk a little more about your son being an experienced climber," she said, speaking so fast that even *she* noticed it.

"He was an avid climber."

"You said"—she swallowed, forcing herself to slow the pace—"he was a member of the American Alpine Club ... since he was sixteen?"

"*Ja,* that's right."

"Where did he climb? From what little I know about Wisconsin's geography," she said, her eyes narrowed, "this isn't exactly the Alps. Kinda ... *flat* ... around here."

"Did you happen to notice the silos on your way in?" Holzinger asked.

"I did. Seven. Seven very impressive concrete silos." She nodded. "I counted them."

"Interesting fact for you," he said, sitting back in his seat, one long, slender arm draped over the back of the sofa. "Wisconsin has more silos than any other state."

"Did not know that."

"I taught my son how to climb when he turned sixteen so he could help me paint *diese* beasts. It was a rite of passage for him. I told him from when he was still just the littlest *moppelchen*—'He only earns his freedom *und* his life who takes them every day by storm.' Goethe said that."

Her head rocked back briefly. "So, he was climbing the silos to help you paint them." She wanted to make sure she'd heard him right.

"*Ja,* silos."

"They *are* concrete, aren't they?"

"They are."

"You paint concrete?"

"*Ja,* we do. You must seal the concrete to keep it watertight."

Her chin lifted slightly at having missed the obvious. "Makes sense." She smirked at her notebook as she scribbled a note.

"*Ja,* you've got to protect your silage from mold *und* rot. *Und* you do this by painting *und* filling in the pores, pock holes *und* pinholes that develop over time. Weather is the enemy; I'm afraid: rain, snow, *und* ice. It takes its toll. Once Wolf got the hang of it, he offered his abseiling services to the other farms in the area."

"Abseiling?"

"'*Rappel*' is *der Französisch* name—you want the definition, it's 'a controlled descent of vertical drop using rope. Comes from *dem Deutschen Wort 'abseilen,'* meaning 'to rope down.' Wolf did well *mit de* abseiling business before he went off to study at UNL. How he made his mad money. Check *mit* Gus—Gus Ambrosia over at Ambrosia Dairy." He pronounced the name casually enough but there was a tinge of disdain, she noticed, as it crossed his lips. Again, for her, or for Gus? It was hard to tell.

"Gus Ambrosia," Lila repeated, making a quick note. She jotted down the three-pronged Greek letter *psi* next to it, some deep *psychology* at play between these two, she suspected.

"*Ja,* Gus. He's a prickly character, but Wolf did a lot of work for him back when Gus was just getting started *mit* his 'Big Milk.'" He turned away with a look of contempt.

"*Big Milk?*" she laughed, "I thought you were the Big Milk around here."

"We're the largest *privately*-owned dairy in the state. Gus's dairy is part of a larger-scale conglomerate. His operation is huge; covers over forty square miles. At last count, I think he had twenty-five thousand head of cattle under management. Twenty-five thousand head makes him five times our size."

"That *is* Big Milk," she said, scribbling. When she was through, she looked him in the eye and said, "You seem somehow less than enamored with the idea."

"What? *Mit* Big Milk?"

"Don't know. With Big Milk. Maybe with ... Gus Ambrosia."

Holzinger got up and poked his head out the door. "Agnes, get Gus on the horn *und* tell him I'm sending someone over to see him." When he returned to his seat, he said, "We're fighting an industry trend developing over the last several decades or so—goes back to the seventies. Large-scale corporate agriculture is taking control of all stages of our business. Corporations running milk-processing plants naturally prefer to work with a few large-scale dairies as opposed to thousands of small ones. On the one hand, we've benefited handsomely. We're not exactly small potatoes ourselves. *Ja, und* on the other hand, the bigger Gus gets, the larger the shadow he casts over our future prospects."

"How so?"

"I don't relish the idea of having built what I've built only to discover it's not big enough, that I'm forced to join the ranks of the smaller farms with fewer places to sell our milk. Prices are falling *und* the industry, in general, is in decline." Before Lila could ask, he said, "Plant-based diets are taking hold the world over. Alternative milks are everywhere these days. Cows are giving way to almonds *und* cashews *und* coconuts. Damned vegans! The milk *und* the meat ... this is not what it used to be." He shook his head, "*Ja*, we've got a tremendous amount of money invested here; this I refuse to lose."

"Cut-throat business. I understand."

"*Ja?* Good. So, now I have a few questions for you."

Lila put her pen down. "Sure. Shoot."

"Your father was a Navy man; do I have this right?"

"During Vietnam, yes. Dad was in the Navy."

"*Und* a surgeon. An orthopedic surgeon."

"That's right," she said. Seeing the scorn lingering in Holzinger's face, she said, "'Strong as a bull, half as bright,' Dad used to say." Lila felt a rush of anger. *This effing guy!* She flipped her notebook and quickly scribbled a four for her shifting mood. She felt her perspective beginning to turn ever so slightly from the clarified center of the looking glass out toward the distorted edges of the funhouse mirror. It was exhausting.

"They both died young, *ja?* Your parents. In their fifties?"

"Yes, they did," she replied sharply.

"So, you were raised in a home *mit* de highest morals *und* values, no doubt."

A quick cough to clear her throat. "As much as anyone, I suppose. Why do you ask?"

"Military background, this is what I mean to say," he explained, affecting the voice of a cartoon commander to add, "*Achtung!* Everything in good military order!'"

"My mother was the one who kept the discipline if that's what you mean. Dad was largely absent. His schedule kept him away from the home front a lot of the time, what with his surgical rotation at the hospital and his business interests with his bank."

"*Und* the securities fraud?" Holzinger's chin rose slightly, as if he were hanging on her response.

She met his gaze evenly. It was unnerving to have a client know more about her than she did about them. She felt that her privacy had been invaded, and was left wondering what his angle was.

"That must have been hard on the whole family," he added.

"It was," she agreed at last. "In fact, in the end, it's probably what killed them both, truth be told."

"Ah, yes. *Stress.*"

She glared at him for a long moment. If he was looking for a fight, she was fucking ready. She didn't care how close a friend he was to her boss.

"Sad. *Und* you come out so well!"

She expelled a sigh through her nose.

"Practically unscathed," he added, eyes still on her.

"I don't know about that. But we soldier on, do we not?"

"*Ja-ja*—we do, indeed. Though sometimes it feels like it kills us to do so." At that, he exhaled softly.

There was a silence.

Holzinger slapped both hands on his knees. *"Ja,* okay. So, what's next?"

"Next?"

"After you meet *mit* Gus."

She snapped herself back into purely professional mode. "I plan to meet with PD to see what they have on the other fellow who fell to his death that night—Louis Breem. See if there's a connection there. Talk to the witnesses of both falls. Right now," she added, her eyes making one last circuit of the room, "we're on the hunt."

"When you do turn something up, you will let me know." His words had an expectant, faintly menacing air.

"Of course," she replied, ignoring the rising hairs on her skin.

5

August 10, 2009

Residence of CIA Associate Deputy Director for Operations
Georgetown, Washington DC ~ Nine Years Earlier

THE SUN HAD SET BY THE TIME HANS AND GUS ARRIVED AT JOHN Alden's gray-brick Edwardian manse in the heart of Georgetown. Hans climbed out of the black Town Car, stuck his hands in his pockets, and followed Gus toward the door, eyeing the ivy-covered two-story carriage house fronting the street—five windows above, five below. The grand estate's curved cobblestone drive was packed with fancy cars.

When they reached the motor court (the main house being set back from the street), they passed through a patch of warm glowing light shining from one of the arched windows one floor up. Hans spotted a high-ceilinged room crowded with smartly dressed women and men, some civilians, some military, all sipping drinks, nodding now and then, smiling, chatting. A lively piano—which, Hans remarked, sounded like someone getting ready to launch into some Puccini—provided a sophisticated backdrop to the otherwise mirthful blend of chatter that spilled out over the cobblestones.

The moment they hit the doorstep, the charcoal front door swung open, revealing a fleeting glimpse of the foyer's grand spiral staircase and black-and-white marble floor before two thick-necked members of the director's security staff stepped forward, blocking the view. Poker-faced, with white coiled-tube earpieces emerging from their starched white collars, they stood shoulder to shoulder, blocking the entrance like a couple of clean-cut NFL linemen.

"Names and identification," one of them said.

"Gus Ambrosia and Hans Holzinger," Gus answered, reaching behind him for his ID. But before he could fetch his wallet, a petite woman with gray eyes and short white hair gingerly squeezed between the two guards and stepped into the ring of amber porchlight. She was dressed for work—dark suit, dark pumps, white blouse, no-nonsense.

Hans recognized her at once as Alden's longtime assistant, Marjorie Ward. *"Guten Abend, Fräulein!"* he said.

She placed her palms flat against her thighs and, with her head held affectionately to one side, greeted her old friends with a wry smile, "Herr Holzinger, Mr. Ambrosia—how lovely to see you gentlemen again. Mr. Alden is expecting you." She turned around and, with an insistent nod, peeled the guards aside and beckoned her two guests to follow her.

Inside the ten-thousand-square-foot estate, swirls and eddies of party-goers packed the halls and clogged the staircase, the whole place abuzz with chatter.

"Quite a party you've got here, Marjorie," Gus said as they climbed the spiral stairs to the second floor. "What's the occasion?"

"We're celebrating his son's appointment as CO of the USS *Themistocles.*"

"Navy captain!" Gus said, then glanced back at Hans, eyebrows up.

"Ring knocker," Hans muttered contemptuously.

Gus choked back a laugh and said under his breath, for Hans's hearing alone, "He could have attended anywhere. The fact that he chose Annapolis—well, I'll cut him some slack."

"You'll be meeting in the library," Marjorie explained as they threaded their way through the lively throng being hushed to silence by the opening strains of a piano concerto.

"*La Bohème*," Hans whispered with piqued interest, "it's Puccini's *La Bohème*."

Another clean-cut young man, this one in a white dinner jacket, was busy at the Steinway grand accompanying a heavyset baritone in black tie whom, Marjorie whispered, was with the Washington National Opera. He stood front and center beneath an enormous crystal chandelier, his rich tenor voice filling the room. At one point, he extended his left hand for dramatic effect, singing the emotional aria: *Che gelida manina*.

When the performance ended, the room erupted into enthusiastic applause, at which time Marjorie opened the door, allowing Hans and Gus to duck into the wood-paneled study. Shortly after that, Alden's familiar laugh echoed outside. Several minutes passed before he finally entered the room, lugging three highball glasses and a half-filled bottle of Pappy Van Winkle's 23-Year-Old Family Reserve.

"I appreciate you gentlemen joining us on such short notice." Alden looked at Hans, then at Gus. "How was your flight in?" But before either one could answer, he glanced down at his hands. "Oh!" he said, "here!" He pushed the empty glasses against their chests. "Take these."

Hans and Gus took their glasses and stood there like a couple of campaigning pols with their hands out while Alden uncorked the bottle and poured into each one a generous measure of dark amber liquid. "*Pappy* is best enjoyed neat," he said with a guilty grin, recorking the bottle and setting it down on his desk.

Hans lifted his glass. "*Prost!*"

"To John Junior," Gus put in.

Alden flashed a smile over his shoulder on his way back to the door, echoing both toasts. He asked Marjorie to wait outside, then quietly pulled the door closed. He bolted it shut, leaving the three in solitude.

Alden turned, his smile gone. He eyed his two friends evenly as he sipped from his glass. "So," he said, thumbing them toward the sofa and chairs. He paused by his desk and fiddled with his laptop until Mahler's Symphony No. 9 in D Major resounded from the ceiling-mounted speakers. "*Why*—I imagine you'd like to know"—he cranked up the volume —"have I reactivated the two of you?"

Alden sat down in the armchair nearest his desk. Gus took one end of the sofa, Hans the other. Alden looked at them expectantly, eyes moving back and forth like he was watching a tennis match.

Hans kept silent, suspecting that Gus was about as "retired" as Alden was.

Gus grinned and went first. "If I had to guess, I'd venture you're planning to use your wife's money to make a move on the Wisconsin dairy business." He twirled his drink, passing it admiringly under his nose. "You probably figure"—he trailed off, squinting—"that your only hope is to get the two of us *leaders* of that particular industry, for lack of a better term ... handily out of the picture."

"Not exactly. But it does rankle that you two bastards get rich while the rest of us poor slobs have to work for a living."

"*Ha!*" Gus laughed out loud. He turned to Hans and said, "This from a guy living in an eighteen-million-dollar estate!"

Hans feigned a laugh and looked around at the luxurious floor-to-ceiling bookcases, noting the life-size oil portrait behind Alden's gilt-bronze Louis XV-style desk depicting a fair-haired beauty—a much-younger Mrs. Alden, he imagined—reclined on a couch with her twin red pharaoh hounds. He looked Alden in the eye. "Come spend a day *mit* either one of us. *Ja,* either one! We'll show you who's working."

Gus's head tilted back briefly as he let escape a chuckle. Turning to Hans, he said, "Tell him how long you've been at it."

"Summer of sixty-three," Hans replied with considerable pride.

Alden held his jaw as if he were about to laugh. "You've had your dairy for forty years?" He creased his brow. "Christ, Hans! And how many cows did you start with?"

"We started *mit* thirty." Hans showed a glint of worn, almost-white teeth. "Now, we have over five thousand Holstein milk cows *und* six thousand replacement heifers."

"Which, as I understand it, back in the eighties," Alden said, shaking his head and lifting his glass in awe, "you somehow miraculously managed to run from halfway around the world."

"*Ja,* so okay, we must be busy *wann* the corn is ripe—this is what we say."

"Easy to say," Gus snickered, "not so easy to do. Believe me, I found out the hard way."

Alden took another sip and looked directly at Hans. "Especially when you've already got your hands full running arms to the mujahedeen."

Hans shrugged.

"Or," Gus put in, "organizing opium caravans sneaking back to Pakistan to pay for them."

Hans should have at least attempted a laugh at the backhanded compliment.

Alden turned to Gus with a canny squint. "Why dwell in the past? What about you, Gus—how long have you been in the dairy business?"

Gus hooked his thumb in Hans's direction. "He's got me by twenty-six years. I didn't get in until after the Soviets left in eighty-nine."

"So you simply retired," Alden said, eyes sparkling beneath ironic eyebrows. "Gave it all up for Big Milk."

Gus let loose a quick snort. "Hey, time to move on."

Hans kept his thoughts to himself.

"Most people swing and miss," Alden added. "You seem to have hit the ball quite squarely."

"It's a gift," Gus shrugged. "What can I say? I've always prided myself on being able to recognize a good thing when I see it. Hans showed me that you don't have to be original in this country to get rich. You know what they say about pioneers—most of them end up face down in the dirt with a dozen arrows sticking out of their backs."

"How's your Pashtu?" Alden asked Gus, leaning a little toward him in his chair.

"*Ba halwa goftan dahan shirin namishawad.*"

Alden looked at Gus suspiciously. "Which is to say what?"

"The mouth cannot taste sweet just by speaking sweetly."

"Ha!" Alden laughed. "True enough! Good to see you kept up with it." He turned to Hans and said, "What about yours?"

"I find it works just as well to let the youngsters do all the *chabbering.*"

"See that!" Gus laughed, "Sixty-three and I'm still a youngster!"

"I'll spare you my mangled Pashtu," Hans offered, shooting a scornful glance Gus's way, "but I seem to recall a Pashtu proverb that says, 'When the wolf turns gray, the young pups nip at his balls.'"

Alden appeared to be assessing them both as Hans sat there stoically and Gus laughed.

"Okay," Alden said as Gus's laughter died down, "time and the Holy Roman and apostolic bureaucracy march on." He leaned forward and put his drink down on the coffee table, ready for business. "A few years back, when forty-three was in office, Erik Prince approached the president with an offer to privatize everything from protection of agency personnel to snatch-and-grabs to running covert assignments. You remember that?"

"Prince *was* a Bushie," Gus said, nodding, seemingly ambivalent.

"It went deeper than Prince being a favorite son," Alden said. "The man does have impeccable timing, you've gotta give him that much. Our operations in Baghdad and Kabul had stretched us thin, as you know. We still are—stretched thin, that is. Which," he exhaled wearily, "brings us to our little get-together today."

His guests sat perfectly still, waiting.

"When we were running guns back in the eighties, you'll recall we all kept our focus on damaging the Soviets."

"Und that's what we did!" Hans blurted. When he looked up and noticed that he was the only one with a smile on his face, he added suspiciously, "The Soviets left, *Ja?"*

Alden quirked his mouth. "If you recall, most of the Pashtun warlords we worked with had been aggressive drug smugglers before we got there, working primarily in the south-eastern part of the country."

Gus showed the palms of his hands. "Our orders were clear. We weren't there to police the drug trade."

"Oh, I know, I know. No, the trouble is, the collapse of the Taliban set the stage for the resumption of widespread opium cultivation, which in turn served to turbo-charge the drug trade. We pretty much expected that outcome—no surprises there—we just didn't expect the scale to mushroom like it has. I don't know if you've been following the news but, ever since the Soviets left, opium production has exploded."

"And that surprises you?" Gus said, squinting sideways.

"No, I don't think that surprised any of us. What did catch us by surprise us was the sudden appearance of fentanyl, which they use to boost potency."

Hans shook his head, frowning, eyes cast downward.

"That's ..." Gus mused, "not good." He and Hans exchanged glances.

"Afghan heroin now supplies over ninety percent of the worldwide market. If you're talking about farm gate value, the figure's 1.4 billion US, give or take."

Gus put his head back and muttered under his breath, "That's startling." He looked up at Alden. "It's a patch of dirt. No education, especially for girls. No mental or general healthcare. What's the GDP per capita? Five hundred bucks?"

"*Und* what have we been doing about it?" Hans asked.

"The usual."

"*Ja,* meaning?"

"Meaning, nothing's been effective. Crop eradication isn't working. Interdiction isn't working. We've tried just about everything we can think of and all we've got to show for it is more poverty, more disease, more extremism, more violence, and, of course, more terror. Which is the whole reason we went back to that shithole in the first place."

"*Forget about it, Hans,*" Gus said, with a laugh, "*it's Afghanistan.*" He lifted his glass.

Hans shot him a confused look.

"*Forget about it, Jake,*" Gus said, "*it's Chinatown.*" He rolled his eyes. "It means there's nothing you can do about it. There's darkness in the world—always was, always will be."

Hans kept silent.

"I want to show you something," Alden said, stepping around behind his desk to reach for his wife's portrait. He pushed a hidden button at the lower right edge of the frame and pulled the portrait away from the wall, revealing a safe. Entering the code, he opened the heavy door and took out a red gym bag marked with a rampant puma and dropped it on his desk. "You know what that is?" he asked.

Gus crossed to the desk, looked to Alden for a nod to proceed, then unzipped the bag. He reached his hand in, squinting as he rummaged. "One, two, three, four ... five," he said, then tilted the bag open for Hans to see. "Five kilos of ... of *what*? Heroin?"

"Five kilos of fentanyl," Alden replied. He reached down, zipped up the bag, put it back in the safe, and locked it away. The portrait closed shut against the wall with a soft *click!*

He turned to his friends, his face set and suddenly tired. "That's enough poison to kill every man, woman, and child in Washington, DC three times over." His eyes shone with steely determination as he added, "That's two million people. Dead."

"Christ!" Gus blurted.

"To the community of free and responsible nations, obviously, we'd like to come across as a force for good in the world—responsible, dependable, respecting the rights of others. Living up to our founding promise."

"So, what's the answer?" Gus asked.

"The answer?" Alden shrugged. "Well, let's just say we've finally come around to the idea that maybe these transnational narco-cartels aren't as innocuous and ... *manageable* as first we thought. The fact that Al Qaeda, Hezbollah, FARC, and a whole host of increasingly violent gangs are now joining forces with them, not to mention the Russians, the Chinese, both of who've been keeping their hands in, stirring the pot ... that's a development that needs to be dealt with as a matter of national urgency. Let me be blunt—there are no easy solutions here. Certainly, no painless solutions."

Hans shook his head. He drained his glass and pressed it back onto the table.

"We've got a violent, metastasizing drug trade valued at a half-trillion dollars worldwide. In Afghanistan, the narco-dollars coming into the country are financing the Taliban and other insurgent groups, protected by officials at every level of government. Production and cultivation are up and the band keeps playing; Afghan people are starving and have no future, and the band plays on. But it's the geopolitical dimension that concerns us most." Alden looked at Hans and asked, "You ever read Gibbons?"

"*Ja*, sure."

He turned to Gus. "You?"

"You bet," he nodded, adding, *"The Decline and Fall of the Roman Empire."*

"Then you know that part of Gibbons's thesis was that Rome fell because of the spread of Christianity."

Hans and Gus listened with grim expressions.

"The clergy successfully preached the doctrines of love, devotion, and surrender. They discouraged society's active virtues and supplanted them with pacifism and weakness. In the end, the empire's military spirit was completely eviscerated, buried in the cloister while vast sums of money were lavished on the useless multitudes whose only social contribution was walking around expounding the merits of abstinence and chastity." Alden's disgust was apparent in the way he held his jaw.

Gus opened his mouth to speak but was cut short.

"Take my meaning—so often in life, it's the most insidious thing that takes down giants. Believe me, our enemies know this as well as we do. In our modern world, it's not the unshod son of a Jewish carpenter, but a few kilos of fentanyl. For those it doesn't kill outright, it enslaves. Changes the way they think; this world no longer matters to them. They lose their jobs, their families, their homes. Next thing you know, they're living in the streets. Millions of them. Then, rotting from within, our once-advanced society begins its slow but inexorable spiral right down the crapper."

There was a heavy pause.

"What's the plan?" Hans asked.

Alden answered with a distinct nod. "Leviticus."

"Leviticus?" Gus echoed, giving Hans a lopsided grin.

"Venezuela's the gateway. Milwaukee's one of the main drop points. You make your contacts. And, uh, gloves are off on this one. Don't worry about Queensberry Rules. The plan is—first we understand it, then we dismantle it."

Gus laughed. "Gotcha—gut it, burn it, salt the earth."

"We're playing in our own sandbox," Alden added. "And we let our enemies see us doing it. What is it the Pope says? *'The shepherd must have the smell of the sheep on him.'*"

Hans stood up and shook his head. "No, not me. I'm too old for this. Besides, this smacks of a project well outside the scope of the agency's charter." He glanced at Gus, his expression removing all doubt of his disdain. "I signed up for the US foreign intelligence service, not US organized crime."

Alden set his drink down on the table and calmly said, "Black ops, Hans. Just another dark project."

Hans, again, emphatically: "No! *Absolut!*"

Alden turned to Gus, who shrugged. "I guess I don't suffer from this one's scruples." Again, he glanced over at Hans, unable to mask his suspicion that there was more to Hans's refusal than taking the moral high ground.

"Good. Let me worry about the scruples," Alden replied, reaching for the door. "You get in there and do what you're good at—get the smell of the sheep on you." He halted halfway out the door. Turning back, he added, "'Our journey has turned out to be an orbital one: because we tore ourselves from the hold of violence, and into the hold of violence we have returned.'"

Hans groaned. Gus chuckled.

Hans waited until Alden had left the room and shut the door before he clicked his tongue and leaned over, glaring at Gus. "What the hell are we doing here? You take my advice; you run this by the director before signing on. When it comes to dark ambitions, Alden makes Thomas Cromwell look like a boy scout. And Solzhenitsyn ... that's a tired old trick. He quotes great men to appear great himself, virtuous men to appear like the prince of peace. Prince of darkness, more like. What he's asking us to do is illegal. Man's a liar. Stay away from him, Gus. This guy has grown more dangerous than he ever was."

"Come on, we're spooks, Hans; we live in the shadows, do we not?"

"Big difference between living in the shadows and blocking out the light." He held Gus's stare until the other man turned away. Satisfied, he stood. "Leviticus my ass."

6

January 28, 2018

Ambrosia Dairy
Kewaunee, Wisconsin

LILA STEPPED OUT OF HER STREET BOOTS AND PULLED ON A PAIR OF rubber replacements. Clasping them shut, she looked out across Ambrosia Dairy's large carousel milking parlor, where she spotted a well-built man of average height wearing a blue patch-pocket blazer over a gray cable-knit turtleneck and faded Levi's.

She stayed put, eyeing him up and down, wondering whether competitive business interests had become a point of friction between Holzinger and this younger, more vital-looking rival. Gus Ambrosia appeared to be in excellent physical shape for a man his age: broad-faced, with blue eyes and graying sandy hair, he was, Lila thought, somewhere in his early sixties, which meant that back when Wolf had worked for him as a teenager, roughly twenty years back, Gus would have been somewhere in his early forties. And now he headed up the most extensive commercial dairy operation in the country.

Nothing particularly flashy about either man, she noted. *Realists, both these guys; both know how to run a business and both obviously have the ambitions of much younger men. Something to prove, perhaps?*

The milking parlor sounded like a busy industrial plant: the massive carousel in the center of the barn space droned away as it made its careful revolutions, fully loaded with cows standing shoulder to shoulder, dairy employees talking while they worked, industrial groans echoing off the metal and concrete and bouncing around the sheet-metal building. Crossing to shake Gus's hand, she counted six rotary carousels.

He watched her lips move, evidently catching her counting. "Eighty cows," he said impatiently.

Lila did some mental math and lifted her eyebrows—480 *head.*

She explained her reason for wanting to meet him and he gave her a brusque nod, showing a begrudging willingness to oblige her in deference to her client, she figured, as it was obvious that he wasn't exactly thrilled by the intrusion.

"One of the questions I asked Mr. Holzinger," Lila said, stepping past her host as he held his office door, "was whether Wolf had been prone to any ... *impulsive* acts in the past."

"What did he say?" Gus asked, following her into his office and leaving the door open.

"He said no."

"Then there's your answer," he replied curtly.

Lila met the void in his eyes, annoyed. "What are you saying? 'No' is right because Hans Holzinger says it's right, or 'no' is right because you know it's right, personally?"

"'No' is right because I know, er—*knew* Wolf Holzinger. It's been a long time, but when he was in high school, Wolf used to come by to do my silos and drying tower. I'm sure Hans told you all about his abseiling business. Hans was very proud of everything his son did. He was the apple of his father's eye. Hell, I admired that kid—my wife and I went to see him in his school plays and musical revues." He cracked an unexpected grin at the reminiscence. "Saw him do 'Baby, It's Cold Outside' with a covey of young gals hanging on him. He was a great hit with the ladies, the wolf." He chuckled at saying it out loud. "And then there were his gymnastic accomplishments—no, Wolf was exceptional. He had a lot of dash. My wife and I have no children of our own, so you might say he was as close to being a son to me as I'll ever get. Can't explain it. Chemistry—we just hit it off."

Perhaps anticipating her next question, Gus said, "Hell, who knows why some people we like while others we can ... I don't know ... do *without*." He held her gaze, his face hard.

But she didn't flinch. She was here to do a job, and the idea that this guy—or any guy, for that matter—might be able to insult his way out of one of her interviews was laughable. She lifted her head into the light and quietly waited for an elaboration that didn't ring so manipulative and self-serving.

"You want the inside scoop on Wolf Holzinger?" Gus relented. "Kid grew up on a dairy farm. His father is a dairyman. A *Wisconsin* dairyman."

Lila looked at him, unimpressed.

"You know what our state motto is?"

Lila shook her head.

"*Forward*. That's resolve, indomitability, and progress all rolled up into one word. *Forward*. That means something around here."

Lila's gaze wandered to the pictures on the wall behind his desk: family photos, mostly; Ambrosia Dairy employee gatherings and barbeques; some old photographs that she guessed probably dated back to the early '80s. In one of the photos, a much younger Gus was standing alone next to a camouflaged helicopter, the flaxen-haired leading man sporting a black baseball cap with scrambled eggs on the visor and an old bomber jacket over his civilian khakis. Hard to determine anything special about the arid mountainous location; the surroundings had been cropped out. Across the top of the photo was an inscription in black felt-tip pen: *From your bros at A/A.*

"Where was this taken?" Lila asked.

"Afghanistan. A long time ago," he said without emotion. "And that," he added, a look of tenderness washing suddenly over him, "is a camou-flaged Russian Mi-17 helicopter."

"You flew Russian helicopters?" Lila leaned in for a closer look. "What branch of the service were you in?"

"I was more of a civilian advisor. Taliban flew Russian choppers. Helped us go in undetected. Besides, the Mi-17s were terrific in the 'hot-and-high' environment over there."

Civilian advisor. Lila considered the implications of those two seem-ingly innocuous words. So Gus had been a covert operator.

"You mentioned your 'drying tower' earlier—what do you do with a drying tower?"

"We produce powdered milk here in the plant."

"People still buy powdered milk?"

"We sell it to the confectionary business, but the bulk of it goes to Third-World countries where they don't have the luxury of refrigeration. Ship it in plastic-lined fifty-pound bags. We do about thirty million pounds a year."

Lila's gaze traveled to the centerpiece on the wall beneath the photo. It was an old walnut, brass, and enamel Air Force plaque, white angel's wings stretching up, wingtips vertical at the twelve o'clock. Between them at the base, a small antique shield with horizontal stripes of red, white, and blue and a motto: *Anything, Anytime, Anywhere, Profession-ally.* She wondered if maybe Hans suspected that Gus had been involved in his son's death. Maybe that was the reason he'd sent her here. It begged the question.

7

January 30, 2018

Headquarters, Chicago Police Department
Chicago, Illinois

LILA FINALLY CAUGHT UP WITH HER OLD FRIEND FROM CHICAGO'S
John Marshall Law School, Deputy Chief Cornell Williams, behind
closed doors in his small corner office downtown. She'd asked that they
keep their meeting and any resultant work product "eyes only," so
Williams (in his role as head of Chicago PD's Special Investigations Unit)
had limited the attendees to himself and one of his direct reports, the
commanding officer of the city's Crime Scene Investigations Unit, Detective Bobby Krzyskowski.

Krzyskowski had firsthand knowledge of the Holzinger case; he had
been the officer on duty the night Holzinger hit the pavement and the
first senior detective to arrive at the scene. "Fallen Man One,"
Krzyskowski had reported after receiving two simultaneous calls
alerting him to the two nearly identical falls occurring less than eight
miles apart. "That was one helluva mess. We put that case to bed and I

damn sure don't want to open it up again. It's done, it's over, we move on."

Standing there in the office in front of both men, Lila couldn't help comparing them. She watched the muscles in Krzyskowski's jaw flex as he narrowed his eyes at her.

Physically, Williams cut a tall, athletic figure in his dark blue slacks and starched white shirt. He looked strong, imposing, like he might have played in the NFL. He was a good-looking, middle-aged man with dark chocolate-toned skin and large brown eyes so bright that they seemed to glow when he looked at you. Add to that a well-shaped head shaved bullet-smooth set off by dark geometric horn rims and the ever-present whiff of soap. The silver oak leaves on his starched white collar indicated his rank as PD's deputy chief. Yeah, she thought, Cornell was imposing all around. While Lila had entered John Marshall right out of college, Cornell had entered law school as an adult student and had already spent years building up his career at the police department.

Krzyskowski was another kind of man entirely. He looked to be about ten years younger, with high, angular cheekbones; intelligent blue eyes; small, perfectly shaped ears; and an altogether disarming smile that was quick to go slightly off-kilter. She figured that he was likely in his late thirties. He came across as a clean-shaven smart ass, with thick dark hair buzzed close on the sides. Unlike his boss's, the oak leaves on Krzyskowski's collar points were gold instead of silver. Thanks to her old man being a Navy orthopod, Lila knew the difference between the ranks of commander and lieutenant commander. Silver leaves, silver calls the shots—her old friend Cornell was the Big Dog. And that, so far as Lila was concerned, was a damned good thing, as she could never bring herself to trust a guy with a lazy smile.

Lila and Krzyskowski sat down on the two wood-slat chairs in front of Williams's neatly arranged desk. Facing them, at the boss's back, was an old cork bulletin board. The deputy chief had hung assorted newspaper clippings, various black-and-white mugshots, and department memos around a large Chicago "heat map" variously stuck with multi-colored push pins. There was a Chia Pet-like concentration of pins on Chicago's

Southside, she noticed without surprise. Urban blight—poverty and despair were responsible for so much pain and suffering in and around the Southside neighborhoods. *Hmm, I like the corkboard idea,* Lila thought.

Williams sat down and rolled his chair up close to his desk. He leaned in and said, "I don't know what to tell you, Lila." His voice subdued, official. "SIG—Special Investigations Group—says it's a coincidence." He looked at Krzyskowski.

Krzyskowski nodded slowly. "Coincidence," he echoed, his thoughts evidently somewhere else. Snapping out of it, he added, "Listen, I'll tell you straight up—this is settled business so far as I'm concerned. There's absolutely no association between the two victims. Besides the happenstance of the falls, you have to consider why each man was outside a highrise in a very precarious position in the middle of a very cold night. What could it be besides coincidence? It's weird, yes, but to see some conspiracy between those two incidents is to let emotion cloud your logic."

"Maybe it is, maybe it isn't," Lila replied in a measured tone, "too early for me to argue one way or another. Look, I'm simply here for a paying client. I have no argument with a 'reasonable conclusion.' Meanwhile, I've got to follow any lead I can find. That's my job."

"You're reaching," Krzyskowski said with a snort. "There's nothing there."

Lila had been gazing at Krzyskowski's mouth as he spoke, watching the flash of his teeth through his lopsided grin. Now she turned her eyes expectantly, eyebrows arched, back to Cornell.

The older man was thumbing through the police report before him, reacquainting himself with the facts. He looked up from the report and glanced over at Krzyskowski. "Just ... give her what she needs."

"Yeah, sure. Why not." Krzyskowski flashed his cockeyed smile. "I'm eager to see what our super sleuth here comes up with—hey, whatever Chicago PD can do to help. We serve and protect."

A more disingenuous offer Lila was convinced she'd never heard. Nonetheless, she jumped in: "I do have a couple of questions."

Cornell looked up from his case file. "Fire away."

"I'd like to talk to any other witnesses who may have seen him fall that night."

"Easy. The principal witness—since she was the last one to see him alive—is a med student—Russian gal," Krzyskowski said. "I'll get you her number."

"Already have it," Lila replied, flashing a tight-lipped smile. "I've called several times already. Can't seem to get hold of her."

"Keep tryin'," Krzyskowski grinned and expelled his breath; it was almost a chuckle. "Nobody ever said police work was glamorous. You don't have to be good, just persistent."

"What else?" Cornell sighed, quirking the corner of his mouth.

"The girlfriend. The deceased's father tells me they met at a gala in DC when his son was at Georgetown Law. Who is she and where can I find her?"

"Name's Sofia Castellanos," Krzyskowski replied. "She works at First Options."

"Thanks," Lila said, before glancing at Cornell. "So, um ... instead of us taking all the time for me to ask questions and you to look it up, any chance I could ... just peruse the file myself?"

Krzyskowski raised his eyebrows as if to say *You believe this woman?*, but Cornell just smirked. "I'm okay with that," he said, closing the file and sliding it across the desk.

Lila tried not to smile too much—not until she added, "And the Breem file too?"

8

January 31, 2018

The Ceres Cafe
Chicago Board of Trade Building

THE CAB PULLED TO THE CURB BENEATH THE TRACKS IN FRONT OF the Chicago Board Options Exchange. Lila handed the cabbie a twenty and climbed out as a passing El clattered and banged noisily overhead. Before she could close the cab door, a pregnant lady rushed toward it, snapping at her distracted child, who was mesmerized by the passing train—*"Get in! Get in!"*—Lila holding the door for them before setting off, weaving her way through a rowdy mob of futures and options traders at the corner, grabassing around until the light changed and the boisterous crowd spilled out onto the crosswalk.

She pushed through the chrome and glass turnstile that opened onto the Options Exchange's foyer. As soon as she was through, she got jostled by another boisterous throng swamping the exit, the rushing constituents a repulsive blur of colorful trading jackets. She threaded her way through the crowd and took the elevator to First Options' seventh-floor offices, where she found Sofia Alejandra Castellanos's private office surrounded by a vacant warren of dull, gray, low-partitioned cubicles.

Popping up from the desk closest to her boss's door, a young woman in a brightly colored traditional African dress introduced herself as Ms. Castellanos's customer support liaison and explained that Ms. Castellanos was out to lunch and wouldn't be back for an hour or so.

Lila nodded and took out her cellphone. Determined to reach the elusive Marina Resnick once and for all, she dialed the number yet again—and when, once more, she got her voice message, she said, as evenly as possible, "Marina, this is Lila Piper. This is the, let's see, the *fourth or fifth* message I've left. Very important we speak. Please call me back at 555-486-5194 and let me know a convenient time for us to meet. I'll come to you, wherever that may be. Thanks!" Lila returned her phone to her bag with perhaps a little more kinetic energy than she'd intended.

Evidently sensing Lila's frustration, Castellanos's liaison gave an apologetic smile. "Look," she said, "if you want to try dropping in on her, you can probably catch her at the Ceres Cafe."

"Is that the restaurant in the Board of Trade building?" Lila asked.

"It is. Did you come in on Van Buren?"

"I did."

"Then right where you came in. Across the street, then straight through the building to the main entrance on Jackson."

Backtracking, Lila once again crossed Van Buren, this time in the opposite direction, and entered the Board of Trade's Art Deco high-rise. She followed the towering marble hall toward the main entrance, her footfalls echoing beneath the vaulted ceiling.

When she reached the restaurant, she spotted two women seated at a small table by the bar, talking to a dark-haired guy wearing a forest-green trading jacket. Both Latinas, one stunning, with a dark complexion and thick dark hair. A little zaftig, Lila thought. The other woman looked like a model, tall and slender, with a gorgeous cover-girl face and luxuriously curled brown hair cascading down beyond her shoulders.

As Lila made her way toward them, she strained to catch the gist of their conversation. One of the women resembled the photo she had glimpsed in Sofia's office.

The trader was well put together, his thinning brown hair casually raked off to one side and, in profile at least, he had a square, clean-shaven jaw.

The model shot her companion an incredulous glance, then turned and gave him a you-gotta-be-kidding-me scowl. "I'm sorry," she said in a heavy Spanish accent, "we're having a private conversation."

"Free country," he replied. "Don't let me stop you." His eyebrows did a disarming little jig as he stood his ground, stuffed his hands in his pockets, rocked back-and-forth on the balls of his feet, and grinned.

Lila snorted at the guy's unmitigated gall.

He looked at the model's companion and said, "Well, Sofie, my dear, I'm waiting. You gonna sit there and let your ol' buddy go down in flames?" Lila gave a small smile—it was definitely the right table.

"Oh, I don't know," the woman replied, her lips parted in a smile, "I'm rather enjoying the spectacle." She chuckled and, seeing his wavering smile, rolled her eyes. "Oh, all right. Orfilia, this is Rafe Dryer. Rafe, Orfilia Campos. We're cousins. She's visiting from Caracas. Rafe is an—"

"Options trading *legend*," he quickly put in, extending his hand.

"Please!" the model fired back, recoiling. When he just stood there, hand falling slowly to his side, she said in a blasé way, "I appreciate the"—she drew in an exasperated breath—"the *effort*, but seriously, we are having a private conversation."

"Then," he said, retreating with a slight bow, "I'll leave you two ladies to your privacy."

Lila stepped out of his way as he passed her on his way out. He shot a final, defeated wave to his buddies slouching around the bar.

The hostess materialized by Lila's side and said in a thick Irish brogue, "Will you be having lunch, dear?" Following Lila's gaze back to the Latinas' table, she said, "Or would you be looking for someone in particular?"

Lila flashed an appreciative smile. "Actually, I am looking for someone." Her eyes surveyed the room once again before settling on the table directly across from the bar. "I think ... possibly, right over there. Sofia Castellanos?"

"Oh, that'd be Sofie, sure enough." The hostess stepped out of the way. "Go on with you then, take the weight off your legs."

Lila let out a small, dry chuckle and went over to introduce herself.

The dark-haired beauty leaned in and spoke in a hushed tone as Lila reached the table. Both women looked up at her.

"Hi, um ... My name is Lila Piper," she said, gripping her bag in front of her with both hands. "I'm—"

"Sofia," the dark-haired beauty replied without rising from her seat. Her eyebrows went up as she waited to hear the reason for yet another interruption.

"Nice to meet you. So sorry to intrude, but ... If you have a few minutes, I'd like to talk to you about Wolf Holzinger."

"*Wolf!*" Sofia said. Her head fell forward and momentarily hung over the remains of her half-eaten Reuben sandwich.

In the intervening silence, the model popped up out of her chair, hastily snatched her outsized shoulder bag from the nearby chair, and said, "I have to run." She turned to Sofia, her chin rising slightly. "We'll finish this up later." When she stepped away, Lila noticed two Hispanic bodyguards—thugs, their expensive suits too tight across their muscled chests—rising from among the crowd to follow her out.

"Call me," Sofia called after her.

Orfilia lifted an acknowledging hand but didn't look back.

Lila rested a hand on the empty chair. "May I join you?"

Rousing herself, Sofia said, "Sure. Why not? Wasn't expecting to hear that name. Please." She motioned Lila into the chair.

"Thank you." Lila plunged her hand into her bag and came out with her gold scrollwork card case. She took out an embossed business card and handed it to Sofia before sliding into the vacant chair. "So, uh ... What's with the goons?"

"What, Orfilia?" Sofia glanced back toward the entrance and chuckled. "What can I say? Orfilia loves an entourage." She looked down at the card. "Savage, Lutz, Finnegan, and Foehl. So, what is it you do? Are you an insurance lawyer?"

"No."

"Following up an insurance claim?"

"No, this has nothing to do with insurance. It's a private matter."

Sofia's eyes narrowed. "It's his father, isn't it?"

Lila set her bag down on the floor. "Probably best to start with some context." She drew a deep breath and exhaled. "Yes, I am working for Mr. Holzinger."

Sofia uttered a little laugh. "Surprised it took him so long," she muttered.

Lila offered a non-committal smile, waited to make sure that Sofia had finished what she was saying, and then launched in. "Mr. Holzinger is troubled by the number of—I guess we could call them 'red flags' surrounding his son's fatal fall. He thinks there may be something odd about his officially accidental death. Something PD may have overlooked."

"What are you saying?" Sofia asked, her head slightly tilted, her eyes narrowed. "You mean that Wolf didn't accidentally fall to his death? That he was ..."

"I'm not advancing any theories or making any pronouncements today. Let's just say we're exploring the possibility that there may have been something peculiar about his death, something the detectives missed. Mr. Holzinger simply wants a fresh set of eyes to look into it, that's all."

"Yeah, well," Sofia groaned, "'peculiar' is putting it mildly. Did he fall? Was he pushed? Did he jump? Was he up there alone? Already beat myself half to death with those chaotic thoughts."

A waitress appeared at the table, nodded to Lila, and said, "You ordering, dear?"

Lila shook her head, prompting the woman to put her black leather bill-presenter down on the table. "No rush, hon," she said with a warm smile.

"Thanks Nora," Sofia replied. She gazed idly at the woman's retreating back before reaching for the bill.

"And have you come to any conclusions?" Lila asked.

"My only conclusion is ... he screwed up," she said with a gentle sadness. "He shouldn't have been up there. It was stupid. He suffered an inexplicable lapse in judgment and he died a tragic death. That's all I can say about it."

Lila absorbed the remark and then nodded. "I've been asked," she continued quietly, "to gather any additional information that might help corroborate or otherwise put to rest Mr. Holzinger's suspicions of foul play. For instance, what can you tell me about Wolf? It would be helpful if we could start there."

Her initial wariness softening, Sofia leaned forward on one elbow, looked down at her plate, and unenthusiastically pushed it aside.

"What can I say? He was a hustler, an entrepreneur. He owned two businesses: a limo company and a tanning salon that he'd just bought."

Lila raised her eyebrows.

"Wolf was doing well for himself," Sofia quickly added. "Things were finally starting to pick up, business-wise."

"'*Finally* starting to pick-up?'" Lila repeated. "Had he been struggling financially, prior to that?"

"No more than anyone else our age, or in his position. You know, launching a new business, working as his own boss. Trying to escape his father's shadow. '*You miss one hundred percent of the shots you don't take,*' Wolf used to say." A wistful smile briefly lifted the shadows from her face.

"One of the news articles I read used the term 'jilted.'" Lila looked at Sofia like an understanding big sister.

"I know, I hate that! I *hate* it! Makes me feel like I'm the one who killed him. You know, if I'd only answered his call." Tears clouded her eyes. "What an awful way to die. I can't get that horrible image out of my head. This whole thing's been an absolute nightmare."

"Had you two split?"

A second's pause for a quick dab of her rapidly blinking eyes. "We did."

"May I ask why?"

Sofia gazed away, beyond the entrance, apparently beyond this present moment. After a short pause, she snapped back into focus. "He was getting clingy and jealous at the end. I deal with these guys every day, guys who make a lot of money. I think Wolf felt 'less than,' if you know what I mean. Things were starting to pick up, but he had only the one car in his limo business when what he wanted was to big-time it with a fleet of vehicles. It just got to where I couldn't take it anymore, the never-ending interrogations, the accusations—*Where have you been? Who were you seeing? Why didn't you answer your phone? Why you always hangin' out with all these fucking traders?*" She looked at Lila and sighed. "It gets old. You should have seen his face when I took back my key. It was like it was the end of the world."

"*Were* you seeing someone else?"

Sofia flashed an impatient expression and looked away. Finally, she straightened up in her chair, brushed her hair with her fingertips, and said, "Truth is, I decided that I prefer the company of women."

Lila's eyes widened involuntarily and, for some inexplicable reason, she felt her face flush.

"Does that shock you?" Sofia asked.

"Nope. Completely un-shockable, that's me." Lila flashed a little smile and tried to recover herself.

"That's a curiously ambiguous response." Sofia grinned as if with newly awakened interest.

Lila pressed on, determined not to let this exotic beauty, sitting so close to her, make her blush again. "Let's get back to Wolf. You said he felt 'less than.' So, would it be safe to say that, although his businesses were doing well, maybe they weren't living up to his expectations?"

"That's a fair statement. As I said, things were only starting to pick up for Wolf. Prior to that ... no, not so much."

"Is it possible that he may have been getting pressured by someone?" Lila leaned closer. "Someone behind the scenes, perhaps. You see that a lot with these self-made types." She remembered bitterly her father's business and legal struggles. "Maybe they had no idea what they were getting into when they started; you know, they're not hitting their targets and it finally dawns on them that they're under the gun, that they're in over their head. That maybe there's no way out. They act out. Then ... well, then comes the inevitable trouble at home."

"What are you saying?" Sofia slumped back in her seat. "That that's why they're not hitting their targets?" Her eyes suddenly lost their sparkle. "Great! Something else to feel guilty about!"

"No," Lila said quickly, "you misunderstand me. It's the other way around. They're getting pressured at work, which they then bring home with them. It's the pressure that causes the problems, not the other way around. Although it sometimes works that way too, I suppose." She paused for a moment to let that sink in, then added, "Like I said, after almost ten years of non-stop investigative work, I feel like maybe I've seen it all." This was the turn of the screw that Lila used to end all her investigative interviews; she liked to leave her interviewees with the nagging thought that she'd been at this a while, that she was experienced and savvy enough to know the difference between a gentle summer breeze and plain hot air.

Sofia glanced down at the opalescent butterfly on the face of her iWatch. "I'm sorry," she said quietly, "I've gotta get back. I told you, it just got too much for me. What can I say? I'm human. I have a human heart." A tight-lipped smile and eyebrows up. "That's all there is to it."

"Okay. I understand," Lila said. Getting to her feet, she added, "I wonder, would it be possible for us to finish this over dinner?"

"Sorry," Sofia said with a pursed smile. "Plans."

"How about this weekend? Sunday afternoon? Brunch?"

Sofia looked at her and hesitated, her face unreadable. Her gaze wandered off towards the entrance before she turned back to Lila. "We could do that."

9

February 6, 2018

Angela Breem's Apartment
Lawndale, Illinois

THE WICKER PARK LOCATION ANGELA HAD PICKED OUT WITH her University of Life sponsor's help was working out beyond her wildest dreams. Situated among the trendy vintage stores, dessert shops, singles bars, and indie shops, Angela's shop, *African Queen Atelier*, sold traditional Ghanaian wedding dresses and headscarves featuring bold, brightly colored geometric patterns. Her sponsor's fundraising skills (honed as the founding member of Lawndale's principal community organizing group) had proven invaluable. Thanks to her skill at finding high-net-worth individuals to finance Angela's dream, the shop had become all the rage among affluent women of color not only in Chicago but, thanks to the Internet, all over the country, and now, for the first time in Angela's thirty-two years of life, she was making money—*real*, honest money. In fact, she was doing so well that, if things continued at the current rate, she would be able to move out of the projects in the next few months.

Angela frequently asked her sponsor to reveal the identity of her shop's anonymous backer so she could send him a letter and thank him personally—the man was, after all, a saint. He had changed her life for the better, that much was obvious, and she wanted to express the depth of her gratitude.

"I'm sorry," her sponsor explained when she broached the subject, "he wants to remain anonymous. You're showing your appreciation by focusing on growing your business and supporting the community. He's big into the whole 'pay it forward' thing."

"I can do that," Angela relented. "I mean, I *want* to do that. Like I told you, I had absolutely nothing to do with Louis's drug trafficking. All I know is that he had some big business contact up in Milwaukee that he was always going on about. I forget his name."

Her sponsor's eyebrows shot up in surprise. "He told you the guy's name?"

"Yeah, but hon, the way Louis could talk, I had to filter out half of what he was saying to keep hold of my sanity. Besides, you know how focused on my work I've been these last few months. That's all I think about, lately—fabrics, thread colors, sewing machines, sergers to prevent fraying—I mean, I had no idea what they were up to. Zero. When I found out he was dealing drugs from one of the guys in the building"—she lowered her gaze, her smile fading—"my reaction was immediate—I locked his ass out of the apartment. That's the night he fell. You know, he was trying to climb back in. He didn't know I'd already flushed his stash down the toilet."

When Angela and her sponsor weren't laboring over her business, they were donating their time to the community's "RJ" team. The concept underpinning "Restorative Justice" was to repair the damage caused by crime and violence by getting all those touched by it, including the criminals themselves, to sit down at the same table, address the causes, and work to put things right. And that's what Angela intended to do tonight—close up shop early so she could get to her weekly RJ team meeting on time and at least try to make amends for all the damage Louis had done. RJ's mission statement had become her own: *The best way to help someone is to restore their dignity by making them able to offer something back to the community.*

Running a few minutes ahead of schedule, she swung by her apartment. She was standing in front of the bathroom mirror, straightening her newly designed bright yellow headscarf, when there was a knock on the door.

"Mercy! Now that just about gave me a heart attack!" she said to her bonneted reflection. "Just a minute!" she called out loud, crossing the clean but dilapidated floor.

A child's voice answered. "Is me, Ms. Breem!"

"Darnell?" she said. She peeked through the peephole at nine-year-old Darnell Grant from two floors down. "What are you doing up here, hon?"

"Mamma says to tell you man's here what's got you a package."

Angela unlocked the door and said, "Ah, my new fabric!"

Looking down at the empty-handed little boy, she smiled and asked warmheartedly, "Where's my package, sugar?"

"I dunno," the child replied, shifting on his feet.

Angela squinted down at the boy and cringed, watching him pinching at his crotch with his thumb and forefinger. He shrugged a few times distractedly, rocking from side to side with stiffened legs.

"Darnell, do you need to use the restroom?"

"Yeah, I gotta pee, Ms. Breem. Real bad."

"Well, don't just stand there, come on! And don't you dare pee on my nice clean floor!" Her eyes tracked him as he scurried off to the bathroom. She waited to hear the toilet flush and then held the door open for him as he headed back into the corridor.

"Thank you, Ms. Breem."

"You're welcome, sugar," she replied with a warm smile. She had the door half-shut when she spotted a short, muscular Hispanic man in a brown UPS uniform pulling a large, mattress-sized box on a four-wheel cart down the heavily graffitied breezeway. When he turned to look at her, the thin cigarillo hanging from his lips dropped ash onto the sleeve of his brown jacket. He flicked it off with his free hand.

"What do you have there?" She craned her neck, sizing up the box's length and width. "What is that? A mattress?"

The man stopped at the door and turned to face her. "Breem?" he asked.

"*Mrs.* Angela Breem," she said with a sober nod.

He reached into his pocket and pulled out a small plastic sandwich bag. Angela squinted as he held it up by one end, letting it unfurl with an uneven, flopping movement.

Angela's eyes shot wide. A finger's width of pure white crystalline powder lined the bottom of the bag. "Drugs!" she said, recoiling, shaking her head, "oh no you don't! Get away from here!" She leaned into the door to shut it, but he pushed his way into the apartment and, before she could let the scream stuck in her throat out, he grabbed her, his hands wrapping around her neck. He kicked the door closed behind him. As he lowered her to the floor, her eyes bulging, she scratched frantically at his arms, trying to peel them away. Within seconds, she gasped, pawed one last time at his hands, and went limp. By the time the drugs forced into her unconscious body took hold, she was dead.

February 6, 2018

1100 North Dearborn Apartments
Chicago, Illinois

HAVING NO LUCK HAILING A CAB, LILA CLICKED OPEN UBER AND ordered a ride to take her back to her office on LaSalle. As soon as she'd buckled herself into the back seat of the blue metallic Prius that had picked her up in front of the CBOE building, she was on the phone, trying, yet again, to get in touch with Marina Resnick.

No answer.

Ten minutes later, she was standing in the building's wood-paneled lobby, telling the doorman that she had come to visit Marina Resnick. While she was talking, the doorman reached for the phone, punched in a number, waited a few moments, then hung up. "She's not answering. I'm sorry, but I don't think Ms. Resnick's here. Fact, now that I think about it … I haven't seen her in a while."

Lila glanced over at the large, modern oil canvases on the walls bracing the seating area before turning again to the doorman. Patiently, she explained the reason she had come, how she was a PI investigating the tragic death that had occurred back in October. "Do you know about that?"

"No, ma'am. But hang on a second," he said with an understanding nod. He picked up the phone, punched in a number, and said, "Patty— James. We've got a visitor who would like to see the place."

Lila gave him an appreciative smile. "Thank you," she silently mouthed.

A moment later, an attractive young brunette, mid-to-late twenties, hair down to her shoulders, came around the corner wearing a gray stretch wool suit and white silk blouse. After a quick introduction, she said, "Let's take a look around."

Lila followed her into the center elevator. She counted one fish-eye camera in the lift and, when she stepped out into the sixteenth-floor corridor, two more, one at each end of the hall.

Marina's apartment was located halfway between them, her guide told her as they disembarked. "I notice you have a camera in the elevator and two more on this floor." Lila quickly snapped pictures. "Same deal on all twenty floors?" she asked.

"Yeah. We have a new full HD CCTV security system," she said proudly.

"How new?"

"Two years. Late 2016 we put it in. Whatever the man's reason," Patty said with a groan as they drew up to Marina's apartment, "it doesn't bode well for his intentions." She smirked and gave the door several loud knocks.

No answer.

She tried the doorbell, which resonated loudly beyond the door.

"Do you think we could have a look at the roof?" Lila asked after a second ring went unanswered. "I'd like to get a view of where the incident presumably took place."

"Sure. Although"—Patty looked at her askance—"I don't know why you would say *presumably* took place. The roof is the spot he climbed down from." She nodded to the security cameras and accompanying

LED lights on the way back to the elevator. "They all work with motion detectors," she added over her shoulder.

Lila snapped a close-up picture as they passed by the CCTV rig in the corner. "So you have footage?"

"No."

That was *not* the answer Lila had been expecting.

Back in the elevator, Patty hit the button marked *Sundeck*.

"Don't you have cameras on the roof?" Lila asked.

"We do."

"Then how did he avoid detection?"

"That ... I do not know."

"You said you installed the new system two years ago. Is that widely known?" Lila asked. "The motion detection, the high-res cameras?"

"You bet." Patty gave an emphatic nod. "It's one of our key selling points. We have a lot of single women living here. Printed right there in black and white on all our marketing materials. You can see for yourself in the lobby. We've got it posted in one of those clear acrylic sign holders on the coffee table. The first thing you see when you're waiting to tour the building—other than the paintings, of course."

Lila nodded absently, trying to envision how Wolf got up to the roof without being caught on camera.

They stepped out onto the windy sundeck. *"Grrr, it's cold!"* Lila said, bundling herself against the chill.

Two distinct spaces divided the rooftop: on the developed side was a sundeck paved with terracotta tiles, a dozen bare trees lining the perimeter planted in clay pots, a scattering of black metal tables and chairs beyond surrounded by a waist-high black iron fence. The undeveloped side featured an open utility space with a large brick smokestack in the approximate center, a squat green TV box off to one side, and a fire-escape, its handrails curling over the edge.

"Cameras on the fire escape?" Lila asked.

"Of course."

"Mind if I have a look at that CATV box?"

"Go ahead."

Lila stepped through the gate in the fence and went over to the utility box. It was neither locked nor frozen shut, so she easily popped the lid open. The mass of cables coiled inside gave her pause; there was nothing long enough to reach five stories down. Of course, she reminded herself, it had been three months since Wolf fell to his death. She snapped a few pictures of the interior and pocketed her cell before snapped the box shut, straightening up, and looking back at Patty, her eyes narrowed. "Were there any reports of any TV or telephone or internet outages that night? Maybe the next morning?"

Patty shook her head slowly. "Don't know. We don't keep those kinds of records. If we get a call like that, we refer it immediately to the cable company. You could check with the cable provider—that's RCN."

Lila thought back on the police file she'd perused in Cornell's office, trying to recall any reference to contact made to RCN Telecom. "Yeah ... yeah, I'll do that," she said at last. "Let me take a couple of pics over the railing before I go." She went to the iron fence and leaned over the side above where she guessed Marina's apartment was likely situated and gazed down the twenty stories to the street below. The view, combined with the fresh memory of the crime scene photos, gave her a touch of vertigo.

"You take a lot of pictures in your line of work," Patty said affably as Lila stashed her phone away and headed for the elevator.

"Gotta cover your bases. A lot of mundane legwork, and ninety-five percent of it doesn't pan out to anything."

Back in the lobby, Lila thanked Patty and James for their help and stepped through the revolving door. Once outside, she walked over to where Wolf had most likely hit the pavement and looked up at the distant towers. She snapped another couple of pictures.

That done, Lila decided to walk home, since the building was, after all, only a half-mile from her place. Something wasn't adding up, she told herself, walking with the crowd down Michigan Avenue, her collar raised against the icy wind. She came away from the building without answers, but with a gut feeling that old man Holzinger was right—there was an enigma in here somewhere. All she had to do was find it.

Later, in her apartment, cupping a hot mug of Earl Grey in her hands and wondering why she hadn't seen any mention of an attempt to contact RCN in the police file, Lila set down her drink and called the cable company herself. When she finally got through to customer service and inquired about the building's service logs, she was told, due to the ninety-day lapse from the date of interest, that it would take "No more than two to three weeks." The customer service rep was chirpy and almost too polite. "Just give us your name and number, and we'll call you as soon as it comes in."

11

February 7, 2018

The Donnelley Biological Sciences Learning Center, University of Chicago
Chicago, Illinois

LILA STEPPED THROUGH THE ENTRANCE TO THE DONNELLEY Biological Sciences Learning Center and tried to duck the mob of students crisscrossing in front of the help desk at the center of the room. She wove her way through the jabbering crowd, coming to a stop in front of the ginger-haired young man with the protruding Adam's apple standing behind the desk.

"Excuse me." When he looked up, Lila smiled and said, "Hey—I wonder if you can help me. Do you know where I can find Marina Resnick? She's a first-year med student."

"Yeah." The young man gave a brief smile before frowning. "No, we're not allowed to do that."

Lila let out an irritated sigh.

"You check the campus directory? Try giving her a buzz?" He turned to acknowledge a passing student. "Hey, dude ..."

"Oh, I've tried. Believe me," Lila said, speaking to the man's profile, turning exasperatedly to survey the passing backpack-burdened crowd. "I've left a half-dozen messages, at least."

A young Asian woman, standing at the end of the counter, near enough to overhear their conversation, threw Lila a glance. "You're looking for Mysh?" She frowned, lips tight. "Marina Resnick?"

Lila nodded.

"What about?"

"I work for a local law firm," Lila replied. "Need to talk to her about the fatal fall she witnessed." When that failed to register with the woman, Lila said, "Some guy fell to his death after rappelling down her building a few months back."

Instantly, the woman's face brightened. *"Jeez, yeah!"*

"So you heard of that."

"Yeah, she told me about that!" She paused and scrutinized Lila more closely. A half beat later, she said, "Try the greenhouse. Mysh loves to study in the greenhouse."

"Greenhouse," Lila murmured, looking around blankly. "And where ... ?"

"Rooftop," the young woman said, motioning toward the bank of elevators across the room.

Lila nodded her thanks and turned away. When she stepped out of the elevator, she followed the yellow arrows painted on the asphalt, zigzagging her way around several large aluminum shelters and a Rube Goldberg arrangement of HVAC ductwork until she glimpsed the greenhouse's panes glinting in the morning sun like cut diamond. She could see no one through the glass, only a fine mist that hung over the mass of plants inside like a tropical rain cloud.

Lila edged into the building, quickly shutting the door behind her to shut out the cold. Inside, the air was warm and damp with a slight tang of manure, but the prevalent scent was sweet and earthy. Other than the hush of sprinklers, the interior was silent and appeared vacant.

"Marina?" she tentatively called out, scanning the apparently empty room.

Venturing in among the rows of raised planters, she called out again, "*Mysh!*"

A pile of books and papers suddenly spilled noisily out into the center aisle. A moment later, a young woman peeked out from behind the planter she'd been leaning against, blue eyes bright over the top of her oversized red readers. She looked a little mousy, but in a good way—cute, with a smallish face and pointed features.

"Yes?" Marina replied before muttering something to herself as she scrabbled for her scattered papers.

Lila crossed to the planter. "My name's Lila. I've been trying to get ahold of you for the last few days. I've left a lot of messages."

The look in Marina's eyes said she had not armed herself against this self-admitted stalker.

"Well, anyway." Lila peered out through the greenhouse's segmented window panes, some of the corners edged with snow and frost roses. "You certainly picked a great spot to study up here."

"I'm liking the view," she replied, still collecting her things. "And, umm, it's quiet."

"No, I get it." Lila nodded, inhaling the loamy air.

With her books and papers gathered together, Marina got up, stretched, and asked, "So, what, umm—you said you were trying to reach me?"

"I'd like to talk to you about the guy who fell from your building. Just a few questions."

"Ah, I see."

"I know you spoke with the police. Filed a report."

"I did." She juggled her papers to get a better grip. "The nice man, the ... umm, *detective* from that night, he comes to see me yesterday."

"Krzyskowski, by any chance?"

"Yes, this is him—Krzyskowski. Yes, umm, in fact, I was thinking of giving him a call."

"I can't believe this guy!" Lila muttered to herself, looking away. She drew a deep breath. "Okay." She gazed back into Marina's uncertain eyes. "So, now you got me curious!"

"I think maybe I may have mischaracterized what I was telling him I see that night. Mischaracterized, umm ... misremembered, misspoke." She rocked her head side to side, cringing apologetically. "The night the poor man when he falls."

Lila had the good sense to keep quiet. A trick Savage had taught her long ago—*"Try more ear and less mouth. More elephant and less hippopotamus."* She followed Marina's gaze out across the eastern edge of the University of Chicago campus, past the advanced physics lab, the particle accelerator, the Army's research lab, out across Jackson Park's dormant brown grass dotted with thick clusters of wiry bare trees, past the Museum of Science and Industry, and out to Lake Michigan's gray, scalloped shoreline.

The young med student seemed momentarily distracted, her face angled down, her eyebrows knotted together. At length, she expelled a breath and said, "It was three o'clock in the morning."

"That's one of the questions I had for you; you're sure about the time?"

"Yes. Absolutely. Three o'clock it was exactly." Marina turned back to face her. "I have wall clock that chimes every hour."

"I hate that!" Lila put in.

Marina nodded. "This is when I see him. At first, I'm thinking maybe he is standing there in my living room."

Lila's brow furrowed as an odd image flashed in her mind—Wolf's silhouette partially obscured by shadow near Marina's apartment window, his body cautiously approaching.

Marina shrugged. "I had turned lights out. I was *soo* tired." She shot Lila a probing look. "Mid-term exams. You know how this goes, burning the candle on both sides. Too much with the caffeine, too little sleep." She paused.

"For me it was law school." Lila grimaced. "Been there, done that."

"So you know." Marina gave another weak shrug. "I guess my eyes, they hadn't adjusted to the dark when I first see his silhouette ... there is

92

pretty good glare of city lights that shines in through my window. I remember thinking, God help me, I'm seeing demon or something. Hallucinating, I think I might be."

"What did you do?"

"I scream," Marina answered seriously. "This is when he tells me that he is most sorry, that he has the wrong apartment."

Lila felt overcome by anxiety as she listened to Marina compare Wolf's boots to black slugs on the window, the same anxiety she'd felt during her psychedelic therapy with Dr. Ross back in Tucson. As Marina's voice faded into silence, Lila had the uncanny sense of time rewinding; again, she was there in Mysh's apartment that night, this time viewing the wave-distorted imagery of Wolf Holzinger preparing to stomp through the glass. The spectral legs of the dandelion-shaped spider lingered and pulsed at the edge of the vision. An icy chill ran down her neck. She swallowed dryly and asked, "And that's when he fell?"

"No."

"Oh?" That surprised her.

"Right before he falls, one of the lines he is using must have snapped or runs out or something."

"Wait a minute"—Lila's face tensed—"what do you mean *one* of the lines? What are you saying? There was more than one line?"

"Yes, this is why I'm thinking I probably ought to give that detective another call. I'm thinking, enough time is passed. I think I've gained perspective. Replaying whole sequence of events over and over in my head since that night, now it strikes me that ... just before the bounce—"

Lila looked slantwise into her face. "He *bounced?*"

"Yes, he bounced. The line stretched, and then he bounced or rebounded or whatever you call it. *Re-bounced.* But just before that, I remember looking up, tracking the line he was using. At first, I thought it was a glint of light that had caught my eye. See, and that's what I told the detective. But the more I think about it now, I mean, I distinctly remember seeing something and then tracking the line up toward the roof, and I *think*—like, I can't say for sure, but I *think*—I may have seen a second line ... like maybe what I saw wasn't a glint of light at all. I mean, since when does light glint off a dark rope or antenna or whatever he was using? So, maybe it was a second line, you know ... kinda loosely snaking itself around the remaining line that was pulled taut, the one that was still there holding him up, the one that snapped."

Lila kept quiet. This wasn't the first witness she'd encountered to alter her story. Maybe there was more she'd misremembered or mischaracterized in her report that night.

"I think that's what caught my eye. You know, I wanted to see what the hell was going on. Like, maybe there was someone up there helping him. I don't know; it all happened so fast. Then again, maybe I'm overthinking it. Probably am. It was *sooo* surreal. Too much time spent with my nose in the books. The line gave way and the guy bounced, that much I know for sure. And I thought he was going to fall, but when he didn't, when he recovered, I remember feeling this overwhelming wave of relief wash over me. Like—*phew! Thank God! That was a close call!* But that didn't last long. Next thing I know, the line just snapped, and I stood there and I watched the poor guy slam into the pavement." She gazed out at the gray, silent lake. "It was horrible."

"You actually saw him hit the pavement?"

"Well, no, not actually. I mean, I leaned on the window and tried to look, but it's *sixteen floors!* Believe me, I saw the whole thing in my head. And seriously, that is a scene that stays with you."

12

February 8, 2018

Law Offices of Savage, Lutz, Finnegan & Foehl
Chicago, Illinois

LILA STOOD AT THE DOOR TO JIM SAVAGE'S OFFICE, WAITING FOR him to finish up with his phone call.

"Yeah, Charlie, I will," he was saying. He gave Lila a summoning nod, took his feet off his desk, sat up, and motioned for her to sit.

As she crossed the threshold, Savage cupped the phone and jerked his chin in the direction of the elaborately carved silver urn on the credenza at the back of the room. "Coffee's fresh," he whispered.

She went over and poured a cup for herself, then came back and plopped down in one of the ivory brocade armchairs that fronted his desk.

"Good work," he was saying, "no, I will. Thanks. We'll be in touch. And Charlie," he said, "keep your powder dry." He hung up the phone and gave her a weary, sympathetic smile.

"What?" she said suspiciously. She knew that look; it always preceded any news he thought might distress her.

"That was Charlie-O. Just confirming receipt. Preliminary report's in."

"Okay," she said slowly, an eyebrow raised.

Savage hit a hidden button on his desk that closed his office door and then reached into his drawer. He brought out a manila envelope addressed to Lila and slid it to her across his desk. She unclasped the envelope and took out the unfolded report. It was typed, single-spaced, on one sheet of lined yellow legal paper. The report's typos, corrected with many sloppy blobs of *Wite-Out,* were par for the course for Charlie-O, who was so tragically "old school" it was almost laughable. The content, on the other hand, was always impeccable and always took up precisely one full page, regardless of the subject matter. She imagined an old Underwood Champion manual typewriter and gave a half-chuckle at what she figured was Charlie-O's two-finger hunt-and-peck labors. "You believe this?" she said, fluttering the *Wite-Out*-scarred page.

Savage lifted his open palms.

Lila began reading the unaddressed, unlabeled report evenly, without, at first, displaying either interest or distress. The bottom line was that the SEC and the comptroller of the US Department of the Treasury had her brother, Ulli, in their crosshairs for ...

"*Smurfing!*" she blurted, the shock of it filling her nerves. She read on with a tense frown. Somehow, her brother had managed to get their family firm, McManus & Piper, tangled up in a massive foreign investment money-laundering scheme. "Oh, this is just perfect," she said before reading out loud, "in violation of Section Five-Three-Two-Four of Title Twenty-One of the United States Code."

Savage sat there looking at her, listening over steepled fingers.

That was the alleged offense, technically speaking. What it amounted to in practice was much more straightforward: many of the mutual funds and commodity trading pools McManus & Piper had underwritten over the last few years had been found to be improperly "structured."

"Instead of coming from a large pool of small- to medium-sized investors," she read aloud, growing more and more distressed, "the money was traced back to a single offshore source that had been subdivided into many smaller sums structured to 'come in under the radar,' as they were all less than the statutory reporting limit of ten thousand dollars US. The pools were distributed among many 'smurfs,' or captive agents of the one larger and sole source of what was very likely dirty money, likely tied to a major narco-cartel, all evidence pointing to Ismael Zaldavar Valiente—*La Ballena.*"

Lila closed her eyes. Her face tightened. It wasn't just the family fortune beyond her control, now at risk; it was the legal jeopardy posed to her brother and his young family. What would her nieces do without their father if Ulli got sent up the river? What would his wife, a stay-at-home mom, do? How would they support themselves if, through some boneheaded move, he lost it all?

"Let me know if there's anything I can do," Savage said reassuringly.

But she wasn't reassured. "I guess my brother and I are going to have to have a little chat. Knowing Ulli," she said almost wistfully, "he probably had no idea what was going on." She gave a weak grin, "My brother tends to manage from a distance." Then, she struggled to add, "Oh, yeah"—touching her hand briefly to her forehead in a distracted gesture —"and please give Charlie-O my thanks for turning this around so quickly. Maybe someday we can actually meet."

"Will do." He leaned back in his chair and narrowed his eyes. "So," he said paternally, "change of subject—how's the Holzinger thing coming along? Charlie-O's available to chip in if needed. I told her what happened to Wolf, as well as Hans's suspicions."

Lila looked up at him. She knew his game; he was trying to get her to keep from going down the rabbit hole. She was thankful, of course, but it still pissed her off. "Made some progress," she said.

"Oh?"

"Holzinger appears to be right. Wolf apparently was *not* alone. There *was* someone on the roof with him that night."

"And *how* do we know that?"

"The med-school witness. The one living in the sixteenth-floor apartment. I talked to her earlier. She's changing her story."

"Yeah, and how many times does that happen?"

"I know, right."

"Did she see the person? Who was it?"

"She didn't. Although she did see a second rope."

"So—have you told Hans?"

"Not yet. I thought you might like to have the honors. Though, as I told him ... until I can figure out *why* his son was on the roof that night, there's not much hope in figuring out what might have happened to him up there. To say nothing of *who* might have been keeping him company."

"Okay, I'll give him a call. Anything come out of your follow-up with him?"

"We met at his office in Kewaunee. That was ... *interesting*. Have you been up there?"

"Kewaunee?"

"Yeah."

"Of course. Many times."

"The Great White Hunter décor threw me."

"The man does take his hunting seriously."

"I guess." She let out a deep sigh. "And—"

Savage looked at her.

"I must say I was a little taken aback with the depth of research he did on yours truly. Man goes through that much trouble, makes me wonder what his angle is."

Savage shrugged. "I wouldn't worry about that."

"Oh—he did put me in touch with Gus Ambrosia."

"Those two go back a few years."

"Yeah, not too big a rivalry there. Something to do with Ambrosia Dairy being a big corporate agri-business sucking the air out of the room for all the smaller operators."

Savage drew his head back. "Hans is hardly a small operator."

"No, but seems he's substantially smaller than Ambrosia Dairy and not too happy about it. I get the feeling Ambrosia's success galls him. That and, my God, he's so damned moralistic—"

"Ha! Yeah, the old dog *is* a straight arrow."

"The fact that he's getting beat at his own game, especially by a reformed alcoholic ... as judgmental as he is, that has got to chap his hide."

Savage furrowed his brow and reached for his coffee. "Who's the alcoholic?"

"Ambrosia. I saw an old photo in his office. It was autographed to him from his 'bros at A/A.'"

Savage let out a wry snicker, "Lila ..."

His admonitory tone earned a sideways glance. "What?"

"'A/A' isn't 'Alcoholics Anonymous.' I think, if you check, you'll find that 'A/A,' in this case, is referring to 'Air America' – you know, the clandestine airline run by CIA? I think it was probably intended as an inside joke, since Air America ceased operations in 1976 since it was primarily working in Indochina—Vietnam, Laos, Cambodia, Thailand. And neither one of them ever flew for them."

Lila rolled her eyes.

"That's what I meant when I said those two go back a few years. Hans was a pilot for CIA for—hell, I don't know—twenty years?"

"No, I got that. Gotta love our intrepid Wisconsin dairy farmers." Falling into thought, she looked up and tried to read his expression. "Odd coincidence, though, don't you think?"

"Hmm? What's that?"

"Two guys ... both ex-CIA ... friends, rivals, whatever, both end up in the dairy business in the same city. The CIA just, I don't know, pings in my ear."

"See," Savage fluttered his hand, "that's that ... bloodhound thing of yours. You see patterns where others see nothing at all. The way I look at it, we live in a random and brutal universe. It's bound to deal you two of a kind occasionally."

"We'll see," she said, remembering suddenly that while she had sleuthed Wolf's mishap, she still had the Breem case to investigate.

Savage cocked his head and reached across his desk. "By the way"—he picked up a pink message slip and waved it in front of her—"what's up with this guy? He's called three times already."

Lila read the name: Mark Morgan. She snatched the message from his hand.

"I'll take that."

13

February 8, 2018

North Lawndale Public Housing Complex
Chicago, Illinois

Lila turned off 19th and parked her 4Runner in front of a redbrick three-story apartment building on Karlov. She got out of the car, locked the door, and then clicked it again for good measure. She looked up at the iron gate and beyond it to the edge of the building, her eye drawn to the pale blue placard that read in block letters,

WARNING: WE CALL THE POLICE

Drawing in a deep breath, Lila made her way toward the centrally located entrance, passing a cluster of thugs slouched against the wall, staring her down, sneering.

Lila felt the anxiety of a woman alone, despite eight years of Krav Maga training she'd taken through high school and college at her father's insistence. The compact Sig Sauer P365 she wore in a concealed holster in the back of her pants only reminded her of a violent threat she'd rather not face (this despite her doctor's gentle counsel to consider refraining from carrying firearms of any kind). Sure, Lila had her depressive moods, but she was definitely *not* self-destructive. She loved her life and she promised Gail that, if ever any bizarre ideations about doing harm to herself *were* to pop into her head, she'd surrender her sidearm at once.

Right now, suicide was the furthest thing from her mind; *survival* was the dominant chord now. Out of the corner of her eye, she saw one of the men push himself away from the wall and fall in close behind her. Too close, by her in-the-moment assessment. She could almost feel his breath on the back of her neck, and her hands began trembling with her runaway heartbeat.

She halted at the door and spun around. "Step back, or I *will* use this," she said, reaching behind her and pulling out her P365, the gun's steel barrel pointing groundward.

Despite her expanding sense of danger, she expelled a loud breath and focused her energy to stay loose, ready to move against the imminent threat. She glared at the stranger hounding her.

He was massive and wore a bulky black leather coat.

"Fuck you doin' up in here?" he snarled in a low, threatening voice, backing down a step at the sight of her Sig, hooking his thumbs nonchalantly on his belt.

"I came to see Angela Breem," she answered steadily, ready to move if he so much as flinched.

He rolled his head slowly, slightly off-center, and narrowed his eyes at her. "You here to see Angela Breem—you're late!"

Her face tightened. "What do you mean, I'm late?"

"Angela Breem OD'd yesterday."

"Checked out on the A train," another said with an evil snicker.

With quick, mobile eyes, Lila took stock of the slowly gathering circle of hooded men closing in around her.

"Take me to see her apartment," she insisted, feeling increasingly exposed with her back against a door that could just as easily be opened—

or shot through—from the inside. One of the men was whispering something into his cell phone.

"Police sealed her apartment." The big man grinned, nodding to his accomplice with the cell phone.

Lila let out a snort like she'd been around a long time and was accustomed to dealing with the likes of these characters. "Not that yellow tape in the Lawndale projects ever seals anything for long," she said.

At this, the big man gave a slow smile and abruptly shifted his weight. "Hold up now!" he said to the wiry fellow manning the cell phone before regarding Lila again, this time as if in a new light. His head moved slightly to one side and then shifted to the other, and he regarded her more closely, seeming to scrutinize every pore on her face. At length, his voice went up an octave: *"That you Snowflake?"*

Lila dropped her chin and looked at him again, mystified—could this hulking behemoth be the very same gangster disciple she used to call "My G"? Could it be? But her "G" had been tall and lanky; this brute, while he was certainly tall enough, was a long, *looong* way from lanky. Built like a brick, more like. "Maurice?" she ventured cautiously, her brow furrowed, her smile tightly restrained.

"Snowflake!" He laughed out loud. *"Damn, girl!*—almost didn't recognize your crazy ass! Where's all your pretty blonde hair?" He looked off across the dead lawn that fronted 1860 S. Karlov at her parked 4Runner. "And your daddy's whip! Come up here in an SUV—you *slummin'* it now!"

"Garaged for the winter," she replied, relieved, re-holstering her sidearm.

"No, I hear that." His chin went up in recognition before he turned to his posse and said, "I got this."

"We good?" Cell Phone asked, still maddogging her.

"Yeah—we a'ight," the big man replied. "Me and my Snowflake here, we did some *bidness* back in the day." He turned back to Lila. "How long's it been, girl? Ten years, I bet."

"More like twelve."

"Damn—that's right! Twelve years." He shook his head. "Time flies."

"Take me to Breem's apartment?" Lila asked, feeling suddenly emboldened by their walk down memory lane.

"Oh, hell yes! Let's get on with it." Maurice shrugged toward a battered door, leading the way into a shadowy building across the street. The entire crew squeezed into the urine-reeking elevator up to the third floor, Maurice and Lila making small talk all the way. The doors slid open and she followed him down the gloomy and heavily graffitied corridor. Finally, he stopped and made a sweeping gesture toward the door criss-crossed with yellow police tape. "The Breem pad," he said.

CRIME SCENE DO NOT CROSS

Lila shook her head. "Why didn't PD tell me about this?"

"And say what?" he laughed derisively. "You know s'well as I do, girl —this entire project's a motherfuckin' crime scene!" He laughed as if he were proud of that dubious distinction.

His crew echoed him with dry cheers.

"Tape us all off if they could," one said.

Laughter all around.

Lila looked both ways down the dark hall; at the farthest end, through the door, a gun-metal sky was showing through a small wire-mesh portal shaped like a coffin. A couple of thugs were hanging around the open elevator, a yellowing neon light flickering off and on above their heads.

She turned to face Maurice. "So, what happened?" she asked.

He shrugged. "OD'd, like I said."

"Heroin?"

He hesitated and looked up at the sky. For a split second, Lila thought she saw his eyes well up. "Your people sell that to her?"

He shook his head slowly.

"But you know who did." Again, Lila glared at him, unable to hide her growing contempt.

He rested his palm lightly against her arm like a concerned uncle. "*Lemme* educate you about survival in this here motherfuckin' jungle. What you know and what you say best have *nothin'* to do with each other." His eyebrows went up as he waited for his words to sink in. When he got the submissive, understanding nod he was looking for, he added under his breath, "Sista got soul. She was like ... havin' Mother Teresa up in here. Angela Breem—uh-huh, and she *was,* too—an angel, I mean. Always lookin' out after her people; problem-solvin'; fightin' against injustice, violations of human rights, legal rights—standin' up for everybody's rights but her own, I guess. We found the bag that killed her on the bathroom flo' by the body. She never used the stuff. But there it was, one full ounce of pure, uncut China White, just short of the tiny bitch-assed amount that mussa kilt her. Tell you somethin' straight up, Snowflake. Up in here, thassa wicked motherfuckin' windfall that blows a stash like that into yo' hands." He lapsed into silence.

Lines appeared on Lila's forehead. "I'm not sure I follow," she admitted.

"Look here, I can cut a gram of that shit into seven thousand hits on the street." He looked at her intently, his face darkening. "Seven *thousand!*" he repeated lustily. "You ask me, somebody wanted her dead. You think about that! An ounce, that's almost thirty grams. Like I said ... thassa motherfuckin' *lotto* win! Now, who'd go and do a crazy-assed thing like that?"

"China White," Lila repeated quietly, mulling it over.

"China White." Maurice shrugged and looked at her sideways. "What do you know 'bout fentanyl?"

"I know it's a problem."

"It's *waaay* more powerful than heroin. Fiddy times. Hun'ert times. Maybe more. Sista never had a chance. Way I see it, highballer what was runnin' her old man, he mussa wanted her out of the picture *real* bad. Fact," he leaned in and whispered into her ear, "you best watch *yo'* back. Hate to hear 'bout my Snowflake slippin' off some Gold Coast high-rise."

"What do you mean? Who was runnin' her old man?"

"That fool was the biggest blower I ever saw," Maurice replied. "He had some shady highballer connections, I give him that. But runnin' round, braggin' he was workin' with CIA ..." He chuckled, *"Shit!"* He pulled a heavily laden keyring from his coat pocket and, without remark, selected a key and slid it slowly into the Breem's keyhole. "Way, *waaay* up the food chain. Guns"—he opened his leather coat and gave the sawn-off inside a slight shake—"supply just about anything you want. Anything. And mo' motherfuckin' Benjamins than you can count. But CIA? Nah, no way. Things changed over the twelve years since you been out here. By the way, you ever need a taste again, I help you out. Top-quality. Pure as the driven snow." He laughed.

"No thanks," Lila replied. "I've turned over a new leaf."

"A'ight. I gotcha!" He smiled, nodding knowingly. "You lookin' for new leaf—I got ya new leaf. Hun'ert get you a Z." Again, the falsetto. "Ol' Maurice knows how to take care of his homies! And I ain't never short of blow, as you well know. Way we been rollin', some say we just might do a hundred mil a year through here." His eyes sparkled. "Fact, if old Louis Breem hadn't started getting' high on his own supply, likely he never woulda stepped off that ledge the way he did a few months back. Know I'm sayin'?"

Lila once again faced the door, her teeth scraping her bottom lip. The death of the other fall victim's wife was certainly unexpected. She was undecided as to whether she should give Cornell a call to get his blessing before entering when Maurice said, "Go on, check it out. Ol' Maurice got yo' back."

She felt a wave of anxiety wash over her as the door creaked open. With a sudden shock, she realized she was half expecting to find that damned dandelion-shaped spider lying in wait for her, ready to pounce. What struck her instead was the lingering reek of cheap cigars and stinkweed that clung to the modest furniture; that and the musty smell of the empty mattress box leaned up against the wall. She stepped around the box and asked Maurice, "Can you show me where Louis fell from?"

"Pad next door. Door's open; check it out if you want. I'll wait up on you."

Lila gave a tight-lipped grin, stepped past him, and went to the neighboring apartment where the door had been left open a crack. She pushed her way inside. The place was a filthy, tumbledown mess—missing floor tiles, holes in the walls, scorch marks on the few yellowing lino tiles that remained. It looked like someone had built a bonfire in the living room. She glanced up at the smoke stains on the ceiling, easing her phone out of her pocket and crossing to the grimy window to have a look at the ledge. The window was loose in its frame and slid open with ease. Poking her head out, Lila snapped several pictures: the ledge—in both directions— and the pavement below.

Returning to the Breems' apartment, she found Maurice leaning against the kitchen counter, looking down at his cell phone. "When was the body found?" she asked, not looking back at him as she peered into the bathroom, flipped on the bare light, and snapped a few more pictures. Unlike the rats' midden next door, the Breems' was reasonably clean, despite the dilapidated facilities.

"Which one?"

"Angela's," Lila called out. "And who found it?"

"Yesterday, like I said. One the little kids she looked after found her."

She switched off the light and rejoined Maurice, now in the living room, and took a closer look at the mattress box. "When was this delivered?" she asked.

"Mussa been yesterday. Least, that's what I told that detective what was here snoopin' round."

Lila crouched low, examining the box from every angle until she found the barcode shipping label in the corner by the floor. She pointed her cell phone at the shipping label and snapped a picture:

IL 006 9-06

Straightening up, she asked, "Wouldn't happen to be Detective Krzy—?"

"That's the one."

"Curious ..." she muttered to herself, still eyeing the label. She stowed her phone away in her messenger bag and took one last look around before she said, "Okay, that's it. Thanks, Maurice. That's all I need to see."

On her way home, she hit the hands-free switch on her steering wheel and called Cornell. The phone rang several times before she got an answer.

"Chief Williams," he said.

"Cornell, Lila. Hey, need you to run down a shipping label number for me."

February 8, 2018

Gibson's Bar & Steakhouse
Chicago, Illinois

WHEN LILA SAW THE CROWD GATHERED IN GIBSON'S, SHE DECIDED against checking in her coat. Instead, she threaded her way through the throng. Peering over the heads of bustling drinkers, she spotted Mark sitting alone at the bend in the bar. She almost didn't recognize him—the faded Levi's and Chukka boots threw her off. He looked much more relaxed in his civvies, not as straight-laced, she thought. Instead, he appeared tanned and rested in a gray V-neck sweater pulled over a white crew-neck T-shirt. Retirement evidently suited the man.

"Sorry to keep you waiting," she said, sidling up next to him. Nowhere in her eyes was there any sign of confidence or enthusiasm. She sighed, fumbling with her coat buttons.

"Not at all." He put down his beer and slid off his barstool to help her shrug off her coat.

She was about to drape it over the back of her barstool when he reached over and snatched it up together with his own dark tweed topcoat and suggested they let the hostess know that they were ready to be shown to their table.

It was after their waitress popped open the bottle of '88 Grand Cru Pinot that Lila suggested they lift their glasses to toast Commander Mark Morgan's retirement.

"This is good," Lila admitted after her first sip. An incipient smile flickered across her lips as she savored the wine. Though she liked the wine selection and liked the booth, she resisted the temptation to surrender entirely to the pleasures of her companion. Collecting herself, she straightened in her seat and looked across the table at him, waiting.

"It is," Mark said, smiling at his glass, "isn't it?" He took another sip as if to confirm his first impression.

Lila waited until he'd put his glass down, her tongue moving lightly across her unpainted lips, before she said, "So, okay, I've got a question for you."

"Shoot."

"Didn't it ever get boring? I mean, my God, twenty years—it *had* to get boring."

"Didn't *what* get boring?" he said, a bemused grin on his face, before turning to briefly eye the selection of as-yet-uncooked steaks being presented to the party of four directly across from them.

She lowered her chin and gave him a cynical look. "You know perfectly well what I'm talking about."

He turned back to face her. "Ah! Subs again," he said.

"From what my father told me about fast-attack boats," Lila said, "you guys play cat-and-mouse the whole time you're down there—six months at sea per deployment, right? That means you spent ten years underwater."

His emphatic nod as he reached for his glass told her she had it about right.

"Searching for enemy ballistic missile subs that you'll target," she continued, filling the brief pause, "in the *hopefully unlikely* event a real shooting war breaks out."

"'Hopefully' is an understatement," he said over the wine, his white teeth gleaming in the candlelight. "And yes, that's the lion's share of the work, but it's definitely not *all* we do." He took another sip and then ruminatively turned the glass in his hands, encouraging Lila to do the same, pointing out the wine's impressive glycerin legs.

Lila's brows went up.

"For instance," he started reluctantly as he set his glass down, "we do a lot of work with the NSA on missions considered vital to national security. *Global access ops*, they're called, designed to penetrate various non-military targets the NSA has interest in."

"The NSA," she repeated.

"National Security Agency. The folks responsible for the global monitoring, collection, and processing of data for foreign intelligence and counterintelligence purposes."

She suppressed a chuckle at the military precision of his reply. "I know what the NSA is." He might be too much of a sensualist, she was thinking, the way he was oohing and aahing over the wine. Or maybe he was just nervous, finding something other than his unfamiliar date upon which to focus.

"And we do quite a bit of work with the CIA, running covert cyber ops."

"CIA." The term struck her as a curiosity. She gave her head a loose shake, pushing back away from the table. *"Again!"* she muttered to herself. Was there really a pattern there, she wondered, or did her sensitivity merely signal the return of her anxiety, the presence of melancholy and despair poised around the next corner?

He shot her another puzzled look. "What? You telling me *you've* had run-ins with CIA?" He chuckled.

"Forget it." She lifted her hand in dismissal.

"What—what'd I say?"

"What's so 'out there' about me maybe having anything to do with CIA? Because I'm a woman?"

Mark shook his head and stared at her. "Seriously?" he said, astounded. "What would that have to do with anything?"

"My point exactly." Lila picked up her glass and took another sip. Then another. Then she put the glass down a bit too hard, splashing wine over the edge of her glass. "Look, maybe this date was a mistake. Maybe—"

He reached out and took her hand. "Lila." He held fast, even as she feebly tugged to free herself. "You are misunderstanding what I said. Or I'm misunderstanding what you said."

She watched his hand release hers. She thought about Dr. Ross's take on her occasional bouts of defensiveness: *You keep your head on pretty straight in professional situations; it's when you get into the personal sphere that things start to fall apart.* "Look, it's nothing," Lila said. "I'm a little tense. Please, go on, finish what you were saying."

"Okay, but first"—he pointed to the drip of wine moving down the side of the glass—"you're about to lose a whole sip there."

Lila smiled—she couldn't help herself.

"Okay, back to what we were saying. NSA, CIA, DIA—that last one's the Defense Intelligence Agency—they're all part of what are called 'forward intelligence missions,' which boil down to getting out there and combing deep waters for vital intel. You gotta remember, the Silent Service is the stealthiest platform we have. One way to think about our sub fleet is as a counterpart to our spy satellites. So, that's a second level of activity: intelligence gathering—a lot of work with undersea cables and listening devices. That's how we get beyond our boat's current crush depth limitations and reach"—his eyebrows went up as he pronounced the last few words almost lyrically—"*deep into the abyss.* Then there's our deep-sea search, rescue, recovery, and salvage capabilities. We're talking everything from surface ships to subs, aircraft, rockets; hell, spacecraft even. Oh, and lost nukes, of course! Can't forget that one!"

"That's a little unnerving, what you said about crush depth. Exactly how deep are you talking about?"

"That, I'm afraid, is classified."

She arched an eyebrow and broke into a loose grin. "Oh, I get it—"

"Exactly: if I told you, I'd have to kill you."

"Ha!"

"But I wouldn't tell you, so we don't have to worry about that."

She had her elbow on the table with her chin in her hand, watching. There was something about the way he was able to defuse tense situations while making her smile. There was something unnerving, but at the same time comforting, about him.

"I remember, a few years back, one of the senior fellows at Stanford University's Hoover Institution said, 'Our capacity to go deep, to go anywhere in the water column without anybody knowing it, and do anything we want there, is the greatest security asset we have.'"

Lila kept quiet. She watched his face as he spoke, his eyes alight. He'd suddenly transformed from this tiresomely chivalrous dinosaur into an engaging, interesting man who, somehow, was still talking about diving deep below the sea. Suddenly, she found herself thinking about sinking deep beneath the sheets. She felt her face flush.

"But enough about the life of the submariner. Truth be told, now that I'm retired, I'd kind of like to put that chapter behind me."

"Yeah, let's do that," Lila said, straightening in her seat. She quickly reached for her drink and lifted it in a toast. "You stay in the water too long, you get all pruney."

"Which is not exactly a good look!"

They clinked glasses.

"So, tell me about you," Mark said. "How's the double life as a lawyer and private investigator?"

"Interesting," she said, gazing into her half-filled wineglass before seeking his eyes to check the real depth of his interest. "Most of the time. Sometimes ... *profitable*. Though, at the moment, maddening."

"Oh?"

"Yeah, I'm kinda stuck in this thing that's been chewing up all my time. Distraction, really. You know, doing a personal favor for our senior partner."

"Bummer."

"No, it's ... whatever, it's work, right?" she said very quietly, eyes lowered, focused on nothing. "Have you heard of frequency illusion—you know, you buy a red hat and everywhere you look, you start seeing red hats."

Mark looked at her curiously. "What do you mean?"

"Those three letters—CIA. I'm telling ya, CIA's become my red hat. It's like every time I turn around, the CIA's popping up in conversation. It's weird! Anyway ..." Her eyes made a furtive circuit of the dining room, and she picked up her glass. "I'm rambling. Sorry."

The waitress came out of the bar and dropped off menus on her way to deliver a round of drinks to the next table. When she came back, she recited the night's specials and then left them to consider their selections.

Deciding on the ribeye, Lila peered at Mark over the top of her menu, her thoughts wandering to Hans and Gus and their secret histories with the CIA. "Can I ask you something?"

"What's that?" Mark replied without looking up from his menu.

"How does one go about ... landing a career in the CIA?" She closed her menu and put it down on the table, pushing it off to one side. "I'm interested in the recruitment and hiring process."

"Okay, well, for instance ..." His facial expression tightened as he briefly averted his gaze; his tone earnest, he said, "there's ... job fairs, I should think. CIA recruits new hires just like any other big company out there. Referrals, too, I suppose, especially from university professors they have in their pocket. And I would think referrals from their field staff would garner a high-priority status. Grad schools, of course. I don't know about any preference for lawyers. FBI likes lawyers. CIA, I don't think so. They like people with foreign language skills—that I know for sure."

Lila thought about his response. Referrals from field staff. Field staff like former case officers, perhaps? Former agency pilots? And then there were Wolf Holzinger's Georgetown Law credentials—he dropped out and never finished. She wondered if he had ever been approached. He seemed to fit the profile: Scholar. Elite gymnast. Law School dropout. She hadn't thought to ask if Wolf had mastered any foreign languages. Put that on the to-do list. Yes, that would be the very next question she would ask his father. Then again, why not ask him straight out if his son had ever been involved with the CIA? Like father, like son, perhaps? And even if it were so, would it have any relevance to the case?

The rest of the dinner passed pleasantly enough. By the evening's end, Lila found that she really *was* attracted to him; when they said goodbye just outside the restaurant, she pressed herself into him and left him with a kiss. Nothing too soulful—it was far too soon for that. But it was uncommonly sweet, she thought as they parted, and as she drove away from Gibson's, she glanced at herself in the rearview and let out a little snort, surprised at herself, at how eager she suddenly found herself to see him again. She'd have to enter that revelation into her notebook. Mark it an eight.

Lila's cell phone beeped with an incoming call. She hit the switch on her steering wheel, her spirits soaring at the thought that it might be the man himself. *He feels the same. Don't go—meet me.*

Her mind was a mixed jumble of possibilities when an accented voice said, "Hi, is this Lila?"

Lila's heart deflated. "It is."

"Hey, this is Sofia."

Lila's eyes opened wide. "Oh, *Sofia*—hi! Thanks for getting back."

"Say, I know it's late—what is it? Nine-fifteen? But I'm free now, if you're in the neighborhood. Stop by for a drink?"

15

February 8, 2018

Sofia Castellanos Gold Coast Apartment
Chicago, Illinois

It was 9:30 p.m. when Lila entered the twelve-story Gold Coast apartment building Sofia Castellanos currently called home. The lobby was sparsely furnished and had the look of a building that had gone to seed and only recently been renovated. Other than the mahogany sideboard she passed on the way to the elevator and the oversized mirror above it, in which she caught a glimpse of her reflection, the lobby was empty and sterile.

She hit the call button and had one last look around, noting the absence of a doorman as a metallic blue BMW M5 with Y-spoke wheels and run-flat tires slowed to a prowl, suspiciously dogging the entrance. When the chime sounded and the elevator's dulled brass doors quietly slid open, she got in, glancing between the closing doors as the BMW pulled away.

Lila reached for the heavy brass doorknocker and gave it a couple of loud raps, her eyebrows rising at the realization that Sofia's new digs took up the building's entire top floor.

Sofia opened the door and greeted her with a wide, welcoming smile. "Lila!" she beamed, her silk kimono lifting slightly at the edges as she leaned forward and gave Lila a light kiss on the cheek. "You made it!" There was a slight boozy slur to her words, at first hard to detect beneath her heavy Venezuelan accent. "Come on in, Li-la!"

For the second time, Lila was taken aback by the warmth she was experiencing, that same Hollywood arc-light glow she'd felt whenever her booze-addled mother had turned that glamorous smile of hers on her fidgety little girl. Lila's heart fluttered as she entered the richly appointed apartment overlooking Lake Michigan. The heavy gold-colored Versailles curtains were held open with sash tiebacks, revealing the lake's vast, dark expanse just beyond the floodlit neoclassical apartment building across the street. "You have a beautiful place!" Lila effused over Lana Del Rey's "Mariners Apartment Complex."

"My cousin's place, actually. And I know! Don't you just love it?" She pulled the door shut and lifted the Waterford brandy balloon she held in her free hand. "Care for a nightcap?" She waved the glass a little too carelessly, spilling a drop on the hardwood floor.

"No, thanks," Lila replied, eyeing the splatter. She looked up at her and smiled. "I'm good." She followed her hostess down the central hallway; halfway there, Sofia pulled Lila into her side office, crossing to the wet bar next to a large salt-water fish tank. "You sure?" she asked over her shoulder, wobbling slightly as she reached for a crystal decanter shaped like a heart. "*Ninety-eight*-year-old cognac. Aged to *perffffection.*"

Lila slipped out of her coat, leaned down, and gazed at a large dark brown fish painted with dramatic orange stipes. "God, this one's beautiful! What is it?"

"Pinnatus bat-*fffish,*" Sofia answered, swaying slightly to the music.

"It's gorgeous!"

"Yesss, it's pretty rare, from what they tell me."

"*They?*"

117

"The"—she swung her snifter in an arc and again sloshed insanely-priced cognac on the floor—"*people!*"

"The people." Lila chuckled.

"The little people I have taking care of the aquarium."

"Oh, the *little people!*" Lila laughed. "And who are you, Marie Antoinette? Or ... Judy Garland?"

"Honestly, I don't know anything about it. Just the names of a few of the fish. Come on in, let's take this to the living room."

Halfway out the door, Sofia halted and spun around. "Sure you don't want something?" Again, the carelessly hoisted glass.

Lila backed away from the spill. "I'm sure," she said with a grin. "Thanks anyway."

The living room had an enormous sofa with two roll-arm chairs arranged in a U-shape, opening up a conversation area facing a large carved stone fireplace. In the corner was a Steinway Louis XIV grand.

"You play?" Lila asked. "Or does your cousin play—I'm sorry, who did you say lives here?"

"No, I play. *Un poquito,*" Sofia answered. "But I do. I try to play. I live here."

"But your cousin owns the place."

"Oh, *ffff!* Or-*fffilia* owns property all over the world. So ... lucky me, right!"

"When did you move in?"

"Just before Wolf *fff*-ell. I wasn't home that night. I was here, taking delivery of that beautiful signed Steinway right *there*. Here"—she reached down to the wraparound sofa and shuffled several large silk pillows into place—"let's stretch out on the couch."

Lila slung her coat over one of the armchairs then sat down beside her and, unable to find anything to do with her newly unencumbered hands, looked up and grinned sheepishly. "You know, maybe I will join you with a—"

"Cognac?" Sofia beamed.

Lila shrugged.

"Oh, good!" Sofia set her snifter down on the coffee table and scurried off to get Lila's drink.

While she was gone, Lila reached into her messenger bag and got out her pen and memo pad. She looked around at the opulent appointments —obelisk-shaped mahogany speakers on the hardwood floor, thick silk tassels hanging from every cabinet knob in sight, outsized Italian Renaissance oils hanging from ornate silk rosettes attached to the white picture rail molding that encircled the beige room and ran down the central hall. She called out to her hostess, "So is it common practice for piano delivery people to work on a Saturday night?"

Sofia called back, "Oh, night, afternoon, I don't remember—*oh, shit!*"

"You okay?"

"Yeah. *Solo un segundo!*" When Sofia returned, she handed Lila a glass and plopped down beside her on the couch. Reaching for her snifter, she lifted it up and said, *"Cin-Cin!"*

Lila lifted her glass and took a sip. Clearing her throat, she put her drink down and said, "So." She clicked her pen a few times. "How about we start at the beginning?"

Sofia let her head fall to one side and gazed dreamily at her over the rim of her glass.

"How did you guys meet?" Lila asked, feeling rather exposed.

"We were both living in DC. Wolf was at Georgetown Law. It was a black-tie gala at the Venezuelan Embassy honoring the birth of Simón Bolívar.

"That's where you're originally from, right? Venezuela?"

"Sí. Nacido y criado en Santiago de León de Caracas."

"Caracas," Lila nodded, jotting it down. She let a moment pass before she asked, "Did you go to Georgetown Law, too?"

"No. No, I was *at* Georgetown," Sofia said, crinkling her nose, "but I was only an undergrad."

"Oh, really? What was your major?"

She swirled her cognac and gazed pensively into her glass. *"Literatura,"* she said a little wistfully.

"Ah! And what does one *do* with a degree in literature from Georgetown University?"

Sofia laughed and took another drink. "You mean other than starve?" A little burp escaped her, prompting her to blush. *"Pardón!"*

Lila chuckled along with her. "Yeah."

"I wanted to be a writer. Someday I will. *Tiempos hay de acometer y tiempos de retirar.*"

Lila looked at her, waiting for the translation.

"There are times to attack and times to withdraw."

"That's a tough racket."

"A vocation, I think. In the religious sense. Something deep inside calls to you, and you have no choice but to put everything else on hold and respond. A gift. From God. I think that's right." The light in Sofia's eyes shifted as she looked at her; they became more earnest, somehow.

"So what was it for you?"

Deep furrows appeared on Sofia's brow.

"I mean, what was your first clue that ... *God* called you to write?"

"Ah," Sofia said, "promise you won't laugh?"

"Now that I cannot do."

Sofia regarded her carefully. "Okay, well at least you're honest."

Lila bared up under the lingering scrutiny and waited.

"I was in high school," Sofia began at last. "International boarding school in Geneva, Switzerland—*Collège du Léman.*"

"Sounds expensive."

"It was ... *muy exclusivo.* Anyway, I was in my junior year and we were reading Djuna Barnes's *Nightwood,* which is supposed to be a cult classic of lesbian fiction."

"Really! You read that in high school?"

"International boarding school, like I said. So, I turn in my book report entitled, 'No Big Thing,' which I'd intended as a play on the seriousness of the journey of people coming to grips with their sexual identity on the one hand, plus a hidden phallic reference—'no big thing'—on the other; you know—for fun."

"Cute."

"I thought so. And lucky for me, my *professeur de lycée*, Mademoiselle Dumonch, thought so too. She hands me my paper back and scrawled across the top of it, in red ballpoint pen, it says—*I very much doubt that you read this, Sofia. But you talk a good talk—A+.*"

"*Did* you read it?"

"No. God no, I never read any of the books she assigned!"

Lila laughed. She took a sip of cognac and looked at the weakly inspired writer. "You don't like to read but you say you felt called to be a writer. Pardon me for saying this, but ... you sound a little bit lazy."

Sofia shrugged. "I blame Dumonch. She's the one who said I talk a good talk. When she said that, I thought, okay, I may as well get paid for it."

Lila shook her head. "So, what was so beguiling in your report that it earned you an A+?"

"I thumbed through the book and picked out this character that had caught my eye—the Duchess of Broadback, Frau Mann. She's a"—Sofia's eyes absently dropped to Lila's lips and stayed there—"aeria*lips*, aeria*lish*, aerial ... *er*—she's a trapeze artist. And the line that stuck with me, I still have it right here." She reached up and tapped her temple, giving a prideful little grin.

"Really?" Lila chuckled. "I'm surprised you can remember anything after drinking this stuff." She lifted her half-full glass.

"Like it was yesterday."

"Okay." Lila waited.

"So, she's wearing these tights they wear, Frau Mann, and she views them not as something covering her, but as herself, her skin. Here's what she wrote:

'*The span of the tightly stitched crotch was so much her own flesh that she was as unsexed as a doll. The needle that had made one the property of the child made the other the property of no man.*'"

Her grin widened in wicked triumph.

"Wow. Interesting."

"I finished up with a riff on Barnes's famous line—*'I'm not a lesbian. I just loved Thelma.'* You familiar with that one?"

"No. Sorry," she frowned. "I was a poli sci major."

"Well, anyway, I started my paper with the line, *I don't know Thelma. In fact, I've never even heard the name Thelma before. But I am a lesbian. And I hold it as a sacred pledge to forever stay that way. I am, and will always be, the property of no man.*"

"Strong words. Especially for a teenager."

"Well, it helped that Mademoiselle Dumonch was gay. That was the rumor, anyway." She lifted her glass in a toast.

Lila looked at her with renewed interest. One who knew her place and was so willing at such a young age to proclaim it to the world would not be so easily swayed from it, she suspected. And if that were true, then what was this supposed long-term romance between Wolf and her? Was it real? Was it a dark charade? And if so, to what end? Sitting there with lifted glass, pondering that question, Gus Ambrosia's words rushed to mind: *"The kid had a lot of dash."* That the girls hung on him, fawned over him when he sang "Baby, It's Cold Outside!" A show tune ... *Show tunes, for God's sake!*

"Oh, before I forget," Lila said, "did, uh, did Wolf *habla español?*"

"*Hablaba.* Imperfect tense—referring to something that used to happen regularly. You say: *¿Wolf hablaba español? Did Wolf speak Spanish?*" she smiled, her head teetering slightly. "*Sí, es verdad,* he did. And German. Anyway, my cousin, *Orfffilia Campos,* you know, she's the one you met at the Ceres Cafe. She's the one who owns this place—she was working as a junior secretary in the consulate. Wolf and I had run into each other a few times by then and we were talking about the 2008 Olympics when she came up with her boyfriend and introduced us. *Lil*—um, *little* did we know he was the Venezuela—er, he was Hugo. Not that we didn't know Hugo, of course we did. Everybody knows Hugo. We just didn't know Hugo was her boyfriend." When that failed to register, she added, "The Marxist President of Venezuela—Hugo Chavez?"

"Well, that's an interesting boyfriend to have for a junior secretary working in the consulate."

Sofia leaned close. "*Shhh*-ugar daddy," she whispered. She straightened and beamed drunkenly. "She stepped out on him all the time, though. Orfilia. Saw other men. *Shhh!*" she laughed. "She s*slipped halhalcyon* into his drink at night. *'Orfffilia!'* I told her, *'¡Eso es envenenamiento!' That's poisoning!* She told me, she said—'I just wanted him to *go to sleep!'* Ha! You believe that? *I just wanted him to go to sleep! El Presidente! Fucking Hugo!*"

Lila was still writing when she asked, "Did you guys hang out or—"

"No," Sofia laughed, "not really."

"Okay." Lila backed off. "I just thought, with Wolf being in law school, that maybe a young law student and the Head of State for Venezuela might have something to talk about." Lila reached for her drink to slow the pace down a bit before things got too sloppy. She wanted answers, but she knew better than to push.

"Oh, they did. Hugo was a perfect gentleman. Ah! That was a *fff*un night."

"I bet. What did you guys do?"

"As you said, hanging out with *El Presidente*," she said, "we had *lots* and lots of champagne, and we laughed! Wolf got to show off his *Español* and his admiration for Marx. It was great—I love your hair, by the way. Do you mind?" She reached over and ran her fingers lightly through Lila's hair.

"No," Lila chuckled, wrinkling her forehead, "that's fine. Although, if I had your hair, I'd wear it long too." She made a few more notes, thinking, *The owner of a limo company and a tanning salon a Marxist? Rather unlikely. Sounds like a pose.* And if he was posing, she wondered, to what end? Was he CIA like his old man? Didn't CIA want Chavez deposed? And what about the rumors that the CIA was responsible for his death? Could Wolf have played some role in that?"

"When did Chavez die?" Lila asked, feigning idle curiosity.

"Oh, Hugo died in 2013. He'd been sick for a couple of years."

Continuing to play with Lila's hair, Sofia pronounced, "I like it short. It looks good on you. It looks ... *muy intelegente.*"

Lila's lips spread in a timid smile. "So why did he drop out of school?"

Sofia finished fussing with Lila's hair. "There. *Perfecto*." She took another sip from her cognac. "After his first year, our relationship was getting pretty hot and heavy, so he decided to quit." She pursed her lips to one side.

"But what about your 'sacred pledge?'"

Sofia ignored the question. Instead, she rambled on: "And after we went to Caracas to meet my family, we moved to Chicago. Wolf grew up on a big dairy farm outside of Milwaukee, as you probably already know. I think his father lent him money to get him started in business."

Lila made a few more notes, one of which she coded—*ITQ—Ignored the Question*. "Did you two travel back and forth to Caracas regularly?"

"As often as we could. My family and I are *vvv*ery close."

"Both parents still living?"

"Yes. They're in their early sixties."

"You're lucky to have them." Lila jotted something down and asked, "I'd like to get back to the reason Wolf gave for dropping out of Law School ..."

"Oh, God, 'Too much red tape,' he said. He told me, 'Why be somebody else's bitch when I can go into business for myself? If I need a hired gun, I'll hire one.' That's when he started his limousine company. I told you about that, right?"

"You did."

"*Rrr*ight. Running conventioneers back and forth between O'Hare, Midway, and Downtown. That was his sweet spot. He made a lot of money doing that."

"Back at the Ceres Cafe," Lila said, "we were talking about how the newspapers used the term 'jilted.' You said Wolf was getting clingy."

"The day before he died, he left me *fff*ifteen rambling messages! Halloween was coming up the following day and he wanted the two of us take the limo out on the town. I had this *sss*uper slutty costume I'd worn the year before"—she gave a wicked little snicker—"very cheeky! I think maybe that memory got stuck in his brain. Me, I just couldn't do it anymore. So ... *nope!* I did not call him back." Again, with the lips pursed sideways. "Hindsight, right! Maybe I should have. Maybe if I'd called him back ..."

"But you kept his messages."

"Yeah."

Lila waited a few seconds and then asked, "Why?" She didn't need to hear the messages; she'd read the transcripts in the police file.

"Because he was starting to creep me out." She popped up from the couch and said, "Tell you what—I'm gonna go pee and get a refill, and then ..." she wavered slightly, "I'm going to show you my costume. You'll get a kick out of it. You need a refresher?"

"No, thanks. Still working on this one." Lila watched her glide unevenly away. "Seriously," Sofia called out from the other room, "wait until you see this."

"Can't wait!" Lila called back. She shook her head and looked around the room, at the tassels, at the paintings.

Several minutes later, Sofia came slinking down the hall in a long, red, Veronica Lake wig, wearing bright red stiletto heels and a strapless, boob-hugging, sparkling red dress slit all the way up to her hip.

Again, Lila's heart began to race and flutter. "Jessica Rabbit!" she laughed, her face flushing.

Sofia drew near and turned slowly about, showing her backless gown. She arched a come-hither eyebrow from beneath her red peek-a-boo hair-style and did a sexy little shimmy. "*¿Sí, te gusta?*" she teased, rubbing up against Lila's leg.

Instead of standing outside looking in, nose pressed against the glass, a child held rapt before a wondrous glamour she could never attain to, Lila was sharing the glow, feeling lifted and renewed, melting just a little. She felt ravished by the sudden warmth washing through her.

Sofia laughed and kicked off her shoes and wig. "*Ooofff,* I forgot my drink!" she said, running on tiptoes back down the hall. When she returned, her nipples were peeking over the top of her dress. Lila blushed, trying to avert her gaze as Sofia plopped down on the couch next to her, leaned over, and abruptly said, "*I'll Never Love Again!* I love this song. Let's dance."

"Oh!" Lila laughed, "okay." When she got up, Sofia wrapped both arms around her and began to sway slowly, rocking back and forth, slightly out of time, singing softly along.

Sofia gently kissed Lila's neck. "Here's the thing about this dress," she whispered breathily. She took Lila's hand, placed it on her still-partially-exposed breast, and kissed her again.

"I need to tell you something," Lila managed to say, "I have been with women before, you know, tricks in a past life, but I'm not—"

"You're not *what?*" Sofia's lips were again on Lila's neck.

"I'm not ... *gay.*"

"Don't be so categorical." The kisses kept coming, gentle, teasing, testing, exploring.

"My point is ..." Lila shivered, the hair lifting on the back of her neck, "this isn't going anywhere. This *can't* go anywhere." She closed her eyes and let her head fall back, felt her heart pounding. "I've moved on," she said breathlessly, fighting the urge that contradicted her words. "Survival instinct."

"From what? *To* what? Just relax," Sofia replied. "*Re-lax.* There's no gender here. No labels. No categories. It's like Djuna Barnes said—we are 'beasts turning human.'"

They danced for a while, but it wasn't long before Sofia stumbled to the sofa, fell back into the pillows, and passed out. Lila stood over her, smiling down at her red dress all askew, then went down the hall to the master, grabbed a blanket from Sofia's bed, and came back to gently tuck it around the snoring woman. Still smiling, she quietly let herself out. When she climbed into the driver's seat of her car, she took out her notebook and, flipping it over to the back pages, scored her mood a "ten."

16

February 8, 2018

Mark Morgan's Lincoln Park Brownstone
Chicago, Illinois

IT WAS WELL PAST TWO O'CLOCK IN THE MORNING WHEN LILA showed up at Mark's house. She banged on his front door before backing off the concrete stoop and looking up, her eyes focused on the snowy second-story bay window.

A dog started barking, and a light came on.

At first, the curtains remained perfectly still. *Do I have the right address?* she wondered. Only after she gave an enthusiastic wave were the curtains drawn open and Mark appeared, bare-chested, clad only in black boxers. He held up a forefinger, then gestured down at the front door.

She stepped back onto the stoop and stuffed her hands deep into her coat pockets, shearling collar up, vaporous breath dissolving in the frosty night air.

Finally, the door swung open.

"Lila!" he said, collaring his dog and bringing him to heel.

"And this must be Bertrude!" she said a little too loudly.

Mark turned to the dog, heeled obediently behind him, and said, "Good boy."

Bertrude, staying put, let out a low *"Woof!"*

Mark sent the dog away with a commanding wave of his hand then quickly pulled shut his ankle-length terry robe. He stepped aside to let her in. "To what do I owe this ... delightful surprise?"

In lieu of a verbal reply, she pressed herself into his arms and gave him a soulful kiss, practically knocking him over. He responded in kind, one hand blindly groping for the door to shut out the frigid night air.

After the door clicked shut, he spun her around, kissing her passionately. His hand found its way to her breast the instant her back touched the wall and she slipped her hands inside his robe, feeling the warmth of his skin as he reached for the button on her waistband.

She gasped when his warm, tentative fingers finally reached her. She drew a deep, longing breath and pulled him closer before gently pushing him away.

He looked down at her and smiled in confusion, scrutinizing her with a subtle shift of his head. He blinked a few times as if to clear the sleep from his eyes, then asked, "What time is it?"

She glanced down at her watch, catching her breath. "Two forty-five." Her hands dropped and quickly re-buttoned her waistband.

"And we said our goodbyes at what," he asked, "nine or so?" He didn't seem angry. "Anyway, how'd you find me?"

"Hello. Private investigator."

His lips spread in a mischievous grin. "Could've saved both of us the trouble if you'd just come home with me."

"I didn't come here for sex." She said it so fast that it didn't sound credible and, when she saw his face fall, she quickly added, "Maybe I did —I don't know ... I'm a little freaked out right now." Seeing the lack of apprehension or remorse in his eyes as he smiled down at her, she added, "But I like being with you." She reached up and gave the lapels of his robe a single gentle tug as if to underscore what she'd said, and then laughed at herself, feeling ridiculous. She didn't like being that girl—the *cocktease*.

"Come," he said, taking her hand and leading her into the kitchen. "You look like you could use a cup of coffee. I know I could."

"You won't be able to get back to sleep!"

"Nonsense. I'm immune to caffeine."

Lila took her coat off and slung it over the back of one of his metal-mesh chairs. She sat down at the table, silently watching him as he filled the pot with water. His robe favored his masculine build: broad shoulders, narrow waist, long legs.

"Whole wheat toast?" he asked over his shoulder, "artisan jam?"

She shrugged. "Sure."

She watched him in silence as he worked. After a moment, a steaming cup and a plate of buttered toast were placed in front of her. Yawning, he sank into the chair opposite her.

She picked up the toast, still watching the serious look on his face as he dipped his knife into the jar and, with surgical precision, smeared jam onto his toast. Something was refreshing about the domesticity of the moment, and she wanted to just sit and watch him work in the quietness of the early morning. Finally, she said, "Sorry I'm such a mess." She put her toast back onto the plate and said, "I've actually got a lot going on right now, and I'm afraid sometimes I'm not very good at dealing with all the balls in the air."

He looked up her as he set the knife down on his plate. "Don't worry about it. I get it."

Lila smiled weakly. Had it always been this hard telling empty signs from omens? It made her feel edgy, and the fact that it was so obvious to a man she barely knew only added to her turmoil. She looked into his eyes. Mark Morgan was every bit as attractive as Sofia Castellanos. Not more, not less—equally. Different. She thought about Sofia. What was it, she wondered, that pushed Sofia to pick one lifestyle over the other? Was it the beast in her, or the human she was turning into, as she claimed? And, as for the scolding side of herself, Lila wondered whether it was a beastly thing, or in fact humane, to be open to both? *"Our capacity to go deep,"*

Mark had told her over dinner, *"to go anywhere in the water column without anybody knowing it, and do anything we want there, is the greatest security asset we have."* That's why she was here. The other side, she decided, was just the dark side of the moon.

"So, it turns out," she said, "the victim spoke Spanish."

He furrowed his brows. "Sorry?"

"Wait," she frowned, "I didn't actually tell you about the case I'm working on, did I?"

"No, you ... did not. First date, right? You never want to say too much."

"Are you really worried about dating rules?" she asked. "At your age?"

"Ha! No."

"Me neither. Besides, you seem like a guy a girl can talk to."

"Well, thanks," he grinned. "I think."

"I mean it." She put her cup down and proceeded to fill in the blanks for him, explaining how she was working two nearly identical "falls from height," taking care to not name any names. "My client is convinced somebody murdered his son," she said, reaching for her cup again.

"And what do you think?"

"At first I doubted it. Now, I'm not so sure." She took a quick sip of coffee, then started sketching the number of areas that concerned her.

"One is the eyewitness's change of story," she explained. "She was there, the witness, standing at the window of her sixteenth-floor apartment when she saw my client's son plummet to his death. At first, she claimed that she saw only one rope. That, it turns out, was a crucial clue. But that's changed. Now she claims that she saw two ropes. Which, if she's remembering correctly, can only mean one thing: that the victim was not alone the night he fell. He had to have someone with him. Why? The police only found the one rope at the scene, and that was a half-frozen TV cable, which was blamed for the accident. So, the question is— what were they doing up there? Why were they up there?"

Mark sat there, listening.

"The second issue is the recent overdose of the other victim's widow.

Recall that I said I'm working two virtually identical falls from height on the same night. Literally, twenty-seven minutes apart. The widow lived with the second victim in the projects—one of the Lawndale apartment buildings. Her deal is peculiar: she accepted delivery of a new mattress the other day. Was it something she ordered? PD's looking into it."

"What are you thinking? A professional hit?" he said, frowning.

"Exactly. The mattress delivery could have been a ruse to get her to open the door. But, if that's the case, then why a mattress box when a shoebox probably would have done the trick?"

Mark nodded.

"The third issue is the news that both my client and his chief business rival just happen to have a history working for ... wait for it ... the CIA."

"Ah!" he said, shifting on his chair, his robe falling open to reveal his smooth chest. "So this is the frequency illusion you mentioned."

"Exactly." Lila averted her gaze. "They were both paramilitary case officers."

His brows knitted, his dark brown eyes a reproach to all the world's uncertainties and disorders. Lila swallowed.

"Fourth: the victim himself. I've learned that he was disgruntled by his injury that dropped him from the '08 Summer Olympics in Beijing. He qualified for the US gymnastics team. Everything I hear about him points to him being pretty squared away. He was a scholar and an elite athlete. He was a responsible kid around the house, helped his dad build up his dairy operation while the old man was away during the war. Then the story gets interesting."

"I don't know, seems pretty interesting already."

"He meets his girlfriend a few years ago while attending Georgetown Law. She's a young Venezuelan expat who lives at the building he fell from. Abruptly, he quit during his second year of school. See, this fascinates me in light of what you said about CIA not being particularly keen on lawyers."

"So, you think this fall victim was a CIA recruit? That he dropped out of law school to be a better candidate?"

Lila shrugged. "And to top that off, turns out his girlfriend's cousin, a former low-level secretary working in the consulate, was Hugo Chavez's mistress which ... I suppose you could simply chalk up to a glandular affair were it not for the rather troubling fact that she just happens to own a number of multi-million-dollar properties all over the world. Where does she get her dough? Chavez died in 2013. Rest assured, checking to see if she has any visible means of support is high on my to-do list. I've met her and believe me, this gal's a piece of work. Adds a little kick by way of sleeping pills to her sugar daddy's nightcap so she can slip out and cat around at night."

Mark scratched the back of his head. "So you've got Hugo Chavez, this gal's rich cousin and ... and *how* is that relevant to the case you're working?"

Lila took another bite of toast and a sip of coffee. After a moment's pause, she went on, "Fifth issue: it turns out my client's son was fluent in Spanish, and his girlfriend says he and Chavez talked about Marx together. So, the way I'm seeing it at"—she glanced down at her watch —"a little after three in the morning, you've got a multi-lingual guy who lives in DC, drops out of law school, attends embassy galas, and ends up one step removed from the leader of a major South American country caught in the grips of a socialist revolution. Is it a coincidence that CIA's headquarters in Langley is close by? Could be. It seems that he hits just about every note you mentioned as far as being a dream fit for the agency."

Mark stared past her, taking it all in. "And there's the legacy factor," he said slowly, glancing back at her, "following in his father's footsteps."

"Oh! Oh!" She began lightly tapping the tabletop with the flat of her hand. "And to top it all off—my informant in Lawndale tells me that the second victim bragged about working for CIA, said that they're likely to run almost a hundred million in narcotics through there this year. A hundred million!"

Mark recoiled as far as the chair would allow. "That ..." he said, "is an enormous amount of money. Is your informant credible?"

"Credible enough. And the second guy that fell that night, my guy says he was gettin' high on his own supply."

"Occupational hazard, I guess."

"That he got from some 'highballer' who was backing him—all while he was running around boasting about how he was working with the CIA. Was the CIA behind the hit? An international drug cartel? Both?" Lila was quiet for a moment. "Anyway, all of this leads me to believe that my client's suspicions are right—that his son *was* murdered, that neither fall was an accident. I don't think I'm reaching for something that isn't there or chasing phantoms because of an old man's suffering—no, he was murdered, all right. Now I just need to find out who killed him."

"Interesting problem to mull over," Mark said.

"You're familiar with Occam's razor?" she asked.

"Sure. Simpler solutions are more likely to be correct than complex ones."

"Exactly. And unless I'm missing something, I don't see a simple solution in any of this."

He took a breath. "So maybe it's time to pull back."

"Too many nagging threads ... oh," she said, gazing down into her cup, "and one last thing."

"There's more?"

"Turns out the son's girlfriend, she's gay. Came out in high school. She told me that she'd broken it off with the victim after she decided she preferred women. But she was a pretty radical teenager, sexually speaking, and if she's as deeply gay as I suspect then it's likely that she and the victim were never an item. So, the question is—was he gay, too? Was she his beard? And, if so, why? What was the real connection? And what is *their* connection to this toxic chick with all the unearned dough?"

"Pretty huge leap, there." Mark sat back in his chair. "'Preferred' doesn't mean 'exclusively likes.' I *prefer* steak, but I'll eat chicken. You ever stop to think she might be bi?"

Lila cocked her head. "Yeah, you're not helping."

"Sorry."

"Another key question."

He listened, waiting.

"To your point, his so-called girlfriend claimed that he'd called and left fifteen messages that night. If they weren't an item, why was he calling? She wasn't lying about the number of calls. PD got all her messages off her phone—I met with an old friend of mine down at PDHQ who showed me the transcripts; I read the victim's actual words. He was either frantic or a damn good actor. Naturally, PD concluded they were hearing an impassioned plea from a jealous and jilted lover. That's one interpretation. There are others."

"You think he needed to get into her apartment for some other reason."

"I do. If the two deaths are related and the second victim was knee-deep in drug-running, maybe the first one had his fingers in it too. I suppose it's possible that he was using her apartment as his stash house. Maybe she knew; maybe she didn't."

"Venezuela is ... intriguing," Mark said, "especially in light of Chavez's opposition to Yankee imperialism."

"Yes, but does it have anything to do with anything?"

Mark fell silent, lost in thought. A few moments on, he said, "Let me tell you something I learned in the fast-attack fleet."

"Go on."

"The best defense is an aggressive offense. For fast-attack boats, it's our entire *raison-d'être*."

"And?" she said, getting up and going to the sink to empty and rinse her cup.

"And"—he got up to join her, putting his cup in the sink beside hers —"I'd be very careful if I were you. Sounds like you're treading in deep waters here. Dark waters. Somebody could get nervous."

"Somebody could get *aggressive* is what you're saying."

"Sounds like you're dealing with some dangerous folks," he said, "and by that I mean the kind of people comfortable with killing one another." He looked at her and held her gaze.

Unexpectedly, she kissed him.

He drew her into his arms and kissed her back. She stood on her tiptoes, raking her fingers lightly through his hair, pressing her body into his. He reached under her arms and lifted her up, whispering in a husky voice, "Let's take this upstairs."

He took her hand and led her up the staircase and into his bedroom. They stood there, just inside the door, holding hands, the king-size bed looming deafeningly in front of them, the white sheets disheveled, several pillows leaning haphazardly against the black leather headboard.

Lila looked from the inviting bed up to his face. "Well?" she said.

He laughed and pulled her over to the bed, lifted her up, and gently dropped her onto it, then pulled her shirt up over her head and found her lips again, kissing with renewed passion.

The morning arrived with a blinding reminder that the drapes had been left open. The light blared into Lila's eyes like a silent alarm. When she finally realized where she was, she found she was alone.

She stretched, got up to pee, and, on the way back, smiled at herself in the mirror. She fussed with her hair. "Mark!" she called out. No answer. Then again, louder this time: "Mark?" Nothing. Spotting his robe draped over a chair, she slipped it on and padded downstairs to look for him, only to discover that she was alone in the house. Even the dog was gone. What was happening? Why did he disappear? She went over to her purse and grabbed her notebook, something familiar—something she could control. Shivering, feeling as if the floor was beginning to give way beneath her, she leaned on the table and scribbled a "four" in her notebook. She was halfway back up the stairs when the front door swung open.

"Hey! You get my note?" he asked. He gazed down into the open bagel bag he held in his hand. When he looked up at her again, he smiled.

"No!" she answered more caustically than she'd intended. Once upset, it was doubly hard for her to shift gears. "And I don't appreciate you leaving without telling me. It's not just rude, it's fucking irritating!" She realized that maybe she was especially on edge due to their "dangerous folks" exchange the night before, but being aware of that didn't make it better.

"I left you a note," he said again, confused. "You were sleeping so soundly; I didn't want to wake you." He held up the goodies. "I just ran down to Bagelers. I'm sorry." He shrugged. "I figured you for a bagel gal."

She looked at the coffeehouse bag, her anger wrestling with relief and the embarrassing awareness of how ridiculous she must seem. She took a calming breath, counted silently to ten, then said, "Did you get cream cheese?"

"Of course."

"Okay then."

17

February 9, 2018

Les Nomades Restaurant
Chicago, Illinois

LATER THAT NIGHT, LILA ARRIVED AT LES NOMADES' TURN-OF-THE-century brownstone a half-hour late.

She had agreed to be Mark's date at a dinner with a prospective employer, the founder of a small tech start-up from Dallas looking to expand into Chicago. The moment she stepped through the door and confronted the crowded room, she regretted coming. Despite the clubby mood and opulent décor—things she normally found stimulating—she felt like collapsing into a gray heap. Too much exuberance and intimacy carried too late into the wee hours of the night had left her feeling emotionally and physically drained. On top of that, it had been a frustrating day: instead of investigative legwork, she'd spent the entire day holed up in her apartment, entering her notes into her computer and working on a push-pin flow chart stringing together the different clues. Very few conclusions had resulted from it.

Passing by the bar on the way to the table, her very first meeting with Jim Savage popped into her head. They had talked about whales, she recalled. A cynical grin lifted the corner of her lips.

Seeing Mark smile back at her as she approached the table only added to her stress level; she wished she'd had enough time to pay Gail another visit. Mark and his two guests were already deep in conversation when he got up and pulled her chair out for her. Their glasses were half-empty and an open bottle of *Rhône Blanc* was chilling in a silver ice bucket.

"Ah! You made it!" Mark said with a warm smile. He motioned for the waiter hovering nearby to pour her a glass of wine. "And bring another bottle," he said.

She smiled weakly at her wine glass. "Sorry I'm late," she said to Mark's guests, then extended her hand. "Hi, I'm Lila."

"Abby," the green-eyed, dark-haired woman (mid-to-late forties, perhaps?) said with an ingratiating smile.

"Jack," her husband said, rising to his feet. He shook Lila's hand and sat back down. He let Lila sip her wine before shooting a smirk her way. "Tough day at the office, kid?"

"Jack, *please!*" Abby protested, rolling her eyes. "At least *pretend* to be civilized."

"That's okay, I don't mind," Lila said, flashing her a tight-lipped smile, already annoyed by the woman's pretentiousness. "Cheers," she muttered.

"*Skol!*" Jack said out loud, glancing between Mark and Abby.

Abby took a sparrow's sip and put her glass down before everyone else. "Now, where were we?" she asked Mark.

"The opera," Mark answered, sending an inclusive glance Lila's way.

"*Yes! Rigoletto!*" Abby gushed, drawing in a deep breath. Jack gazed down at his watch. His wife turned to Lila and effused, "My husband took us to the Winspear Opera House in Dallas when Mark came to visit. We saw *Rigoletto.* Did Mark tell you?"

"No, he didn't mention it," Lila said with an indifferent smile over her wineglass.

Abby reached over and gripped Mark's arm and gave him a squeeze through his jacket. "My God!" she almost cried, lunging toward Lila, "the *ending!* Are you familiar with *Rigoletto?*"

Lila shook her head. "I'm not really up on opera." She chuckled and shot a sympathetic glance Jack's way.

"Well, it's just *sooo* tragic, as these things are." Abby leaned further forward, as if sharing a secret. "You see ... Rigoletto, he's the hunchback court jester; well, he gets cursed early on by the Duke of Mantua for making fun of one of the Duke's cuckolded courtiers. It seems the Duke enjoys cuckolding his courtiers—sort of a hobby of his.

"Anyway," she went on, "later, when the tables get turned and Rigoletto's beautiful daughter, Gilda, becomes the Duke's lover, Rigoletto pays a hitman to assassinate him. When the murderous deed is done, he receives the Duke's corpse in a sack as proof, which he then begins weighing down with stones, you know, to toss in the river ..."

Lila sat there in troubled silence, darting the occasional impatient glance at Abby's hand as it continued to grip Mark's arm. The sound of the woman's insufferable voice, her unending monologue on operatic drama ... well, it was beginning to grate. She drew in a recalibrating breath, struggling to keep at bay the encroaching darkness. From the folds of Abby's taut fingers, a distorted, half-there spider leg slowly emerged, caressing Mark's folded arm, elongating impossibly. It rose further, a glinting, graceless orb perched upon a hundred-odd legs, and Lila felt her jaw stiffen, her fingernails dig into her palm. It wasn't real, of course; a hallucination caused by stress and lack of sleep, she thought, probably inspired by that flow-chart she had just slaved over. Abby had paused, she realized with a start—she smiled, nodded, and said "Wow!"

If Abby had noticed her unease, she gave no sign of it. "Now, just when Rigoletto is about to drop the sack into the river," she said, green eyes bulging, "he hears the voice of the Duke, singing '*La donna è mobile*' in the distance ..."

The thought of an ad-hoc visit to Gail's clinic shot into Lila's head unbidden—it was as if her doctor was sitting right there in front of her. Drawing another calming breath, Lila imagined the TMS hood lowering over her head. The clinking of cutlery became the reassuring clicking sound of the sea creatures in her beach-side happy place, soft but clear.

Abruptly, she froze. It was no longer her, Lila Piper, staring out over a white beach, the velvet sea beyond—no, it was Louis Breem, his blood-curdling screams shattering the peace, the effort not restoring his body, his equilibrium, but rather propelling him through incomprehensible violence, his body splitting, trembling, contorting. It was as if somehow she had switched places with him; it was his head that was whipping back and forth, his voice that shrieked from the bowels of his soul.

"Amazed that he hears the Duke's voice," Abby continued, her voice a sickening shriek, "Rigoletto rips open the sack and, to his absolute horror—and I mean *horror!*—he discovers his dying daughter. For a moment, she opens her eyes and tells him she's glad to die for her beloved. *'Father, I deceived you,'* she says. Then she dies in his arms. Rigoletto cries out in horror ... *'La maledizione!'*"

Mark and Jack joined in, both in high spirits: "'The curse!'"

Lila heard the word "Curse" but, in her fevered mind, the thoughts were going by so fast that she couldn't control them; they were no longer hers to manage. They weren't talking about *Rigoletto,* she realized, but about *her*—laughing at *her.* An icy shiver shot through her. She was no longer the person she saw reflected in the glass partition just beyond their table; the identity known as Lila was becoming inconsequential, erased, and something alien yet horribly resident was taking its place.

The sensation was exacerbated by sneering thoughts: *He's forgotten you; it's obvious!* Mark was doubled over laughing, Abby still clutching his arm. At once, Lila shot out of her chair. "I can't!" she spat, "sorry!" She grasped at her head. "So sorry, I have to go." She turned and hurried out of the restaurant.

Mark caught up to her by the valet stand outside. He gently grabbed her by the crook of her arm and forced her to look him in the eye. "Okay ... what was that about?"

Now it was definitive—she'd lost her mind. She could see it in the way he was looking at her. Shaking her head, eyes welling up, she said, "See what's in store for you getting involved with me? I don't *do* relationships. Just ... just let me go." She jerked her arm free. "I'm ... not equipped."

"Let me be the judge of that," he said quietly, pulling her closer. He gazed out at the blackened street, wet from the snow, at the passing cars *swooshing* by, and, after waving off a yellow cab pulling to the curb, whispered, "I don't know, maybe I should nix those season tickets to the opera."

The remark caught Lila completely off-guard. She burst out laughing in spite of herself and, in that unexpected moment, began to reassemble the scattered molecules of her former personality.

"Maybe," he said, his hand on her chin, gently lifting her head, "instead ... what say we focus on developing a plan for figuring out this ... Holzinger thing that's got you so ... *upset*."

"Absurd and pathetic, you mean," she said, looking back at him, longing to rise above her maddening agitation, her eyes tearing against her will. She rested her head on his chest and let her gaze drift briefly to the passing metallic blue BMW M5, the second time in as many days she'd seen the suspicious sedan—Y-spoke wheels, run-flat tires.

"*Upset*," he said again with an emphatic nod. He leaned down to kiss her forehead. "*Upset* is enough. No virtue in piling on."

"Okay."

"So how about we finish the evening with our out-of-town guests?" he asked.

She nodded and relented, glumly following him back toward the restaurant.

Then, just two steps from the door, she stopped suddenly. Again, the encroaching darkness. "Why did you say 'Holzinger thing?'"

"Hmm?"

"I didn't mention any names last night. How did you know my client's name was Holzinger?"

He stared at her for what was maybe a moment too long, then dipped his head in puppy-dog guilt. "I confess—I was curious. I Googled news articles about simultaneous falls from apartment buildings in Chicago."

She scanned his eyes for sincerity.

"The victim's first name was Wolf, I believe? Owned a ... tanning salon. Or something."

"Oh," she responded sheepishly, "okay."

"Hello. Former naval intelligence."

"Touché," she conceded with a slight grin.

She really needed a good night's rest.

18

February 10, 2018

McManus & Piper Securities
Chicago, Illinois

LILA LOOKED AWAY FROM HER BROTHER AND PICKED SILENTLY AT her *salade niçoise,* her thoughts wandering to Mark. She wondered whether he'd received the bouquet of flowers she'd sent to him, whether he'd read the note she'd included:

> *Dear Mark,*
> *I am so sorry for embarrassing you last night. I can't tell you how*
> *worried I am that I may have thrown a wrench into the works for*
> *you, ruining the impression left on your potential employer. I can't*
> *promise it will never happen again, but I do hope you can*
> *forgive me.*
> *Lila*

She'd find out soon enough. Right now, she had her brother's issues to address.

Although Ulli was four years younger than she was, the heavy bags under his eyes were beginning to resemble the anemic oysters that had hung under their father's eyes when he'd had one foot in the grave. Ulli was thirty-four years old, but he looked like a beleaguered old geezer—now, he was quietly chewing his ribeye steak, a faraway look in his eyes. Lila didn't say anything. Instead, she sat there, playing the patient companion, watching him take the last bite of steak followed by a gulp of *Beaujolais*. When he put down the empty wineglass, he snatched up the white linen napkin he had tucked into his collar, dabbed his mouth, and, barely missing a beat, launched into his usual rationalizations. Predictably, everyone around him had apparently been making a hash of things. *Yeah*, Lila said to herself, *everybody else's fault but yours*.

The story he gave her was pretty much what she'd expected—the now-infamous drug lord and leader of the Sinaloa drug cartel, Ismael Zaldavar Valiente—*La Ballena*—had been the bank's best client and therefore had merited "extra attention." In retrospect, Ulli posited, maybe he'd given the complex Mexican businessman more leeway than he should have. "We're a boutique investment bank, Lila," he said, clutching his dessert fork between his forefinger and thumb and indiscriminately stabbing the air around him. "We can't compete with the big boys." *Stab*. "The only edge we have is the concierge-level personal service we provide our clients." *Stab*. "It's all about high touch, our business." *Stab*. "All of it."

The final grumpy stab he reserved for his cheddar-smothered slice of hot apple pie.

"That doesn't justify breaking the law, Ulli," Lila replied, idly skewering a black olive before putting her fork down, the olive still attached. "And what's this about *smurfing?*"

Ulli glanced down at the olive and back to his sister. "I had no idea what Señor Valiente was up to. Money starts pouring in, you take what you can get."

She looked at him, her face tightening. "Whatever happened to due diligence?"

"So you obviously heard about his arrest," he said, speaking over a mouthful of pie.

"I did."

They looked at each other then for a long time. Behind the mask, in her brother's rebuked and exhausted eyes, she saw an unfamiliar depth of loneliness and despair not that far removed from the terror she had seen in his eyes that day in the pool. Maybe he'd been hoping she hadn't heard about the big customs bust in Tampa, or perhaps that she hadn't seen *La Ballena*'s name mentioned in the report or else wasn't well-enough acquainted with Valiente to place him in her floundering brother's company. Wrong on all counts. It would be interesting to hear the excuse he came up with as to why he was so deeply involved with a man indicted for trafficking thousands of kilos of narcotics and bulk quantities of US currency. And who knew how many millions had ended up on their balance sheet? Lila held her brother's gaze and waited.

Finally, Ulli broke the silence. "Look, when you have the kind of dough Señor Valiente throws around, you can't help rubbing shoulders with a few colorful characters. Flies to honey, you know? It's entirely possible that Señor Valiente wasn't aware that his friends were that ... *shady*. I suspect he merely figured they were as generous and free-spending with their pals as he was with his. I'll tell you what I think"—he pointed his fork at her—"I think he got caught up in the glamour of it. What can I say? Man likes to party. So, the feds nab him on guilt by association. I'm sure his lawyers will get this cleaned up in no time."

"From what I've read in the news about Tampa, he'd better hope so."

A more repentant tone overtook her brother's former confidence. "We *all* had better hope so."

"Don't think we can hope our way out of this one, Ulli. What are your plans?"

He slammed his fork down, playing his characteristic role of mean-spirited prick. "Okay." He leaned aggressively over his dessert plate. "I'm not taking any more of your shit! You forget to take your meds again? I know what you're trying to do here!"

She looked at him dumbfounded. "What are you talking about?"

"You think you can use this trumped-up money-laundering BS to finally wrest control of the bank away from me. Ain't gonna happen. I'm warning you right now—*we'll go to the mattresses.*"

Lila's mouth gaped open. "*Still* defensive?!"

He almost threw himself back in his chair, his lip curling. "What do you mean *still?*"

"You pulled this same crap when I used to help you with your math homework. Always thinking I was putting you down when all I ever wanted to do was help."

"Yeah? And you think that's not a put-down? How many fucking times do I have to hear that same fucking story—how you were so gifted and I was so slow, how you just *had* to chip in and lend baby brother a hand instead of going outside to play with your friends? Cause Mom was shitfaced again, taking her daily *nap.*"

"Our mother was *sick,* Ulli. Dad was always working; who else was there to pitch in?"

"Oh, I know. You never fail to hold that over my head."

"You're my brother! We're supposed to be on the same side. And for God's sake, the last thing I want to do is take over the fucking bank! Jeez! Where's your head? You take a hundred thousand dollars a month in uncontested comp and you pay me sixty a year, do I complain?"

"You don't *do* anything!"

"The bank picks up the tab for your five-hundred-thousand-dollar twin-engine plane, did you ever hear me object to that little sweetener? Or any of your other spiffs and perks?"

"No, but you certainly seem to be keeping score."

"It's a fucking *business,* Ulli! That's the point—you're *supposed* to keep score!"

"Dad set up his foundation with Len Seidman and I controlling and with you holding non-voting shares. And you—you just can't get over it." He snorted past his sideways smirk.

"Oh, do *not* get me started with Len Seidman and the Dr. Frank Piper Foundation he engineered specifically to freeze me out. Just so you know, I may hold non-voting shares, but if I wanted to—*if* I wanted to—I could sue Mr. Len Seidman up one side and down the other for all the so-called 'legal' work he's done and the egregious amount of money he's stolen from our family while pitting one against the other to serve his own self-interest. He's not a lawyer, he's a parasite. Man's as corrupt as the day is long. The sooner you recognize that, the better off we'll both be."

"He kept Dad out of jail; he's worth every penny we pay him. You're just mad at him because you two have a past—"

Lila shot out of her chair. *"A past!"* she erupted, throwing her napkin down on the table. She jerked her head back and looked at him sideways, "The man paid me to fuck him. That's not exactly a past."

"And you took the money," he said under his breath.

"Fuck you!"

His eyes flew to the closed boardroom door. "Come on, *language!*"

"Yeah, I took the money. It wasn't romantic, it wasn't erotic, it was a cut-and-dried business transaction. That's on me—my bad. Act first, pay the consequences later. I've since come to terms with my demons ..."

"Oh, *really?*"

"There is another side to the story," she went on, "let's not forget that Mr. Len 'Svengali' Seidman, Esquire, is a piece of shit who was not only Dad's friend but his *lawyer* and, as such, he owed him a fiduciary responsibility. And he used that, he used my ... admittedly *colossal* immaturity and emotional ... *challenges*, of which he was all too well-aware ... to drive a wedge between a dying man and his only daughter just so he could line his fucking pockets.

"*That,* my dear brother, is unforgivable. I know Seidman's the one who came up with the non-voting shares idea. You think a court might be interested in hearing about that little detail? How Len paid your troubled sister for sex and then used that information to alienate our father's affections from me to get closer to you? Keep you fat and happy with a big plump comp package while he goes about his business, manipulating the wishes of a dying man and quietly robbing us both blind?"

Ulli reeled back, eyes wide. "So *that's* your strategy! You're going after Len and, once you've eliminated my *consigliere*, you're gonna come after me!"

"Oh, *jeez—nooo!* And will you cut it with the never-ending *Godfather* references."

"Then what *do* you want?"

"I want some information."

"Yeah, I bet you do."

"You do business in Venezuela?"

"Yeah, so?"

"At the Banco de Venezuela?"

"BDV, yeah," he said quickly.

"I'd like you to see if you can get them to give you a comprehensive ... financial snapshot on somebody I'm investigating."

He glanced down at his watch and then looked at her. "What you're asking for is called their 'total wallet.' Who is it?"

"Her name is Orfilia Campos. Caracas is her home base. I'm betting she keeps at least one account with BDV. I want to know everything there is to know about her finances—how much she has and where it comes from. Everything they have on her. You think you can do that for me? Despite my callous regard for your hurt feelings and, God knows, the manifold errors of my past."

"Like I said—*total wallet*. And this has nothing to do with the bank or—"

"You have my word. This has nothing to do with us. It's a case I'm working."

It took a minute, but finally he gave his familiar little grin. "Okay, let me see what I can do."

19

February 10, 2018

Sofia Castellanos's Gold Coast Apartment
Chicago, Illinois

HE'S JUST PARANOID, LILA TOLD HERSELF, THINKING ABOUT HER brother. *He's got a family; he's under a lot of pressure.* There was their painful past to contend with and, even though trying to make sense from the senseless usually got her into trouble, she couldn't stop herself. Holzinger had spotted it right off. She'd been raised in a military family where discipline, good order, and high moral values had constantly been reinforced. Trouble was, through the jaundiced scrim of booze and pain meds, it had proven rather hard to live with.

Lila had tried to save her mother but, in the end, probably only ended up quickening her death. She'd always been an anxious woman, and the last thing she'd needed was her daughter running wild at the Chicago O'Hare Hilton—her husband's drawn-out legal battles had been bad enough.

One side of Lila's mind understood that her family's troubles had left an indelible stamp on her kid brother, just as it had on her—for the longest time, she hadn't known who the hell she was, and had enough trouble just trying to corral her thoughts. Her efforts to explore the boundaries between romantic and erotic feelings had been nothing more than callow attempts to figure out not only who she was, but who she *should* be—attempts to get to the center of the funhouse mirror she too often saw as her reflection.

The other side of her mind, the *"open sea"* side, refused to lay her life's choices on her chaotic family. There were different depths to a person just as there were different depths to the sea. From the surface to the abyss, there were zones defined by the light that could reach them —*sunlight, twilight, midnight, lower midnight.* She asked herself the age-old questions: Can we not conquer ourselves? Can we not become free agents, reimagine our identities, and ultimately gain control of our destinies, living out meaningful lives in the illuminated zone? Or are we all merely bottom feeders, forced to feel around in the dark, transparent and eyeless? She recalled something her father had told her: *"Damn lawyers picked me clean. Your brother's going to run the bank. It's best for both of you—he's stable; he knows the business. Don't worry, Len Seidman and I have been bringing him along."* Sensing her disappointment, he'd added, *"It's the best thing, you'll see. You, on the other hand, should get a law degree. Keep the two of you from going broke like your old man, paying the goddamned lawyers every time you turn around."*

So, Lila became a lawyer; just not the kind that her brother had wanted. But maybe, she was beginning to suspect, the kind he ultimately needed; not one who practiced law or worked for the bank directly, but one who concentrated on getting concrete answers rather than artful explanations, one with a real talent for getting people to say what they'd rather not."

Lila got into her car and started the engine.

She followed Lake Michigan, the frozen waves whipping by along the fringe of the shoreline, and mulled over her options. She would resist being provoked into what her brother and Seidman could point to as irrational and self-destructive behavior. The wound Ulli had opened up had left her nerves feeling raw and exposed, and a plan, fully formed, flashed into her mind. Savage was right about her "bloodhound gift." A dry smile curled her lips.

She knew exactly how to get Sofia to talk. She let out a soft snort at her sudden flash of brilliance. Experience had taught her that it was gloom that always preceded a breakthrough. That was her true gift—her ability to dance on the stark divide between her darkest moments and the dawning of the light. Now, it hit her like a 1200-watt strobe.

Sofia was quick to invite her over for drinks and, as soon as they were seated comfortably on the couch, Lila opened up about her brother's legal troubles and his appalling behavior toward her, alluding to her troubled past.

"What past is that?" Sofia asked, eyes widening innocently over the rim of her glass.

At first, Lila played it coy, feigning a preference not to get into the gruesome details. It wasn't until Sofia reassured her that her secrets were safe with her that she finally relented. She proceeded to describe her affair with a European man in her senior year of college, the one who'd introduced her to cocaine.

"He was the director of food and beverages at the Chicago O'Hare Hilton when I met him. He was a lot older. European. You know the type. Magnetic. Dashing."

"Works for me!"

"Yeah, maybe not ..." Lila let out a deep sigh. "I ultimately ended up ... and I'm not proud to admit it ... I ended up chatting up strangers at the bar, trading sex for money. It started out as a game, you know? I put myself out there as a high-end call girl. I'd sit at the bar and guys would sit down next to me and strike up conversation. I'd make up names and tell them that I was a trade-show model or whatever. My father was dying of colon cancer and didn't have any money to speak of; he was spending every cent he had paying his legal bills. He was indicted for securities fraud."

"*What!*"

"Yeah, my father was an orthopod whose curse was he hated his profession. *Hated* it! What he wanted to do was run an investment bank, be a mogul, 'sit back and clip coupons,' he used to say. So, he started borrowing money to buy up as many Chinese penny stocks as he could, all on the advice of an old acquaintance from the Navy. Bought low, sold high. Worked for a while. Made enough dough to buy McManus Securities. Anyway, long story short ... there was a host of problems. Big, *big* bucks for a time. Then, news of widespread accounting fraud hit—"

"And your father was caught up in that?"

"Yep ... something about stock manipulation on the Canadian stock exchange."

"Wow!" Sofia shook her head, "How did that all turn out?"

"Hung jury. Dad was eventually acquitted by mistrial. Five others, the guys who were actually involved in setting up a web of fictitious 'suppliers' so they could inflate their balance sheets, they all went to prison. This was back in ninety-nine, right before the dot com crash."

"So your father, he dodged this bullet, looks like."

"No, not really. Within seven years, he was dead from colon cancer. He didn't dodge anything. The whole ordeal took years to finally resolve and basically ruined his and my mother's life. Obviously, I didn't want to put any more pressure on him than he already had to contend with, so I started sneaking off to the airport and did tricks to support my weekend drug dalliances."

Sofia reached her hand out and began gently massaging Lila's shoulder. "So much sadness. You were trying to numb the pain."

"Maybe," Lila replied unconvincingly. "I was out of my mind there for a while, I'm pretty sure." She took a drink and silently stared down into her glass. A moment on, she added, "Where I really went off the rails was jumping into the sack with this guy named Len Seidman, who just so happened to be the old Navy acquaintance who'd got my dad into this whole mess to start with ... and who ultimately became his personal lawyer."

Sofia drew a little closer and motioned for Lila to turn around so she could access her back. She began digging in gently with her thumbs, her hands smallish and warm.

"The case was still ongoing and Dad wasn't very forthcoming about his legal prospects at that point," Lila continued, letting her head fall back, moving from side to side as Sofia worked the knots from her muscles. "My brother and I were scared to death for him."

"What about your mother?"

"My mother had died a couple years earlier from lung cancer," Lila explained with a pursed frown. "Nobody was telling us anything. Brilliant me, I thought by fucking his lawyer I could get the inside scoop. Was he going to prison or not? Was he going to lose everything he and my mother had built up over the years or not? Were we going to have a family left or not?"

"What did he tell you?"

"He told me that they had a good case, that Dad's purchase of McManus would stand. That's the investment bank my brother now runs: McManus & Piper."

Sofia stopped massaging and leaned off to Lila's side. "But ... ?"

"But ... they ended up freezing me out. Dad and Seidman. Dad made me promise to get a law degree, which I did, but they never had any intention of letting me in. They pay me a pittance and keep me at arm's length." When the massage began again, she said, "I'm pretty sure that bastard Seidman told my dad right before he died that I was a coke whore, that I was hooking at the airport to support my drug habit."

Again, the massage stopped, and again, Sofia leaned round to Lila's side. This time she reached for Lila's face and held it tenderly in her hands.

Lila gave her a self-conscious smile. She let a moment pass before she said, a little awkwardly, "Honestly, I can't talk about it anymore. I just ... *can't*." She shook her head, exhaled slowly, and fell silent. Sofia leaned over and gave Lila a long, lingering kiss, finishing by lightly kissing the tip of her nose, before leaving a gentle kiss on each of Lila's eyes as if to release the hurtful images of her troubled past. After several moments of silence, Lila looked at Sofia and said, "What about you? Tell me about you and Wolf."

Sofia reached for her drink. She took the last sip from her nearly empty glass and said, almost apologetically, "Let you in on a little secret"—she put her glass down—"Wolf ..." She smiled at the empty glass as if considering what she was about to say.

Lila waited.

Sofia looked up and caught Lila's eye. "Wolf and I were never lovers. Never even came close." She shook her head and winced slightly.

"But you lived together!"

She gave an earnest nod. "We did."

"His idea?"

"He said he needed a beard."

"For his father?"

"For his father, sure, but mainly for Gus. Some work he was doing with Gus. He told me that if they found out he was gay, they wouldn't be able to work together. Company policy, he said."

Lila came forward on the edge of the couch, returning her glass to the coffee table without taking her eyes off Sofia. "I don't get it," she said at last.

"Wolf was closer to Gus than he was to his own father. Gus used to visit all the time when we lived in Georgetown."

"This is when Wolf was attending Georgetown Law?"

"Yes, then. But when Wolf dropped out, even more. Almost every weekend, it seemed. Sometimes through half the week. I used to wonder what they were up to. They spent so much time together."

"Intimate time—is that what you're getting at? Gus is also—"

"No. *Lord no!* Gus is a straight arrow. And *sooo* boring!" She rolled her eyes. "In fact," she said, getting up from the couch, "wait here."

Lila watched her pad down the hall and disappear into her office. When she came back, she was carrying a small book. It was Kahlil Gibran's *The Prophet.* Lila recognized the title.

Sofia handed her the book. "Read the inscription."

On the inside cover was a message written in heavy black ink:

To Wolf—
Here's to the millions we're going to make!
—Gus

Lila looked up from the book. "What kind of work were they doing? Did Wolf ever say?"

"Gus's business attracted a lot of South American investors, so I gather they were putting together private-placement deals." Sofia looked steadily into Lila's eyes. "I never asked—it didn't much interest me. When we moved to Chicago, he just stopped coming by. Which was, admittedly, a little odd, especially since he lives in Wisconsin. I just figured they had a falling out. But, truthfully, what did I care? I had my own life to live."

Lila gave a noncommittal shrug. If it didn't interest Sofia, she certainly couldn't let it show that it interested her. She looked away and feigned a yawn, thinking meanwhile that she'd have to get Charlie-O to run a check on Mr. Gus Ambrosia to see if he was still active with the agency and, if so, find out what the hell he was up to.

20

February 11, 2018

Lila Piper's Streeterville Condo
Chicago, Illinois

THE SUN HAD JUST BEGUN TO SET WHEN LILA HUNG UP THE PHONE. It was settled: Savage had agreed to ask Charlie-O to run a report on Gus Ambrosia. The orange sky flared through the floor-to-ceiling window of her Streeterville condo on East Ohio Street, casting long shadows over her desk. Her head bent over a legal pad, Lila wanted to get her thoughts down on paper for what would eventually be a preliminary report detailing her initial findings in the Holzinger case. The bulletin board on the wall beside her desk was covered with photos and scraps of paper and a maze of interconnecting twine.

A sudden trill from her cell startled her. "Hello?" she said, catching her breath.

"Hey," Ulli said. "If you've got a few minutes, I heard back from a woman I know at BDV. You said you wanted whatever she had on that Orfilia Campos chick."

Lila could hear shuffling papers in the background. "Great!" she said, leaning back in her chair. "So, what's the verdict?"

"This coming from a financial statement she filed with them about eighteen months ago."

"Okay."

"Total wallet is interesting. Turns out she has *several* numbered accounts with BDV and a few with BGP in Paris."

"What's BGP?"

"Banque de Gestion Privée."

"Okay."

"A few with PBP—that's *Paribas Banque Privée*. A few more with a small, Saudi-financed boutique bank in Geneva. A couple in the Caymans. On the real estate front, she owns a slew of multi-million-dollar properties here in Chicago, in New York, DC, Paris, Florida, and Caracas, of course. High-rise commercial buildings. Multi-million dollar estates. Here's the kicker—you had her dead to rights. The woman has no income, no visible means of support, nothing that could possibly justify her assets."

"Which means—"

"What do you mean, 'which means?' Which *means* organized crime. Like … neck-deep."

"How much are we talking about?"

"How much *what?*"

"How much money."

"Big, *big* bucks. Tens of millions in almost all the accounts." His voice suddenly became muffled, as if he were cupping the phone while he spoke to someone nearby. When he was through, he asked, "Did you order something for us?"

It took Lila a second to realize that the question was intended for her. "What?" she said distractedly.

"A *package*," he repeated. "Did you order something for us? Julie says there's a large package at the front door."

"No."

"Then what is it?" Lila could hear him talking to his kids as he moved through the house and opened the front door. "Jesus! A *mattress* maybe?" he said playfully, "gauging from the size of it."

Lila's breath caught. She glanced down at her legal pad, scarcely hearing his voice. There: *Mattress delivery—A. Breem.*

"Ulli," she said, "listen to me. You need to get out of there."

"Oh, wait a minute," he said. Lila heard shuffling noises as her brother moved around. She heard him open the door and close it again. "Yeah," he said, "The truck'll still be out front."

"*Ulli!*"

"What? Why?" More muffled voices; more garbled chatter in the background.

"*Listen to me!*" Lila shouted.

"*What?*"

"You *need* to get out of there! Can you see the driver?"

"No. Looks like the truck's empty."

"You are *all* in danger! Don't ask questions, just get Julie and the kids into the car and *get the fuck out of the house!*"

There was a moment of silence, and Lila could almost picture her brother's conflicted face. Finally, she heard him say, "Get Mommy! Go get in the car!"

"And where are we supposed to go?" he said to her. Before she could answer, he called out in a commanding voice, "*Julie!* Get the kids and get in the car. *Now!*"

"Go to PD's headquarters downtown. Don't stop anywhere—just drive. When you get there, ask for Chief Cornell Williams. *Do it now. Go!*"

Lila grabbed her coat and rushed out to the elevator. She hit the button several times before the door finally slid open.

She waited until she was in her SUV and headed down Lake Shore Drive before she called Cornell. Unable to get him on the line, she left a message with one of his lieutenants, giving him a heads-up on her brother's imminent arrival.

Then she tried Sofia. No answer.

Turning onto Stone Street, Sofia's red brick and concrete building came into view. Lila could see strips of yellow police tape and TV news vans forming a perimeter around several police cars parked at odd angles in front of the building, blue lights flashing. She pulled up next to a police transport van with side-markings that read:

MEDICAL EXAMINER.

Before Lila could even get out of the car, Detective Krzyskowski was at her drivers-side window. His face descending, tightening. Lila let her window down.

Instantly, the SUV filled with the racket from the street—shouted commands, police radios blaring, news reporters preparing live broadcasts, a small crowd forming nearby.

"What's going on?" she asked.

"Shooting in the penthouse." He glanced down at the notebook in his hand. "Your fallen man's girlfriend ... Sofia Castellanos."

21

February 11, 2018

Sofia Castellanos's Gold Coast Apartment
Chicago, Illinois

LILA CLIMBED OUT OF HER SUV, SHOVED HER KEYS INTO HER COAT
pocket, and followed Krzyskowski into the lobby. They snaked their way
through the crowd of uniformed police and waited for the elevator to
arrive.

"Coroner still up there?" Krzyskowski asked the first man to step out,
a plain-clothes cop wearing his department badge on a chain around his
neck.

He nodded. "Dictating his report now."

"Move the body yet?"

"Not yet," the man said over his shoulder, not breaking stride.

Krzyskowski stepped aside and ushered Lila past him. Once inside,
they stood there in grim silence facing their distorted reflections in the
brass doors.

When they finally slid open, Lila stood there, staring at the splintered front door dangling from its warped center hinge, half-in, half-out of the apartment. Krzyskowski gently guided her toward the door.

Once inside the apartment, it was the sight of the mattress box leaning against the wall that knocked the wind out of her; she sucked in her breath.

"You sure you want to see this?" Krzyskowski asked.

Lila swallowed hard, blew out a breath through pursed lips, and nodded.

Other than the wreckage in the vestibule and foyer, everything else in the apartment seemed to be just as it had been the last time she was there. The pillows were in their usual spots on the sofa. The Persian carpets looked freshly vacuumed. The dining room's dramatic Chippendale table was set with fine china like a high-end department store display. They went slowly down the hall, entered the master suite, and confronted the scene in the master bath. Lila gripped her messenger bag tight to her chest, the rapid flutter in her throat threatening to choke her.

Sofia's bare body was sprawled out on the pink marble floor as if she had been caught mid-stride while jogging. A large pool of drying blood had spread out like a dark red quattrocento halo. The back of her head had been blown entirely away, the entry point a cavernous hole in the center of her forehead. Her eyelids were at half-mast; eyes staring, blank, the skin around them a pale gray.

All at once, like a fire grenade in her brain, Lila saw a kaleidoscopic zigzag pattern arc across the side of her left eye—her had went up to her temple and, just as quickly, it was gone. Then, eerie, multi-colored polygons—spider legs drifting gently, rising, disappearing. Lila blinked. She was no longer standing in the doorway to the master bath, staring at Sofia's corpse. The space around her shimmered and swam, as if she'd opened her eyes underwater.

First come the ripples of a loud pounding knock at the door, Sofia leaning over the sink, applying make-up. She straightens and glances one last time in the mirror before cinching her kimono shut and padding down the hall.

Instantly, the henchman. Slamming his shoulder—the door splintering. Sofia running into her office, pulling from the desk drawer a gleaming pistol. The noise in her head so loud she can almost make out the voices, a thousand people all speaking at once.

Sofia there in the enshadowed hall, pistol pointed toward the door. But he is in, it's too late, the lock cracking, everything thunder—and she fires then spins, tripping, falling to her knees. She scrambles to the master bath and he has her by the hair. She hits the wall hard. Again. Again. Red.

Lila's hands flew to her head and she staggered, the throbbing behind her eyes almost unbearable. Then, above the voices, the screams, Sofia's image went black.

Lila's head shot back as she swallowed a huge gulp of air. She pressed her hand over her mouth and uttered, "I ... I can't ..." then abruptly turned on her heels and rushed out of the room. She stumbled, grasping at the arm of the sofa, and sucked in hot air. *What the hell is happening to me?*

And there, on the table: *The Prophet* still lying there. Lila grabbed it, stashed it into her bag, and ran out the door.

Krzyskowski caught up with her out on the sidewalk; she was sitting alone on the curb, her head in her hands, gripping her hair with fists clenched.

He kneeled beside her.

"Well," Lila finally managed, "I did not see this coming." She looked up at him, tears streaming down her face. "Oh, God—Sofia."

Krzyskowski's gaze wandered off toward the vast black expanse of lake visible between the apartment buildings bordering Lake Shore Drive. When his weary blue eyes returned to her, he said, "So you had a relationship?"

Lila felt her head spin. It was not just that she had lost her grip on the external circumstances surrounding her, but on her own essence. She felt like some alien entity had taken up residence in her brain and was calling the shots while she watched from beneath.

She wiped away her tears and gave Krzyskowski a weak smile. "You're gonna want to question me, aren't you?"

"Have to."

She pulled herself together enough to contend with the threat still facing her brother and his family. *That* she would keep to herself for the moment. She stood up from the curb, her face devoid of all expression. "I'll only talk to Cornell."

He stared at her for a long moment. Then he lowered his head, shook it, and let out an exasperated sigh. "Fine." He slapped his knee and stood up. "Can one of my men drive you?"

"I know my way." She turned and walked back toward her car.

22

February 11, 2018

Headquarters, Chicago Police Department
Chicago, Illinois

An hour later, Krzyskowski rapped on his boss's office door.

"Enter!" came Cornell's voice.

Krzyskowski strode into the room, pulled the door shut behind him, and grabbed the chair next to Lila, who was already seated. He nodded to her. "You okay?"

She gave a weak smile, her eyes cold. "Headache."

Cornell cleared his throat, looked at his watch, and said, "To start off, there's been a development."

Krzyskowski's eyebrows shot up.

"We've taken your brother and his family to a safe house, Lila."

"*Why?*" Krzyskowski asked. A quick glance back at Lila. "What happened?"

"Another mattress delivery," Cornell said.

Krzyskowski seemed genuinely disturbed. "Christ."

"They're fine." Cornell shot a quick, reassuring look Lila's way. "That's under control."

"Well, that's a relief." Krzyskowski sat there a moment, his arms crossed. "Well, this adds another dimension to the case, doesn't it?" He looked up at Lila. "Why would your brother be involved?"

"We'll get to that in a moment," Cornell said. "I'm going to let her get her questions out of the way first."

Have to see Gail as soon as possible, Lila told herself. *Something seriously wrong, needs fixing ASAP.*

Krzyskowski frowned. "*Her* questions?"

"I'm sorry, I really do have a splitting headache," Lila said, absently plucking her notebook from her messenger bag and leaning forward, squinting at the new page. "Okay, so ... when did the shooting happen and how was it reported?"

"A little after eighteen hundred hours," Krzyskowski replied. "We got a 911 call from the victim's neighbor one floor down. She reported hearing a loud crash followed by yelling and what sounded like a loud gunshot."

"Witnesses?" Lila asked, wincing.

"Other than our caller, we're going door-to-door in the building, canvassing the neighborhood, interviewing everyone within a three-block radius to find out if anybody saw anything unusual. That's gonna take some time to get that all wrapped up."

"Security footage?" Cornell asked.

"Building's kind of a one-off work-in-progress deal. Twelve stories. Hundred years old. Recent rehab. No video; no doorman. Not *in* the building, anyway. We're looking at all the surrounding street-view cameras."

Cornell nodded. "In the meantime"—he came forward, looking Lila straight in the eye—"the bigger-picture question is *why* was Ms. Castellanos targeted?" He gazed down at his desktop at a single sheet of paper that bore Lila's signature on the bottom. "You'll recall we have an agreement?"

Lila nodded, her expression exhausted, pained.

"So talk to me. Share your observations."

Lila shifted uncomfortably in her chair. Reluctantly, she began, "The Breem overdose—the mattress thing didn't add up. Seriously, why take the trouble to haul in a big, cumbersome box when a jewelry box would do? But then another mattress at the scene of another hit, and a third delivered to my brother's door. With Breem and Sofia ..." she paused, swallowing hard. "Drugs and a gun. With my brother, a delivery and no violent follow-through. I read that as a direct threat against me. Anyway, I guess Breem was taken in by the mattress delivery ruse; Sofia was not. Breem likely allowed her killer into her apartment. Sofia ..."

Krzyskowski nodded. "Makes sense."

"He's angry, and she's fighting every inch of the way. He pulls the gun and shoots her—execution-style." Lila squeezed her eyes shut for a moment.

Cornell and Krzyskowski exchanged glances.

"Obviously, the two murders are related. Which means the threat to my brother and his family ..."

"And to you," Cornell put in.

"And to me ... is a real and present danger. We've all spoken to both victims. Maybe that was enough to mark them for elimination. Common thread is big-time drug trafficking—that's my theory."

"What do you base that on?" Krzyskowski asked.

Lila took a breath. "Castellanos is a Venezuelan expat. She was living in her cousin's penthouse apartment. One of the *many* multi-million-dollar properties her cousin owns all over the world."

"Name of this cousin?" Krzyskowski asked.

"Orfilia Campos." She waited while both he and Cornell wrote it down. "Turns out she was Hugo Chavez's kept woman. I had my brother run a background check on her, research her total wallet. She has no visible means of support. That's *my* person of interest."

Cornell straightened in his chair and shot Lila a troubled look. "What are we saying—you think her own cousin had her killed?"

She shrugged. "Wouldn't rule it out."

Cornell sat back, astonished. "Well, that's ... very interesting." He paused a moment. "Is she in the States?"

"Who knows—she moves around a lot," Lila answered. "But she was here in town a few days ago."

"Which was?" Krzyskowski asked.

Lila looked down at her notes. "January thirty-first. I encountered her briefly at the Ceres Café the first time I met Sofia." She waited while Krzyskowski scribbled something in his notepad. "She had bodyguards."

He arched his eyebrow at her.

Cornell asked, "How many conversations did you have with Sofia?"

She thought a moment. "Total of three—one at the café, two in the apartment where she got killed."

Krzyskowski took over. "Who else was mentioned during these conversations?"

"Well ... Wolf Holzinger, obviously. He was the reason I was there."

"Surely other names came up."

She hesitated. "I'm not sure they would be relevant."

Krzyskowski glared at Lila, eyes narrowing. "*Everything* is relevant."

Cornell sighed. "Everything you've been telling us suggests a conspiracy. We need to pursue every lead, Lila, no matter how tenuous."

Lila leaned her head down and rubbed her forehead. "I will say this— other names that were dropped—they should, like Orfilia, be considered a high flight risk. If PD starts snooping around, we might lose them. I ask that you let me pursue my own leads my own way and, if anything more than a half-baked hunch turns up, I'll rush over and let you know."

The two men exchanged looks. After a moment, Krzyskowski turned back to Lila tersely. "You are a private investigator for a personal injury law firm. This is a capital murder case. You are required to turn over every name, every lead, every bit of information you have to the proper authorities."

"Thank you for putting things into context for me. But no."

Krzyskowski shot Cornell a look of outrage.

Cornell squinted, looking suddenly very tired. He peered into his hands for a long moment before finally turning to Lila. "He's right, you know."

Krzyskowski gave a smug grin.

"But I'm going to defer to her"—he raised his finger to stop the inevitable backlash—"for the simple reason that, jurisdictionally, we're gonna have to turn this over to the FBI. I'd like to keep this in our purview for as long as possible. Our priority is and should be Ms. Campos. See if she's still in town and get her in here for questioning pronto."

Krzyskowski stared at Cornell, his jaw clenched. Clearly deciding against an outburst, he glanced at Lila and slowly closed his notebook. "Yes, sir." With that, the commanding officer of the city's Crime Scene Investigations unit got up and left the room.

"As for you," Cornell said, turning to Lila, "I expect you to keep your word. Now go home and get some rest."

She forced a smile and nodded.

"And for God's sake, don't get yourself killed."

23

February 12, 2018

Highway 94, Eastbound
Chicago, Illinois to Ann Arbor, Michigan

LILA WAS IN HER 4RUNNER, HEADING BACK TO THE LASALLE
Street office, when she got a call on her cell.

"Lila, Jim," Savage said. "Where you at?"

She looked out the windshield at the weather swirling like some
dismal holiday snow globe then reached for the Chicago dog still
untouched in the box on the passenger seat. She'd just boosted her
lithium dose; the stabbing pain in her head told her she was going to need
it, and she didn't need the side effects of taking it on an empty stomach.
She picked up the hot dog and took a bite.

"Just turned *m'*onto—wait a *sh'*ec," she said, swallowing. "Sorry," she
took a swig of her water bottle and got into the right lane, waited for the
traffic to clear, and turned north onto State Street. "On State. Headed for
the garage. Why?"

"Forget the garage. Come around front and pick me up."

"What's up?" she asked, detecting the urgency in his voice. "What's going on?"

"I'll tell you when you get here."

Minutes later, Lila rounded the corner and spotted Savage standing under their building's canopy. He was in his familiar olive-green trench coat, his collar turned up against the slanting snow. One hand was deep in his pocket, while the other, wrapped in a cognac-colored glove, gripped the handle of his black leather catalog case.

"Eager to leave are we?" Lila muttered to herself.

She curbed her SUV and glanced at herself in the rearview, wincing at the mustard smeared on her chin. Savage opened the back door, collapsed the handle on his case, and slung it onto the back seat. She snatched the hot dog box off the passenger seat and tossed it in the back just in time for him to climb in. "Where to?" she asked, peering into her side-view mirror, easing out into traffic with blinkers flashing.

"East. Take the ninety-four."

She looked at him sideways. "East! What's east?"

He was silent for a few seconds, eyes focused on the road ahead of him, before he replied with a scowl, "Ann Arbor. And why's it smell like ... *hot dogs?* Crack a window, for God's sake, get some air in here!"

"*Ann Arbor!*" She let down the windows a crack; instantly, the SUV filled with chilled winter air. "What's in Ann Arbor?! That's like, what, a three and a half-hour drive?" She looked at him like he'd slipped a gear. "I can't go to Ann Arbor, I'm right in the middle of this thing!"

"Yeah, well, you're going."

She jerked her head back, stunned at the uncharacteristic obstinacy. "In a snowstorm."

"Yup."

"And am I entitled to know *why?*"

"Two reasons."

"Do tell."

"*One*—I'm getting you out of harm's way."

"*What!*" she erupted. "Come on, Jim! We've got the police involved; it's not like I can't handle myself." She shook her head, eyes fixed on the long black line of road that cut through the vast, flat expanse of snow ahead.

"And *two*—Charlie-O rented a house bordering the Nichols Arboretum, not far from the main campus. About time you two met."

She glanced at him. "What? I thought Charlie-O was at Stanford."

"Sabbatical."

"*Sabbatical.*" A slow nod of recognition. "And whatever happened to email or fax or ... hell, getting on the phone?"

Savage shrugged. "You get a chance to meet someone like Charlie-O in person, you take it." As the 4Runner pulled onto I-94, moving along at a good clip, he reached back, clicked open his briefcase, and took out a three-inch-thick fastener file. "Now, if you don't mind, I brought some work along."

Unbelievable. Lila drove on, lost in her own thoughts. Forty minutes later, as they passed the industrial smokestacks of Gary, Indiana, she said, "Check this out."

Savage looked up, frowning. "Check what out?" When she didn't answer, he asked, "What are you looking at?"

"I can't ... tell ... if we're being followed or not."

He turned and looked through the rear window. "What—the Beemer? Get out of the fast lane."

Lila changed lanes and said, "There was a car that looked just like that when I stopped to get a hot dog. And I've seen it at least twice before. Metallic blue BMW, same fancy wheels, low-profile tires."

Again, Savage turned around, watching as the BMW sped up and passed them, a man and a woman gabbing away in the front seats.

"I think we're okay," he said, settling into his seat again. "Besides, whoever heard of a tail driving a high-performance BMW? The idea is to be *in*-conspicuous."

They followed the road in silence for a good half-hour more before Lila, with a little prodding, recounted Sofia's story of Orfilia Campos playing mistress to Hugo Chavez. Abruptly, she stopped, struck. She shot Savage a glance, her face darkening.

"What?" he asked. He turned and looked out the rear window but found no one there.

Lila stared at the white-speckled road, the wipers going full-bore to clear the thickening snow. "Sofia Castellanos," she explained slowly, "told me that Campos used to poison Chavez when she wanted to sneak out at night and, you know, 'hit the town.'"

"She *poisoned* Hugo *Chavez?*" he erupted with an incredulous smirk.

"That's what she told me. She said Orfilia would slip him a mickey and later, when Sofia called her out on it, rationalized her devious behavior by telling her, 'I just wanted him to go to sleep.'"

"'*I just wanted him to go to sleep,*'" Savage repeated. "And this is a critical piece of the puzzle *how,* exactly?"

Lila shot him an insistent glance. "*The mattresses!* You want a *list?* Let's see, you've got as big an *in-your-face* move as you could imagine. Obviously, the killer feels invulnerable, thinks they can do whatever the hell they please. The mattress itself says a lot—the *big sleep;* you guys are *asleep at the switch; I could do this in my sleep.* No, there's no unconscious killer's signature here—she's *consciously* leaving a trail." She let out a chuckle. "Just about as bold as slipping a mickey to the president of Venezuela. She thinks she can get away with murder. This time, she's wrong."

And then, Lila thought to herself, there was Gus Ambrosia's involvement—was he behind it all, lurking in the shadows, pulling the strings? *The Prophet,* again:

> To Wolf—
> Here's to the millions we're going to make!
> —Gus

That she would keep to herself. For now.

"Interesting theory, but it's not enough to build a case," Savage said.

"Yeah, well, the shipping label didn't help either."

"What shipping label?"

"I got the number off the shipping label from the mattress left at Angela Breem's Lawndale apartment."

"Okay, so you went online and looked up the tracking numbers."

"Couldn't get it online; had to call customer support."

"Why couldn't you get it online?"

"Stolen shipment. They said it's under review."

"*Humph!*" He frowned, stroking his chin absently. "So I guess that's a dead end."

"No, it's not a dead-end at all—it's a question of who's been stealing shipments from a legitimate mattress company, where they're doing it, at what point in transit, and what the mattress company and UPS or FedEx are doing to identify the thieves and stop it."

"Okay, so what are they doing about it?"

"I don't know yet. But once you find the thieves, you follow the money trail to see who hired them. We've got a murder investigation on our hands and it's looking more and more like a serial killer, and I, for one, intend to follow those lines of inquiry to see if a case can be built against Ms. Orfilia Campos."

"You need to forget those lines of inquiry for two reasons: one, for your own safety and the safety of your family, and two, it's *waaay* outside the purview of our original case. Wolf Holzinger, Lila. Focus on Wolf Holzinger."

"What the hell do you think I've been doing?" she snapped.

They were silent for several miles before Lila added, "So, no, it's definitely *not* a dead end."

24

_____

February 12, 2018

Charlie-O's Sabbatical Rental
Ann Arbor, Michigan

ROCK SALT CRUNCHED AND CHURNED BENEATH THEM AS LILA pulled up Charlie-O's long drive. The house was a simple two-story redbrick with black shutters, white trim, and a black asphalt roof dusted with snow. Lila parked and they both climbed out, allowing themselves a quick, frigid stretch before trudging up the front porch steps.

The woman who answered the door was old—seventy-something was Lila's assessment—and had short, snow-white hair and rheumy dark eyes magnified by extra-thick horn-rimmed glasses. "James!" she said with a welcoming smile, immediately throwing the door open wide and spryly stepping aside. "Come in! Come in! Quick, get out of the cold!"

"Charlie!" Savage replied, leaning forward to give her a hug and a kiss on the cheek as he passed. "Good to see you again."

"You too!" She shut the door behind Lila. "I trust your drive was uneventful," she said, adjusting her white turtleneck and bundling herself against the chill in her green cable cardigan. "Here, give us your coats."

"It was," he said, shrugging off his coat, "very pleasant. A regular winter wonderland." He brought Lila forward. "I'd like you to meet Lila Piper."

"Lila!" Charlie beamed. "We finally meet! Give us a hug!"

Charlie pulled Lila into her arms and hugged her like she'd known her for years, coaxing a stifled laugh from Lila. She was still chuckling when Charlie led them to the kitchen.

"Joe," she called out from the doorway. "Joseph!" When no one responded, she yelled, *"Joseph, ya bastard!"*

At that, her husband turned. When he saw they had company, he smiled. "Just about through with this, dear."

Savage walked over and extended his hand. "What are you making, Maestro?"

"James!" he said, quickly wiping himself off on his apron before clasping Jim's hand. "Soup and sandwiches," he said, returning to his work. "Grilled cheese and tomato basil."

Charlie dropped the coats on the bench and added, *"Four-cheese* grilled cheese."

"Yum!" Lila effused, prompting Charlie-O to quickly introduce her husband. Once that was out of the way, she led them into the family room and ushered them over to the crackling fire where the comfortable chairs were.

Charlie disappeared back into the kitchen, returning promptly with three glasses of Guinness.

Accepting the drink, Lila said, "So Jim tells me you were a field officer with CIA."

"I was."

Lila forced a smile. "How was that?"

"The work was interesting, if sometimes unbearably boring. Sometimes." She gave an ironic smile and sipped her drink. "I understand you met Gus Ambrosia recently," she said.

"I did."

"He's a company man, you know."

"I knew he *was* a company man." Lila and Savage exchanged glances.

"So far as I know he is. Here—"

She turned toward the kitchen and hollered, "Joe!" When no answer followed, she shouted, *"Joseph!"*

Befuddled by all the commotion, her husband came around the corner at a good clip, mumbling, "Here here, what's all the fuss about?"

"Ambrosia."

"Who?"

"*Ambrosia!* Gus Ambrosia."

"Ah! Good man!" He nodded. "Top drawer."

"Is he still with us?"

"He is. Last I heard." Then, apparently impatient to get back to his kitchen wizardry: "anything else? Don't want to burn the cheese."

"No dear. That's it."

"Good. Good. Oh, uh"—he paused at the kitchen door and looked back at his wife—"soup's almost on."

"Interesting," Lila said after taking a sip. "That would seem to confirm what I was thinking."

"And what is it you were thinking?"

Lila looked over at Jim. Once she got the go-ahead nod, she said, "Based on some information I got recently, it seems that Wolf may have been a spook," Lila explained, "and that Gus may have been the one who recruited him. Pretty obvious it wasn't his father. Hans had plans for his son to take over the family business."

"Gus did recruit him, darlin'. He recruited, trained, and handled him."

"Wow ..." Lila looked up to the ceiling for a moment, then said, "you're telling me I did all this investigating when I could have just picked up the phone and asked you?" She shot Savage a searing look. "Why didn't you suggest I talk to Charlie earlier? I was here thinking that Wolf operated almost exclusively out of Chicago."

"You're wondering what could be going on in Chicago that CIA would consider vital to our national and strategic interests? Or our military and operational interests?" Charlie paused as if bursting with information that she could not or would not divulge. "Come." She got up from her seat and shepherded everyone into the dining room. "Well ... now we're touching on the reason I finally left the company." Lila and Savage sat across from each other; Charlie took a seat at the head of the table. "Reminds me of something Nietzsche said. At least, I think it was Nietzsche. 'Whoever fights monsters should see to it that in the process he does not become a monster.'"

"If only that were possible," Lila said. "What 'monster' are you referring to?"

Joe came in carrying a platter with the sandwiches. "If you're talking about monsters, it *was* Nietzsche."

"Ah, good," Charlie said, passing around the platter, "Haven't lost it yet! CIA, it seems to me"—Charlie shot Jim a look of disgust—"has become a monster. We've moved from wholesaling drugs internationally, for reasons that occasionally *do* serve our national and strategic interests, to the domestic retail business. It's a violation of our founding principles!"

"Hmm," Lila uttered. This seemed to confirm the drug angle of the Gus/Wolf story. She picked up her sandwich. "And that's why you quit?" She took a bite. "Oh, this is terrific!"

"Retired. I retired, I didn't quit. Did you hear that, Joseph?" she called out to her husband, who'd returned to the kitchen, "the grilled cheese is a hit!"

"What?" Joseph called out.

"The grilled cheese is a hit!"

He brought out a soup tureen shaped like a lobster and placed it by his wife. "What's not to like?" he said, handing her the ladle.

Charlie grinned and rolled her eyes. "I realized I worked for a group of people," she said as she ladled out the soup, "who hold tight to the opinion that the advent of the Internet changed the rules of the game." She passed a bowl to Lila. "With the rise of new technologies and the continual dissolution of national boundaries, we can no longer trust anything—not the texts we read, not the photographs we see, not the people we meet. This new protocol, my friends, is operating within our own borders and violating our own charter. My boss sat me down when I started to raise Cain about spying on our own people, and he told me, straight out, 'Charlie, we've entered a whole new era of aggressive, politically subversive warfare. Yes,' he says, 'we're exceeding our original charter.' Then something like, 'If you're waiting for me to offer my apologies, you'll be waiting a very long time.' Then, of course, the 'It's a dirty business' spiel—'but,' he says, 'it's a necessary business.'"

Lila's sandwich hung in hand.

"Eat! Eat!" Charlie commanded as Joe finally sat down. "Plenty of time to talk shop."

After lunch, Savage went over and sat down in the leather armchair nearest the fire. Lila and Charlie settled in on the couch. All along, Lila had pondered what it was that Charlie had to offer that would justify the long drive in the snow and, other than confirming the Gus-Wolf-CIA connection, their host seemed to be short on particulars. When told about what had happened to Sofia, Angela Breem, and Ulli, Charlie said only that she had "no specific operational awareness" of any of those matters. When Lila turned to the original question of why Wolf Holzinger was trying to rappel down from the roof to break into Sofia's apartment, Charlie said, "Your guess is as good as mine." But the overarching question was whether Gus Ambrosia could have been involved. If so, had Wolf's death had anything to do with the CIA's domestic drug trade that Charlie had referenced earlier?

When that subject came up again, Charlie launched into a monologue about the CIA's long history of drug trafficking, which went all the way back to 1949, when arms had been supplied to Chiang Kai-shek's defeated generals in exchange for opium, heroin, and intelligence.

"The agency's involvement in the drug trade," Charlie said, "naturally opened our eyes to developments in that area. Specifically, the use of psychedelics. Did you ever read Carlos Castenada's *The Teachings of Don Juan?*"

Lila squinted her eyes and nodded. "I vaguely remember reading that in college. Probably under the influence."

"Well, it caused quite a stir in the defense and intelligence communities that were investigating ESP and psychokinesis. Castenada's subsequent books prompted the agency to begin looking into *non-ordinary realities* and *remote sensing* in a serious way. This was the so-called 'Stargate Project.'"

"My dear, it went by several different names," Joseph said. "Started with 'MKUltra' and, as I recall, 'Mushrooms.'"

"Well, as *I* recall, it was decommissioned in '95." She tossed her hand in the air. "At least, that's the official position. But I'll tell ya—what happened is that, over time, *physicists* shouldered the *psychics* into the ditch and Stargate took a big ol' turn to non-ordinary reality. Horoscopes are gone—it's all quantum mechanics now. Same interests, different tools."

"So it wasn't shut down," Lila said, "it actually branched off into something much more advanced?"

"Oh, my dear, yes! Considerably," Joseph responded. "Rather than wasting time chasing crackpots and staring at goats, they focused on the science of consciousness." He looked over at Charlie and winked. "And the discoveries that have occurred behind closed doors over the last twenty years? Lemme tell you, the technologies that have been developed, well, we're talking about the capacity to go *deep*—deeper into the realm of the mind than anyone thought possible."

Charlie nodded emphatically. "And they can do practically anything they want down there without anybody knowing."

Go deep—without anybody knowing—why did it all sound so familiar? Of course—Mark's comments about the water column. "The CIA ... are they the only ones doing this?"

Charlie and Joseph looked at each other soberly. "It was very important to keep it contained," Joseph explained. "But that didn't happen."

Charlie took a deep breath. "Some of the researchers were lured away from the company by a very well-financed international cabal."

"A cabal?"

"They wanted to control the science and the technology themselves," Charlie said, "outside the auspices of any government. It's been a source of great ... consternation ... for the CIA and other US intelligence agencies."

So much in the world regular people know nothing about, Lila mused. Her thoughts drifted back to her conversations with Mark, who, she recalled, had been a member of one of those intelligence agencies just mentioned. *What secrets might he be holding?*

To say nothing of ... she shot a glance at Savage, who had been hearing all of this without so much as batting an eye. *What's his connection to CIA? Obviously, he's old friends with these two, and with Hans,* she told herself, *so he's associated. But how far does it go?*

"Jim," Lila said, "did you know about all this?"

Savage looked up from his file and shook his head. "No, I didn't know about any of this."

"Really."

"Lila, we're in the middle of trying to figure out why Wolf fell off the roof. How the hell would I know what the CIA's doing?"

Glancing silently at one another, Charlie and Joseph rose and disappeared into the kitchen. When Joseph reemerged, he was struggling to fit his arms into his coat.

"Where you off to, Maestro?" Savage asked.

"I've been sent to the grocery."

"*What?* It's snowing!" He jumped up from his chair.

"You think a few flurries are going to halt the wheels turning in the kitchen?"

"Let me go. I need to stretch the old legs out anyway."

Joseph stopped and pulled his coat back off. "I'm not going to turn you down—exercise, that's important. Kroger's just down the road a couple of miles."

Savage chuckled. "I'm not going to walk, Joe," he said, turning to Lila. She was sitting on the couch, lost in thought. "You wanna take a ride?" Lila craned her neck and looked out through the picture window behind him. The snow was blowing sideways, coming down even heavier than when they'd arrived. "Seriously?" she said with an involuntary shiver, "you sure you're hungry?"

Savage crinkled his brow. "Come on, a little freezing snow won't kill you."

She got up with a groan and reached into her pocket for her keys before wandering to the window. "Let's at least get the beast warmed up before we go." She looked at Joe and grinned, giving her key fob a little shake. "Technology, right?"

She pressed the button.

Lila didn't see the window shatter, but she glimpsed the fireball and felt the heat of the shockwave. Instantly, she was in the air, thrown back against the fireplace like a rag doll. For a moment, there was no pain—only the overwhelming pungent intrusion of gasoline in her lungs and the acrid reek of burning rubber.

She lay corpse-still against the hearthstones, everything muted and strange—and then came the searing pain in her head. She blinked frantically and, slowly, her sight began to return. Blood beneath her—on her clothes, the stones. Dust, smoke rising—and there, in her side, the source of the stabbing pain. She tore the chunk of glass out with a shaking hand, trying to apply pressure, but blood oozed out onto the carpet.

Across the room, Savage was standing over Joe, who was in a heap, moaning softly. Lila pressed hard on her side, swallowing, eyes flickering, voice gone. A throbbing in her throat, her ears.

When she finally opened her eyes again, Savage and Joseph were leaning over her, their expressions grim, their mouths moving in silence. She looked at them for a long time, their bodies fading in and out of focus, ash mingling with their silhouettes. Her mind was a pandemonium of ghoulish impressions—the deafening blast, the frightful intensity of the white-orange fireball that had launched her SUV into the air, the thick black smoke belching into the sky. She gazed up into the foreign, piteous faces of the men hovering over her, their mouths still moving noiselessly. At once, Charlie was there, her hand over her mouth, her eyes misted. Lila looked at Savage one final time. The room went dark.

25

February 13, 2018

Michigan Medicine Hospital, University of Michigan
Ann Arbor, Michigan

LILA SPENT THE NIGHT WITH AN ARMED GUARD STATIONED OUTSIDE her door. After the medical staff had debrided her wounds, slathered her face with a pungent antibacterial, and applied a dressing, she'd slept only intermittently, shocked awake every so often by unrelenting night terrors that left her gasping for air. Early in the morning, unable to get back to sleep, she sat in bed, gazing out the window to the snow-covered grounds below. She turned her head slowly at the soft knock at the door and watched as a uniformed officer with the Ann Arbor Sheriff's Department came in.

"Can we get you to look at something?" He was holding a photo.

"Suspect?"

"Person of interest."

"Sure." She waved him over, plumped up her pillow, and sat up straight in bed, feeling guardedly eager to hear what the man had to offer.

He sat in the chair next to the bed and, as he handed over the photo, said, "Red-light camera. Intersection of South University and South State."

The picture was blurry, as such photos usually are, but she knew the face immediately: one of the bodyguards she'd spotted with Orfilia at the Ceres Cafe. She recognized the salt-and-pepper hair, the buffed-out build, the eyes.

Over her silence, the cop explained, "We found security footage of his vehicle with DC plates leaving the neighborhood a couple of hours prior to the blast. Fortunately, because of the weather there wasn't much traffic, so it was easy to narrow down."

"What was he driving?"

"Black Dodge Hellcat."

"Really?"

"Were you expecting something else?"

She'd been expecting "blue BMW M5," hoping it would explain her recurring sightings. She sighed. It was probably just her imagination. "No."

"So, do you recognize him?"

Just then, Savage edged into the room carrying a brown paper bag. "Yes, I've seen him," Lila replied to the officer and, to Jim, said, "It's time to bring the FBI in."

Savage seemed taken aback. "Not surprised."

"But I need to talk to Cornell first."

He reached into his pocket for his phone. "I'll, um ... see if I can get him on the line."

Lila turned back to the cop. "Did you run his plates?"

"We did." The officer opened his notebook.

"Who is it?" Savage asked, phone already in hand.

"Hector Velez," the officer said. "Hispanic male. Forty-three years old. Venezuelan passport."

On that last fact, Lila smirked at Savage.

"Care to fill me in?" the cop pressed.

"He's a henchman." She proceeded to brief the local deputy that she had spotted the suspect escorting one Orfilia Campos; her vision of Sofia's murder she kept to herself. She added that Campos was the prime person of interest in a string of orchestrated hits and a threat to her own brother.

Abruptly, Savage handed her his phone. They didn't speak for long; Cornell agreed promptly to contact a trusted associate of his at the FBI and asked to speak to the deputy about coordinating a dragnet. Lila handed it over and lay back, feeling oddly content. She'd been right, and no failed assassination was going to spoil that.

After sitting through a battery of tests, Lila signed her release and got ready to go. Savage returned to find her already wearing her slacks under her hospital gown. "Here," he said as he reached into the brown bag he'd carried in earlier, "I brought your coat and one of my shirts to wear."

"Oh, good. My blouse was ... a lost cause." She grinned. "See! Here you are again, always looking out for me!"

"And you'd do the same for me," he said with a warm smile.

Once she was completely dressed and ready, he ushered her out the door and down the hall, following behind the security guard, the Michigan officer in step behind them. They took an elevator up and, when the door opened, exited into a large open hall with double doors. Soon, they were on the hospital's rooftop, an AS350 executive helicopter waiting there for them.

Savage sat in front with the pilot. Twenty minutes into the flight, as the Windy City's skyline came into view, glimmering like Oz under a cloudless sky, he said over his shoulder, "I don't want you staying at your place."

Lila hollered over the engine noise, "I called Mark. He'll pick me up."

Savage jerked his head around, brow furrowed. "The guy who called for you at the office? The three-messages guy?"

"Yeah. Why?"

"Hey, you're a big girl—you make your own decisions."

Lila snorted, gazing out the window at Chicago's skyline and Lake Michigan's dark blue waters beyond.

"Just ... try to keep a low profile," he added. She saw him wince and wondered whether it was because he didn't like the idea of her seeing Mark or because the bandages on her face and neck reminded him that she could've taken a worse hit—died, even.

Lila ducked away from the spinning blades, trotting in a low crouch toward two approaching men: Cornell Williams and FBI Special Agent Daniel Ortiz.

Lila didn't know Ortiz personally, but she had run into him a few times on those rare occasions when he'd shown up to check in with Cornell. She'd met him first, briefly, at law school—he'd given a speech on Career Day, presenting the FBI's Criminal Investigations Division as a possible career path for those with an interest in law enforcement. Lila recalled Ortiz's disappointment about Cornell's disinterest—the FBI just wasn't in the cards for him.

Cornell grimaced at the sight of her injuries. "Are you sure you're okay?" he shouted above the roar from the helicopter.

"I'm fine," Lila shouted back. "Thank God for remote ignition is all I can say." She snorted out a dismissive chuckle.

Lila followed Cornell downstairs to his office. Ortiz had apparently already been briefed on the case notes compiled by Cornell and Krzyskowski, as well as those written up by the Ann Arbor sheriff.

Lila got busy reading him in. "I know you've got the perp identified, but you should know there's a bizarre set of elements here that just don't square ..."

"Go ahead," Ortiz nodded as he opened his notebook. "Kick it off, I'm ready."

Lila took a deep breath and then told him all about the Holzinger case, about Wolf Holzinger's death and his father's rivalry with Gus Ambrosia, explaining how both men—both operating large-scale agri-businesses outside of Milwaukee, both wealthy dairy moguls—had been CIA case officers during the Soviet occupation of Afghanistan from '79 to '89.

"Hold on. CIA? You sure about your source on that?"

"Absolutely," Savage put in.

"I'm sorry, and your connection to this is?"

"My boss," Lila put in with a quirked grin.

Savage replied, "I've known Hans Holzinger, and to a lesser extent Gus Ambrosia, for over twenty years. So yes, I'm familiar with their covert backgrounds."

"And how's that?"

Savage shrugged. "They told me."

Ortiz raised his eyebrows as he made a few more entries in his notebook. "Interesting," he muttered.

Lila added, "But at least in the case of Gus, I don't believe he ever ceased his involvement in CIA activities." She filled in the details of Wolf's curious relationship with Gus and his connection to Hugo Chavez and Chavez's mistress through Sofia Castellanos. Lila told him she believed the mistress was likely behind Sofia's murder as well as the murder of Angela Breem.

"There is a tremendous amount of money at play here. Huge volumes of drugs flowing through the Lawndale projects, Orfilia's substantial assets despite no discernible source of income, and two curious 'fall-from-height' deaths on the same night. And orbiting around everything is the elder Holzinger's chief business rival."

At that, Ortiz stopped writing. "It is a curious link between Venezuela and *Milwaukee*."

"Bottom line, I believe Gus's dairy farm is a front for a domestic drug-trafficking and money-laundering operation perhaps sanctioned by the CIA itself."

"Do you have any direct evidence to support that conclusion?"

"No—it can only be considered hearsay at this point—but everything points in that direction."

Clipping his pen to his inside breast pocket, Ortiz leaned back in his chair and looked up at the ceiling. Finally, he said, "More likely a rogue operation, exploiting the contacts they made from the agency. I've seen it before." He sat up again and nodded sharply. "But you're right, Lila, it's an intriguing set of circumstances. And disturbing. Worthy of a closer look, for sure." He shared a look with Cornell. "I think I'll call our friends over at DEA and the Organized Crime Drug Enforcement Task Force. Of course, I'll keep you posted on what ATF turns up regarding your bombing suspect. In the meantime"—he pulled out a business card and scribbled something—"here's my cell number and a secure email. If you come across anything else or recall anything you might have left out, don't hesitate to reach out to me, twenty-four seven."

26

February 14, 2018

Mark Morgan's Lincoln Park Brownstone
Chicago, Illinois

LILA COULD HEAR HER BREATH MOVING IN AND OUT THROUGH HER nose. She reached up, pinched her nostrils, then glanced self-consciously at Mark and let go. An image of her meltdown at the restaurant swirled around in her head. *Your irritability is a feature of your illness and this is the way you're presenting,* Gail had frequently counseled her; *erratic moods, depression, hallucinations. Features of rapid cycling—you're cycling, that's all.* Yeah, Lila told herself, *cycling.* Mark deserved better from her, she decided as they approached the stoplight.

He pulled the car to a stop in front of the crosswalk and gave her a quick over-the-shoulder glance, listening carefully while she again apologized for her behavior at the restaurant. "No need for that," he insisted, "just tell me exactly what happened in Ann Arbor."

She explained in excruciating detail how the car bomb had blown out the front window and knocked her across the room. When she finished, he said, "You're scaring the hell out of me."

"I'm sorry."

"Don't be sorry, be careful." He glanced up at the light, still red. "Look, I know we just met, that we've only just ... had a little time together, but I feel like there's something here." He gazed into her eyes, unaware that the light had changed. "I mean, hell, I've never had a woman send me flowers before."

A shy smile pulled at the corner of her mouth. "The light's green," she said demurely.

As they left the intersection, he divided his attention between the road—intermittently crossed by wispy strands of snow—and his injured passenger. "Who did this to you? Do you even know?"

"I have a pretty good idea."

"Care to share it?"

She looked over at him and said, "Let me ask *you* a question."

"Anything," he said, his hands dropping from ten-and-two to the six o'clock position on the wheel.

"What would you think if somebody sent you a mattress?"

He laughed. "Well, now wait a minute! What's the matter with my mattress? Believe me, the flowers are more than enough!"

"No, that's not where I'm going with this," she replied. She stared out the side window. "This case ... has my brain tied up in knots. It's taking every ounce of energy I have trying to make some sense out of it." She filled him in on the circumstances surrounding the two assassinations and the threat against her brother.

"Again ... you're scaring the hell out of me."

"I'm sorry."

By the time they finally pulled into his basement-floor garage, her stress and anxiety had peaked and her headache had returned; she'd said too much, given too much away. Watching the gray steel door roll slowly open, she blinked back surprise when an immaculate two-car sanctuary done in gleaming gray and white came into view. "This place is spotless," she said, one eye scrunched shut, "what are you, a freak?"

He laughed. "I hope not. Guess I haven't been here long enough to mess it up." He cut the engine and leaned over to give her a kiss. "I'm glad you're here."

His warm, self-effacing words helped to put her at ease, and she felt something akin to a second wind come over her as they got out of the SUV and climbed the stairs to the kitchen. When he unlocked and opened the door, Bertrude was waiting for them, panting, tail wagging, his goofy pink tongue hanging out like a cartoon character's.

After ruffling the fur around the dog's studded collar, Mark quickly kibbled some scraps of meat together from leftovers in the fridge and dropped them into a chrome bowl. With Bertrude nose-down in the bowl, Lila followed Mark upstairs to the master suite, her overnight bag slung over her shoulder.

She sat on the edge of the bed, Mark's words *"I feel like there's something here"* replaying in her head. Meanwhile, her host busied himself opening a fresh bar of soap and stacking two bath towels on the stool by the tub. Lila wished she could lessen the fretfulness she was feeling at being bandaged and exhausted in a place not her own, but only managed to stand and begin pacing at the end of the bed.

Mark looked at her quizzically. "I take it there's something you want to tell me, Lila?"

She stopped and sighed heavily, turning to face him. "There's something you should know about me."

"If it has to do with how good it feels to be with you—*that* I already know." He smiled.

His attempts at charm were endearing, but only went so far. "It's this thing, this ... *curse* ... I have," she said quietly.

"*Curse?*"

"It's a ... mental thing. I can't even ... describe it accurately. Everything is great, then this soul-crushing despair ... and *weirdness* ... sort of creeps in and"—she stopped for a moment and swallowed dryly—"and sometimes I find myself wishing that this ongoing drama—that everything would just ... *cease.*"

"*Lila!*"

"Not cease like I'm going to end it all. I'm not suicidal ... at least, I don't *want* to be. But I do get overwhelmed, and I want the *overwhelming* to end. And so—you see my reluctance to commit to any long-term relationship."

"Oh ... is *that* what this is all about ..." He approached her, reaching out tenderly.

She rolled her neck to release the stress she felt tightening and, after a moment, peered imploringly into his eyes. "It's hard enough to make things work with people who are normal," she said softly, "let alone attempt it with one as ... *imperfect* ... as I am."

"Your imperfection is what makes you lovable," he said, gently pulling her down to sit on the bed next to him. "I happen to think it's the source of your heroism."

She narrowed her eyes at him. "What does that mean—*'source of my heroism?'*"

"You didn't let it stop you from getting your undergraduate degree at the University of Arizona, did you?"

"No."

"And you didn't let it stop you from getting your law degree at John Marshall, did you? Even though you wanted nothing to do with it."

"Well, no."

"And you didn't let it stop you from showing up to work every day to help Jim Savage, or from helping him become the most successful personal injury lawyer in the business, did you?"

"No."

"And you didn't let it stop you from jumping into the sack with the likes of me either, now did you?"

That one made her laugh. "No. Although that may have more to do with charity than heroism."

"Well, there you go!"

This level of affection was an unfamiliar and not altogether pleasant surprise. There was no posing, no performance—none of the things Lila was used to dealing with. After gazing into his eyes for a long moment, she found she had nothing left to say, so she turned and picked up her bag and started sorting out her belongings. There, under some folded tee shirts, she found the pilfered copy of *The Prophet* she'd snagged from Sofia's apartment.

Mark wasn't quite ready to drop the conversation. "Look, I'm a hopeful kind of guy," he continued. "You know, forever hoping for that lasting thing, that authentic connection ... the 'irreducible absolute.'"

Lila shook her head. "What is that, a mathematician's hook-up line?" She dropped her voice several octaves in pointed mimicry: *"Ooh, the irreducible absolute."*

He laughed heartily. "The categorical imperative," he managed to put in before standing. A smile still lingering on his face, he said, "I just think a shower, a comfy bed, and"—he glanced at the book she held in her hand—"maybe a good book will help you rest."

Maybe that's a good idea, she thought. *See what Gibran has to offer.*

Mark went back to the bathroom and opened the shower door. "Let me get this going for you." He reached for the controls and, at once, water burst forth from a half-dozen showerheads set along the walls and overhead. "You need anything, you let me know."

When he turned to go, she faced him and said with an almost child-like pout, "So, you're not going to undress me?"

It was an invitation he did not refuse.

The first thing to go was her facial bandage, which he removed as gently as possible. Her clothes seemed to drop to the floor, almost on their own. Soon, they were both naked in the shower, the water streaming down over them as they embraced. He held her gently but firmly; she could feel his heartbeat as his skin pressed against hers. When they finally dried off and climbed into bed, they finished what they'd started, his hands gliding over her bruised and wounded skin.

Later, while he lay next to her, naked, gently snoring, Lila found herself wide awake. She reached over and plucked *The Prophet* from the sideboard before flicking on the bedside lamp.

Despite the archaic language, it was a pretty easy read. Almustafa is preparing to leave the city where he's lived for the last twelve years. The townspeople gather around him, already mourning his departure, when Almitra, a seeress, calling him Prophet of God, says:

In your aloneness you have watched with our days, and in your wakefulness you have listened to the weeping and the laughter of our sleep. Now therefore disclose us to ourselves, and tell us all that has been shown you of that which is between birth and death.

As she read, Lila wondered, why *The Prophet?* What was Gus trying to communicate through this particular gift? She started flipping through the pages, all the way to the end. There, on the last page, she saw something scrawled in faint pencil in the upper right-hand corner:

dropbox.com/s/...

A URL. A Dropbox link. Had this been this jotted down by Wolf? Where did it lead, and what was contained there? She threw the covers off, reached for her messenger bag, and hauled out her computer, startling Mark awake. She took advantage of the moment to ask for his Wi-Fi credentials.

While she straightened, rearranging her laptop, Mark slid out, wrapped himself in his robe, and disappeared downstairs. Meanwhile, Lila entered the URL exactly as it was written, hoping against hope it wouldn't be password-protected. No such luck. She stopped to think; if Gus sent this link to Wolf, what password would he use that would be easy for Wolf to remember? Then, thinking about the inscription, it struck her: *millions.* She typed that in. No dice.

Mark returned lugging a pot of herbal tea and a plate of shortbread cookies. "Thought this might hit the spot," he said, placing the wooden platter down between them. He reached for a book on his sideboard and climbed back in next to her.

Lila shot him a beguiling smile before turning back to her passwords. She entered password after password—all variations on the *Prophet* theme, Gus's inscription, or their respective names—but was getting nowhere. She exhaled slowly, the air squeezed between her teeth. What if this URL had nothing to do with Wolf? Could it have been Sofia trying to convey some kind of message? If that was the case, though, why would the link be password-protected? She closed her laptop with a sigh; she'd consult with the IT folks at work, see if there's a way to hack in.

Mark shifted next to her. His book looked less like a commercial novel and more like an industrial textbook. "Is that a technical manual of some sort?" Lila asked.

"Not as such. More of a primer."

She looked closer. "*Artificial Intelligence and Big Data: The Birth of a New Intelligence.* Is this related to that high-tech job out of Dallas you were interviewing for? What's the status of that, by the way?"

He gave a slight shrug. "We're still talking."

She felt the remorse for her meltdown of that evening creeping back up. "So I didn't totally ruin it for you?" she asked sheepishly.

"*Nooo!*" he replied with a don't-be-silly grin. "They loved you!"

She leaned back on her pillow, feeling a little relieved despite her better judgment. "They were a couple of characters, weren't they? Especially the wife."

He slipped his bookmark into his book and rolled to face her. "Yeah, Jack's an interesting guy. He came up from the oil patch where he made millions in profit and turned it around to start his AI company—"

"Wait"—Lila grabbed his arm—"what did you just say?"

"Um—Jack ... came ... up ... from ..."

She stopped him, not really needing to hear it again, and glanced over at the cover of the book beside her. Her eyes widened. She lunged for her laptop, almost falling off the bed, and clicked through to the Dropbox link. Scrambling for a flyer with the email address *wolf.holzinger@gmail.com*, she typed:

millionsinprophet

Bingo! She was in. After a moment, the file list flickered up on-screen.

Jesus—a gold mine. Hundreds of documents going back nine years—Excel spreadsheets, Word documents. She picked one at random and opened it: a letter from Ismael Zaldavar Valiente—*La Ballena*. As she read, her jaw began to drop. Then another one, and another, and each time her mouth fell open a little more. But it wasn't until she found links to McManus & Piper that her heart began to pound in her chest. Frantically, she jumped to the side of the bed and searched her bag. There: Daniel Ortiz's business card with the handwritten cell number and email address. "Twenty-four seven," he'd said to her. She glanced feverishly back at Mark, who sat, wide-eyed, waiting for an explanation, and asked, almost breathlessly, "Do you have a thumb drive I could borrow?"

27

February 15, 2018

Ambrosia Dairy
Kewaunee, Wisconsin

LILA GOT UP BEFORE DAWN, DRESSED QUIETLY, AND LEFT MARK with a kiss on the cheek and a note on the nightstand. She Uber'd home, despite her boss's warnings, for a quick change of clothes, then headed to Chicago's Midway Airport. Two hours later, she arrived unannounced at Gus's dairy. He was on the phone when his receptionist delivered her to the open door of his office.

The ease with which she was being ushered in unsettled her; it was almost as if he'd been expecting her. Ignoring the twist in her stomach, Lila strode in and stood in front of his desk, waiting while he wrapped his call.

"Let me call you back," Gus told the person on the other end of the phone, interrupting what sounded like some kind of land negotiation—evidently something less important, in his view, than dealing with Lila. Hanging up, he winced at the wounds on the left side of her face and said, "You're upset—I get it. You want answers. Take a seat. I'll have Audrey bring us something to drink."

Lila reached into her bag, came out with the tattered copy of *The Prophet* she'd lifted from Sofia's apartment, and tossed it across the desk at him.

Surprised at first, his expression turned philosophical as he took the book and pondered its cover, front and back. "*The Prophet.* I remember this."

"Did you give it to Wolf?"

"As a matter of fact, I did."

She finally sat down across from him. "What did you mean, '*Here's to the millions we're going to make?*'"

He scowled. "What are you talking about?"

"The inscription!"

His brow furrowed, he opened the book to the first page. "To Wolf," he muttered, "here's to the millions we're going to make ... Gus. *Hmm.*"

"Did you not write that?"

He closed the book and laid it down. "You got this from Sofia, didn't you?"

"Are you trying to tell me she forged that message?"

He leaned back in his chair and gestured to the book. "Do a hand-writing analysis."

"Why would she do that?"

His eyes drifted around the room. "Who knows?" He shook his head and turned back, scrutinizing Lila. "Let's just say she didn't like me very much."

"Why not?"

"Myriad reasons."

Since that appeared to be all he was willing to give up, Lila turned to the next glaring question: "Why did she die?"

He sighed. "*That* should not have happened."

"And Angela Breem? And why was my brother threatened?"

"You're talking about the mattress thing?"

"What did *you* have to do with it?"

"Trust me," he smirked, lifting his open hand to slow the interrogation, "if I were to order an assassination, I would not be so ... *blunt* about it. I wouldn't leave *clues*, I wouldn't drop ... *metaphors*." He regarded the wounds on her face once again—another sympathetic wince. "And Lila ... at the risk of sounding like I'm threatening you, for which I apologize ... if I had wanted you dead for any reason, you would not be here right now."

She glared at him warily. Indeed, he was a professional. And part of that, Lila knew, given his background, was being a professional *liar*.

"Listen, in this particular case," Gus continued, affecting a more uplifting tone, "the simplest and most obvious answer *is* the correct one."

An echo of her earlier conversation with Mark—had he been listening in all along? Shaking off the paranoia, she pressed on: "What's your relationship with Orfilia Campos?"

He scratched the side of his head. "*That,* I'm not at liberty to discuss."

"Is she a CIA asset?" Off his refusal to answer, she continued: "Is she, or, rather, *was* she, a key contact in Venezuela? Is there some reason the agency or the US government is indebted to her? Did she help facilitate the death of Hugo Chavez in 2013?"

"Now you're just spinning conspiracy theories, kid."

"You never left CIA, did you?"

"No one ever 'leaves' the company. Not really."

"Charlie-O did."

"Charlie-O?" He let out a throaty laugh so vocal it took Lila aback. "That old battleax ... she's run with the best of them. But I'll tell you something about Charlie-O—if I were you, I wouldn't take what she says as gospel."

"Really? Well, gee—she and her husband seem to have a pretty high opinion of *you*. '*Top drawer,*' I believe they said."

"'Her husband'?" He chuckled some more. "Yeah, that's a good one ..."

She looked at him perplexed. "What do you mean by *that*?"

"Look ... Lila ..." He leaned forward at his desk. "Spooks are called spooks for a reason. We're ..." his head rocked side-to-side, "*ephemeral.* We exist 'between' realities—not quite this, not quite that. It's not a life most people would want to live, but it's how we affect outcomes. Here today, gone tomorrow."

"'Effect outcomes'? That seems morally ... indifferent."

"Moral judgments are not a luxury we can afford in our trade."

"Your 'trade' is *milk!* How can you run a dairy farm, *and* work for CIA, *and* expand your business, and God knows what else, all at the same time? When do you find time to *sleep?*"

"Don't worry," he grinned coyly, "In spite of it all, I manage to keep myself well-rested."

She narrowed her eyes—was that comment drug-related? After a failed attempt to reign in her anger, she demanded, "What happened to Wolf the night he fell? Was that your handiwork? You recruited him. He reported to you, didn't he? Did you tell him to break into Sofia's apartment that night? Was it your idea to use her place as his stash house? *Your* stash house, as you doubtless had planned it. Entangled him in your vile schemes." She saw him beginning to squirm under her relentless barrage. "Hell, you were probably there on the roof with him! You're certainly slimy enough—you probably let go of the rope on purpose!"

"Enough!" he shouted, his hand coming down hard on the desk with a loud *BANG!* "Enough ..." He leaned back in his chair, a pained look coming over him. "Take to heart what I'm telling you—Wolf was *not* attempting to break into Sofia's apartment under my direction. I promise you. How he ended up on the sidewalk that night ... *that,* my dear, remains as much a mystery to me as it does to you."

"You'll pardon me for not taking your word on that."

"Fair enough. But you can take my word on this: Orfilia Campos is a bad actor. She needs to be brought down. And for a lot of reasons I can't get into, *you* are in a particular position to do that."

"Funny, why do I feel like you're manipulating me?"

"Maybe I am." He lifted his head with an almost self-satisfied air. "But it's the right thing. Besides"—he leaned forward with a down-to-business shrug that made her uncomfortable—"CIA has its eye on you."

"How so?" Lila said slowly.

"Your skills, your instincts, your ... *unique* abilities ... would be very valuable to our team."

She let out a derisive laugh. "Are you trying to *recruit* me?"

"Not directly, but I can pick up this phone right now and set you up."

"Uh, I'll take a pass."

"Don't dismiss it out of hand. You want answers? This is a way to get them."

She leaned forward, took the book back, and waggled it in his face. "I think this conversation is over." She stood and turned toward the door.

"We'd very much like you in our corner," Gus called after her.

She stopped and looked back at him. "*Our corner?* As opposed to whose? Who's in the other corner?"

He hesitated. "*That* we can divulge once you sign the dotted line."

"Sorry. I've got other plans."

They stared at each other for a long moment. Then, ominously, he said, "Do what you must."

Gritting her teeth, Lila finally turned away and stalked from the room. On the way to her car, she grabbed her phone and touched Cornell's name. "Hey," she said, "so here's a disturbing bit of info you might need to hear."

Three days later, the following headline ran in *The Chicago Tribune*:

Ex-CIA Officer Indicted in International Drug Trafficking
Conspiracy

28

February 15, 2018

Stone Mental Health Center
Chicago, Illinois

LILA THOUGHT IT UNUSUAL TO FIND DR. GAIL ROSS SITTING AT HER desk, seemingly waiting for Lila to arrive, but, sure enough, there she was, head down, a sheaf of paper in one hand, a pen in the other. Lila rapped on the door and waited.

Looking up from her work, a warm smile spread across Gail's lips. "And on the third day she rises," she teased as Lila gave a sideways smile. She slid her paperwork aside and said, "Come, sit."

"If you're referring to me rising from the dead," Lila said, plopping down in the chair fronting Gail's desk, "you pretty much got that bass-ackwards. I feel like shit."

Gail leaned forward on her desk, frowning slightly. "You said you took a three-day break. No work, no phone ..."

Lila cocked her head. "I took some time off to recover, get some rest."

"And?"

"And ... nope, not the least bit rested. Although, I did manage to spend some time with Ulli and his family."

"How are they?"

"Well, I see why they call it a *safe*house rather than a *fun*house. Sucks that they're all stuck there, living under a microscope with a bunch of people they don't know, but they're fine."

Gail glanced down at the pen she held by both ends and allowed it to roll briefly forward. "How are you? Emotionally."

"Exhausted. Agitated. Overloaded. That's why I felt compelled to come in." Lila let out a deep sigh. "Oh, and to top it off, I had this ... remarkably vivid dream." Her eyes drifted off to the side. "Last night I was wandering aimlessly through the channels when I found what looked like a perfectly benign nature program on the Amazon rainforest."

"Oh, I like those."

"They were zooming in on these leaf-cutter ants, showing how they carve up the leaves from the surrounding trees—but they don't eat the leaves, they use them to grow the fungus they *do* eat. So they flash-cut to this murderous *zombie ant-fungus* thing. I'm watching as it takes control of this hapless little ant, shutting down its brain and compelling it to climb a nearby plant stem at a height where the fungus grows best. Once in place, it forces the ant to clinch its mandibles into this leaf in a death-grip. Next thing you know, the ant's body erupts with furry white filaments until it's completely covered like a chunk of moldy bread, and a long, disgusting stalk sprouts from its head and grows a bulbous capsule full of spores that bursts open and rains down on the colony's foraging trails, ultimately zombifying them all. And I just about die—I mean, I'm screaming at the TV—*Ewww! Yuck! Nooo!*"

Gail laughed good-naturedly at Lila's revulsion. "And this induced a dream?"

Lila looked at her with a deadpan expression. "I dreamed it was happening to me."

"Interesting."

"But it wasn't really 'me.' I mean, not a human me."

"You were the ant?"

"Not even that. I was ... something that didn't belong in this world. Something more ... spider-like."

"Oh, well that makes perfect sense. The spider image has been a recurring motif in your dreams and hallucinations."

"Yeah, I guess so."

"It's easy to see the symbolism. The spider weaves an intricate web to trap its prey, and you've been feeling trapped by this complex case you've been working. Only this time you're the spider, which reflects your anxiety that no matter how much you take charge of your circumstances, you still feel powerless."

"Except ..." Lila put up a cautionary forefinger. "*Except* ... I got loose. I broke free. Reclaimed my selfhood."

"Really? Was there a particular, um ... catalyst for that?"

"Just my own determination. The force of my own will."

"Huh. Well ..." Gail sat back and crossed her arms. "That seems positive."

"And it felt so ... *real*. Like ..." She paused, groping for words. "Like my true identity was finally busting out of the constraints of this existence. It was like I was seeing things from another dimension. It's ... it's hard to put into words."

"Well, it *is* a dream after all." Gail sank into silence, staring blankly past Lila. Finally, she looked up. "And how have you been feeling since? How are you sleeping?"

"I wake up and it's like, crap, back to the life I was in. My head so cluttered it's ready to explode. Feeling like shit. Headaches getting unbearable."

"No, I get it. You need a tune-up." Gail got up from her desk and, patting Lila on the shoulder on her way to the door, said, "Let's get you back there and hooked up."

Forty-five minutes later, Lila was shrugging on her coat, feeling an unfamiliar sense of calm. She felt as if her mind had been backed up for weeks and it was only now, after her TMS tune-up, that she could move forward again, processing, analyzing, managing whatever the facts threw at her. Just then, her cell phone went off. She glanced at the caller ID— Jim Savage. "Hey, Jim," she answered.

"Just got off the phone with the FBI," he told her. "They caught the mattress thief."

"Really?" Lila replied, her calm rising to excitement, "same guy who planted the bomb?"

"Same guy. And you're going to love this: the money trail leads back to—"

"Orfilia."

"Yup. Took her into custody this morning. He had one of her credit cards in his wallet."

"What are the charges?"

"Suspicion of conspiracy to commit murder."

"Yes!" Lila exclaimed, her free hand punching the air.

"Try to keep an even steam," Savage cautioned.

"I'm good. In fact, I'm very good."

"Your, uh, soaring spirits wouldn't have anything to do with Gus Ambrosia, would they? I take it you're not entirely dissatisfied with his arrest last night?"

She chuckled—Savage always could read her mind. "No, though I did catch the article in the Trib. Bizarre. You think they'll be able to make a connection between Gus and Orfilia?" Hearing her own words spoken out loud, she wondered if exposing Gus had been the right thing to do in the grand scheme of things.

"Who knows? As it stands now, they appear to be entirely separate cases. In other news, our friend, Hans Holzinger, called this morning. He's evidently less ambivalent than you; he instructed me to shut down your investigation. Effective immediately."

Lila stopped in her tracks. Just when it looked like everything was finally starting to snap into place, this bombshell. "Well," she managed, "that's abrupt!"

"I guess with Ambrosia on ice for a while, an opportunity has opened up for him to step in and make some acquisitions of his own. I'd bet he'll be buying up a bunch of neighboring dairy operations Gus had in the works."

"We still don't have the answer he hired me to get—*why* was Wolf on the roof that night, and *who* was there with him?"

Savage fell silent for a moment.

"So, what are you saying? He's more interested in making a land grab than solving his son's death? What happened to his impassioned plea to find his killer—if, I recall, it was the *last thing he does?*"

"You know the game, Lila. We work for our clients. We're at their mercy. When they're done, we're done. On to the next challenge."

She stood there, amazed at how he could so easily transition from go to no-go. Savage could turn away without a second thought; Lila could not. There was still a road ahead—she could see it narrow and disappear into the distance. "Let me call you back from the car," she said in a decidedly less upbeat tone.

Sitting alone in the rental with the engine off, she took advantage of her restored mental clarity, thinking through everything she'd learned while working this case, every fact she had encountered, every relationship and every entanglement that had surrounded Wolf's death. The web —as Dr. Ross had referred to it—had become so sprawling and the strands so tangential that she realized she needed to simplify, simplify, simplify. Pare away the Breems' murders, pare away Orfilia Campos and all her shenanigans, pare away all the dubious assertions and misdirections thrown at her by various players, and return to the underlying question: why did Wolf feel the need to rappel down to Sofia's apartment, and who had a stake in it?

And then she had a Eureka moment.

But, before she could act on it, she needed more information. She opened a browser on her phone and Googled "climbing consultants." She found a guy, got him on the phone, and arranged to meet him first thing in the morning at 1100 North Dearborn.

Bright and early the next day, she met the climber in the Dearborn lobby and brought him to the roof, where she asked him to explain the logistics of how a climber might attempt to rappel down to the fifteenth floor but hit a snag one floor short. As she listened, goosebumps rose along her arms and back, slowly creeping up her neck.

After she thanked and paid the consultant, she called Savage. "Any chance you can ask our client to come in for a final report? Tell him I know what happened to his son."

29

February 16, 2018

Law Offices of Savage, Lutz, Finnegan & Foehl
Chicago, Illinois

HOLZINGER ARRIVED AT THE MEETING A HALF-HOUR LATE AND found Lila and Savage standing by the floor-to-ceiling window, talking quietly. Savage looked over at his old friend and, after a moment, went to shake his hand.

Lila did the same and, followed her boss's nod, took a seat on the couch.

"The sooner we can get to your conclusions, the better," Holzinger said, sitting down in one of the armchairs, checking his watch. "Jim tells me that you've reached a conclusion, *ja?*"

"I have," she said.

He spread his hands expectantly.

"Right. Are you familiar with the term 'frequency illusion?'"

"No."

She looked down at her notebook and read, "The frequency illusion is a cognitive bias which describes our tendency to see new information, names, ideas, or patterns 'everywhere' soon after they're first brought to our attention."

Holzinger looked at her doubtfully. "*Und* what does this have to do *mit* your findings?"

"So, almost immediately after you hired us, the odd subject of the CIA began cropping up. And by 'cropping up,' I mean almost everywhere I looked, there it was: somebody was either mentioning the CIA or had a background with the CIA. It's like when you buy a red hat and suddenly, everywhere you look, all you see are red hats. So I ask myself—naturally—what could this mean?" Her eyebrows went up with the playful curl of her lips. "What I came up with were three possible explanations: One, the world is random and I just never noticed all the red hats that were always there; two, red hats tend to cluster together the way people cluster around major cities and, sparked by the evidence linking my brother's indictment to the CIA and a certain international narco-cartel under investigation, I simply observed one such cluster—"

Holzinger looked at her, bemused. "*Und* what does your brother have to do *mit* any of this?"

"Stay with me—or three, some diabolical bastard has some devious reason for purposely dropping red hats in my path." She looked him straight in the eye.

Holzinger recoiled from her accusing demeanor. "You've lost me."

"You said you hired me to find the truth, to find your son's killer."

"*Ja, und* you said you had something to report."

"Yeah, well, when I accidentally stumble onto something beneficial to you financially, exposing your business rival's criminal activities, you abruptly cancel the investigation. *Why,* I ask myself."

Holzinger's face began to redden.

"One answer is: maybe this was your objective all along—to get one over on your competition."

Exasperated, Holzinger turned to Savage. "Is this going anywhere or are you just wasting my time?"

"I don't know," Savage replied. "Let's hear her out."

"But if this was only ever about gaining a leg up on your competition," Lila continued, "that would mean that you never wanted to find the killer at all. Why would that be?"

Holzinger sat there, unmoving, his arms locked across his chest.

"And the only answer I could come up with is: maybe because you already know who the killer is. And then I realized that the only way you can know who it is ... is because you were there, on the roof that night. I think Wolf told you about his work with the agency, with Gus, whom he had looked up to as a mentor since he was a kid, which I think has bothered you for a very long time."

"You have quite an imagination," he said, turning once again to Savage, "even if it is completely unmoored from reality."

"And I believe he told you about my brother Ulli's entanglement with Ismael Zaldavar Valiente—*La Ballena*—and their smurfing money-laundering scheme through McManus & Piper for his narco-cartel, exposing the CIA's scandalous involvement and the risk to Gus's operation that it represented. The risk to your son."

Holzinger remained silent.

She glanced over at Savage, who was listening intently. "And I think you panicked. You told him Gus was crooked, that he'd gone rogue since Afghanistan, skimming money from his days trafficking opium. You lied to him, told him Gus was going down this time, probably warned him that he needed to get whatever remained of his stash and clean it out—right away, that night—before Gus got popped and ruined his life. You told him Gus couldn't be counted on, that he'd disappear and Wolf would be left holding the bag.

"So, that night, the two of you went to Wolf's stash house, which, unbeknownst to Sofia Castellanos, happened to be her apartment at 1100 North Dearborn. It was two nights before Halloween and Sofia was at her cousin's place on Stone Street, waiting on the delivery of a Steinway Grand. You thought your son had a key, that he and Sofia were lovers. But, when it all came out that he not only didn't have a key but that he was gay, *that* staggered you. So you followed him to the roof, where he planned to use a couple of acces-

209

sory ropes he had in his car to rappel down to her fifteenth-floor apartment.

"I spoke to an experienced climber recently. He told me most climbers don't lug around full lengths of climbing rope with them, which I understand run from sixty to seventy meters in length. Sixty meters is almost two hundred feet; that's a lot of rope, takes up a lot of space. He told me that he typically keeps some shorter bits in his car—maybe a couple accessory ropes, thirty feet each. So I'm guessing maybe Wolf did the same, and maybe you didn't want him to tie two short pieces together. You wanted him to be safe and make a Swiss seat, use the TV cable as a back-up. But you were so distracted, so entirely staggered by Wolf's homosexuality and whether your rival, Gus Ambrosia, had anything to do with that, that you forgot something that to you, at your level of experience, should have been second-nature—you forgot to tie a stop knot."

Holzinger clicked his tongue in disgust. "What, *und* you're a climber now? What do you know about stop knots!"

"I just told you, I contacted an experienced rock climber. Met with him; we had a long talk. When you told him to use the TV cable, you were feeling beside yourself and didn't factor in the temperature. The frigid night air made the copper core brittle. So, when the accessory rope ran out at the sixteenth floor without the required stop knot, the TV cable snapped under Wolf's full weight and you stood there, unable to help, as your son plummeted to his death.

"In the rush, Wolf hadn't tied the stop knot or even bothered to check because he was relying on the one person he trusted most on Earth to do that for him. Gus is not a climber, Hans; you are." She looked at Holzinger and watched his eyes well up with tears.

"So, the way I'm seeing it, you're not only complicit in your son's death, you're getting beat up in business by the very man you're convinced is crooked to the core, professionally and otherwise; the very man you believe got Wolf involved in this corrupt drug business in the first place. In your mind, Gus is the guilty party. Without Gus, Wolf wouldn't have been on the roof that night. Without Gus's influence, Wolf would have been at home, working in the family business. So, you take your wife on a cruise and begin casting about for a way to get even.

"But you're bored out there, and you keep up with the local news. That's when you see a name you recognize in the Chicago paper: *McManus & Piper*. You read the article about how my brother, Ulli, was indicted in a fifty-million-dollar international securities fraud and money-laundering scheme. 'Piper,' you remembered, was the name of your best friend's PI. He told you all about me. Maybe he brags about the cases we've won when you two are alone in the backcountry on your Alaskan hunting trips. So, you do a little research and, lo and behold, it turns out McManus & Piper and PI Piper are not only related, we're siblings.

"So, immediately upon returning home, you contact your friend, Jim Savage. You ask him for a favor, and he obliges. He puts your son's case in my hands and tells me to set everything else aside.

"And then you wait for me to put two and two together. When I do, and your rival takes a fall, your business reaps the benefits. It puts you in position to play the white knight, stepping in and rolling all the remaining small dairy operators Gus was about to acquire into your own company. It turns out you're a greedy bastard, Hans. You had it all figured out—except for the danger involved. What you didn't account for was the can of worms that would open up, causing innocent people to die, get hurt"—she gestured toward her own still-healing face—"or have their lives disrupted, or that your dancing puppet, me"—she shot Savage a rancorous look—"would take that personally."

She stared at Holzinger, breathless. He sat with his arms crossed, poker-faced, staring back at her—but not with an air of anger or defensiveness, but rather more of curiosity. Finally, he softened.

"*Chimmy* was right," he said, "you certainly have an agile mind. *Ja,* but there's nothing that can be done." He looked over at Savage, then back to Lila with a downturned smile. "Attorney-client privilege." He stood, nodding to Savage. "I'll send you your fee. Payment in full for a job well done." At the door, he looked back at Lila as if he wanted to say something else. Instead, he simply turned and left.

3 0

February 16, 2018

Law Offices of Savage, Lutz, Finnegan & Foehl
Chicago, Illinois

LILA WAITED TILL SAVAGE PULLED HIS DOOR SHUT AND THEN ROSE, spreading the vertical blinds that fronted the office and watching Holzinger's back disappear beyond the outer doors of the suite. Finally, she turned to her boss. "Did he just tacitly confess?" As Savage returned to his chair, she walked back across the office, a little shaken. "I mean ... he didn't refute a thing I said."

Savage stared at her for a long moment, neither agreeing nor disagreeing, then, absorbed in thought, looked down at his desk littered with case files.

Lila gripped the back of the chair in front of the desk. "Shouldn't we tell someone?"

Savage glanced up from his work, eyeing the vague figures passing back and forth in front of his office. He cocked his head. "Despite Hans and I being old friends, believe me when I tell you, Lila, we get crosswise with that old buzzard, he won't hesitate to sue our asses off."

"*But—*"

"But nothing," Savage said as he leaned back in his chair. "You just keep your mouth shut. We're professionals—we got paid; we're done." He grabbed some paperwork and turned away from her, staring pointedly at the page.

Lila stared at him, astounded.

He glanced back up at her. "You've got several pending cases on your desk requiring attention. Go tend to them."

After a moment, Lila shook her head slightly. "*Okaay,*" she said, then turned and walked out.

On her way to her office, where she had spent very little time of late, she did a quick run-through of all the possible contacts to whom she might "accidentally" let slip the revelations just expounded and implicitly confirmed. Cornell Williams? Daniel Ortiz? Krzyskowski? But she knew she would never do such a thing—she was indeed a professional, under the employ of a law firm with a sterling reputation and a certain standard of conduct, and she would not risk that relationship. No, it was incumbent upon her to move on and put it behind her, to shift her head back into the space it had been the day before Hans Holzinger had walked into the firm and into her life.

As she was rifling through the files that had been collecting dust on her desk, a forgotten calm settled over her—she'd missed the comfort of mundane work. She was just getting immersed in a personal injury file when her cell phone rang. Distracted, she grabbed the phone with her free hand.

"Yeah?" she said gruffly.

A feminine voice, friendly but no-nonsense. "I'm trying to reach ... Lila Piper?"

"Speaking."

"Hi Ms. Piper, my name is Ruby Hampton, I'm with Technical Support at RCN Chicago. You submitted a request for information regarding a cable service outage on October twenty-ninth last year at 1100 North Dearborn apartments?"

"Yes."

"Sorry for the delay in getting back to you. Our records indicate there *was* a service interrupt logged on the morning of October twenty-ninth at three fifty-three AM for several customers in that building. Would that be what you are looking for?"

"Three fifty-three?" *Not* what she'd expected to hear. "Now ... is that the time somebody called in to report an outage?"

"No, ma'am, that's from our internal data. We did get calls the next morning, and a technician responded that Sunday, but the actual time of the interruption was recorded by the system. Every interaction with a customer's cable box or modem is logged with a timestamp. Sometimes we just have to go digging for it, especially when the data is a few months old."

"So there wouldn't be a ... a *delay*, say, between the time the interruption occurred and the time it was logged?"

"Correct, there wouldn't be."

It didn't fit. Lila clearly remembered from Holzinger's file at CPD that the first 911 call had been placed at 03:06. Why would the cable cut occur at least forty-seven minutes *after* Wolf fell to his death? An hour earlier would make more sense ...

"Okay, let me ask this: We were still in daylight savings time in October. Is that timestamp based on standard time?"

"No, the system logs use local time—consistent with the time shown on the cable box, which is always automatically updated."

"So ... it's not on Eastern Time either?"

"No. Current local time."

Something was not lining up. Lila picked up her pen and started jotting down notes. "So ... three fifty-three AM, *Central Daylight* Time, Sunday October twenty-ninth, 2017."

"That's correct."

"Are there any other outage incidents logged on the twenty-eighth or twenty-ninth at that address—any whatsoever?"

"No, that's the only one."

"And what did the technician find when he came out?"

"Report says 'cable damage due to vandalism.'"

"Vandalism ..."

"Yes ma'am. Don't know if you've ever noticed it before, but high-rise buildings rarely have exposed electrical wire running down the sides. Almost always, the wire—or, in our case, the cable—is run through an electrical conduit. A conduit is—"

"I know what a conduit is."

"Yes, ma'am. So the, uh, the conduit was found dangling from the side of the building with the cable removed."

The technician's word choice—"*dangling from the side of the building*"—conjured in Lila's mind the image of Holzinger's crazy son suspended above the street. What was it Hans had said? *"My son would know better than to trust his life to an unrated, untested line. Especially one that's* chimmy-rigged *from cable made from cheap molded plastic* mit *a thin copper wire core inside."*

"Say," Lila said, "you wouldn't happen to know what kind of cable is installed at that address? The brand, I mean."

"Yes, ma'am. We use *CommScope QR 320 JCAR* coaxial cable." Lila wrote that down. "It's top-of-the-line coax cable with a flame-retardant polyethylene jacket."

Lila's mind was racing—none of this added up. After a prolonged silence, the technician finally added, "Anything else I can help you with?"

"No. You've been more than helpful. Thank you."

After hanging up, Lila turned to her computer and Googled *QR 320 coaxial cable*. She snooped around until she found a broadband catalog to skim, and within that found various tables that listed products by catalog number and description, with measurements describing "physical dimensions," "attenuation," and the like. But it was the table labeled "mechanical characteristics" that struck her—the final sub-category simply read, *Minimum Breaking Strength: 1,800 lbs.* Lila shook the cobwebs from her mind and read it over several more times, wondering, *How on Earth does an average-sized gymnast, weighing less than 200 lbs., possibly snap a coaxial cable rated over nine times his weight?*

Lila tried vigorously to reconcile the facts facing her. Whatever degree of confidence she had lacked going into the meeting with Hans that morning had been made up for by his lack of rebuttal. But now, the apparently indisputable timing of the cable cut, combined with the unlikelihood of the cable snapping, cast a different light on the whole scenario. Under what circumstances would the cable get ripped out *after* the fatal fall? The only conceivable answer was: a cover-up. But a cover-up for what? Wolf's body had indeed been on the pavement that night, as multiple 911 calls would attest. How had he ended up there?

She looked back at the personal injury case file she had started perusing, sighed, and closed it. *Fucking investigation's* not *over—not until I get some fucking answers.*

She wished to God she had a hard copy of the police file and not just her own notes—then, maybe, she'd find some telling anomaly. She thought of calling Cornell, but a sudden thought struck her: what if Cornell was complicit in the cover-up? Hard to fathom—more likely someone under him, but she couldn't risk making that call. She was disinclined to bring this up with Savage, and she certainly couldn't approach Hans, who had to be involved in some way. Ironically enough, the only person she felt might provide some light in this present darkness was Gus Ambrosia.

After all, he *did* ask her to join his "corner."

Lila sat at Mark's dining room table, a simple cup of hot tea, untouched, in front of her. Ortiz had told her to expect a call, so she sat, elbows braced on the table, head in her hands, and stared down at her phone. Mark was across the room reading a newspaper—an actual *paper*, so old-school, this guy—and going on about an article regarding an Army research lab that had started operating on the University of Chicago's campus a few months prior, right next door to the advanced physics lab and the particle accelerator.

"China and Russia developing their hypersonic weapons systems, gonna take some high-tech weapons to defeat them," he remarked. "Advanced physics labs, particle accelerators—sounds like a good place to start."

While she appreciated that he was comfortable enough around her to let out his inner nerd, she was simply too preoccupied to entertain idle conversation. Minutes later, the phone rang.

"Lila Piper!" Gus said tauntingly, "I wondered how long it would take you to reach out to me." Lila grimaced—he sounded way too snarky for a man behind bars. "You wouldn't happen to have anything to do with my being in this lovely facility, would you?"

His attempt at feigning ignorance was almost charming. "Well ... if for some reason I'm called to testify, I'm sure you'll find out."

"So, to what do I owe the honor?"

"I need some answers."

"Don't we all."

"I'm trying to figure out why—if Wolf used a television cable ripped from the roof to rappel down the side of the building—why that cable was disconnected nearly an hour *after* he took his fall. You wouldn't happen to have an explanation for that discrepancy in the story, would you?"

He paused for just a moment too long. "Well, if I did, my dear, I certainly wouldn't talk about it on a *prison telephone*."

"Would you be willing to talk about it in person?"

"I have nothing to offer."

"What was in Sofia's apartment that Wolf needed to get to so badly?"

He chuckled slightly. "I *will* tell you this much—watch your assumptions."

"Watch my assumptions," Lila deadpanned.

"But more importantly," he added, "watch *other people's* assumptions."

"What assumptions are you referring to? What other people?"

"I really can't *staaaay*," he said far too airily, and then abruptly hung up.

1. I   real - ly can't stay _____

Lila looked at the phone—now *that* was an odd way to end a call. Was he being snarky again, or ... was there more to it? It sounded weirdly familiar: *I really can't staaay ...* At once, the response popped into her head: *Baby, it's cold outside ...* Gus had referenced that song in her very first conversation with him. *"Saw him do 'Baby, It's Cold Outside' with a covey of young gals hanging on him, fawning over him. That was a hoot."*

What was Gus trying to tell her?

"Watch your assumptions. But more importantly, watch other *people's assumptions."*

Maybe Wolf *hadn't* been targeting Sofia's apartment, as had been assumed all along. Instead, he was trying to enter *Marina's* apartment ... *but why?*

She pocketed her phone, grabbed her coat, and bolted toward the door.

Mark looked up from his paper. "Where are you off to?"

"Back to school."

31

February 16, 2018

University of Chicago Campus
Chicago, Illinois

No surprise to Lila that Marina once again refused to answer her phone—but she hadn't expected *this:* instead of the usual voicemail message, Lila heard:

> *"The person you are trying to reach is unavailable at this time,*
> *please try your call later."*

Lila needed to question her again. She needed to determine the real connection between

Mysh and Wolf ... assuming that such a connection existed in the first place. Was Marina really a medical student here on a legitimate visa, or something more nefarious? A Russian spy, perhaps? Could that explain why Wolf and Sofia lived immediately beneath her—they were running surveillance on her for the CIA? Or was Marina involved in something even more underhanded, herself another CIA asset? None of the scenarios Lila ran through her head quite fit the byzantine jigsaw puzzle scattered before her. If Marina had been lying that day in the campus greenhouse, she had done an awfully convincing job. Unless she *hadn't* been lying—or, perhaps more accurately, she'd *thought* she was telling the truth. Lila sighed. That would make things even *more* complicated.

Though it was Saturday evening, Lila guessed that Marina might still be at school rather than at her apartment. As she approached the Michigan Avenue drawbridge which spanned the Chicago River, something off to the left caught her eye. She glanced over and shrieked, jerking back—a large black spider was clinging to the outside of her window. After an uncontrollable head-to-toe shiver, she tentatively reached up to tap the window to dislodge the thing, only to discover that the unnerving arachnid wasn't outside the window, but *inside!* It dropped onto her lap and quickly scuttled away down her leg and into the shadows.

Lila let out a shrill, piercing screech, swerving all over the road as she frantically slapped at her lap. When she glanced up, she slammed on her brakes and jerked the wheel just in time to keep from crashing head-on into the bridge abutment. Halted on the curb, half on and half off the road, she scrambled out of the rented SUV and gave another full-body shiver, partially blocking traffic, cars honking and passing her with shaking heads and one-finger salutes.

That's when it dawned on her ... one thing that had been troubling her about

Marina's account of Wolf's fall that night that she'd never quite managed to put her finger on: Marina had said that, *at first, she'd thought she was seeing things, then screamed when she thought Wolf was inside her apartment. But when she realized he was outside hanging from a cable, she went to the window to have a closer look.* Was he inside or outside? She shivered again, wadded up a paper napkin, checked the seat and then smashed the offending spider as it ran across the floor. Relieved, she slid back into the SUV.

. . .

Lila arrived on the E. 59th Street campus a half-hour later and parked in front of the Donnelley Biological Sciences Learning Center. Unable to locate Marina in the center's study hall, she headed straight for the building's rooftop greenhouse. Strange—it was empty.

Standing among the plants, surveying the dazzling lights in the surrounding buildings, Lila gazed down at the cluster of buildings directly below: the Advanced Physics Lab, the particle accelerator, and the new Army research lab. Staring at the illuminated building below, she remembered Mark commenting about this very addition earlier that day. Interesting that Mysh's hangout of choice was immediately adjacent to these facilities. Lila squinted—below, mobbed people were queuing in front of the main entrance to the ARL. Not students. Well-dressed, important-looking people. *What's going on?* she wondered. She turned and headed to the staircase.

Out in front of the physics lab and particle accelerator, Lila ran into a rail-thin

teenager lugging a bulging backpack over one shoulder walking in the opposite direction. She asked, "What's going on in there?"

He shrugged. "They're kicking us out again."

"Again?" she asked, keeping an eye out for Marina as people passed them by.

"Every now and then the Army folks take over the whole physics department for the weekend. We get kicked out every three or four months. Kinda sucks."

The timeframe struck a nerve. "Really?" Lila remarked. "You remember the last

time this happened?"

"Oh yeah, sure. October. Everyone dresses up around Halloween. I remember one of the Army dudes saying, 'Look at all the spooks, how apropos is that?'"

Lila shook her head and stared at the suits milling around in front of the lab, all getting ready to enter.

"Best not go that way, they get edgy," the student advised with a grin. "Unless you've got one of those special badges."

Lila smiled at the kid. "I'll watch my step." She thanked him then headed back toward the parking lot. This could wait—she still had to find Marina.

An hour later, Lila entered 1100 North Dearborn, where she was greeted by the same accommodating doorman she'd met the last time she was here. After engaging in some friendly banter while she waited for the elevator, Lila got in and rode to the sixteenth floor. She approached Marina's door and rang the doorbell. After a few seconds, she started knocking. She leaned in against the painted wood: "*Marina ... ! Mysh ... !* Are you there?"

"She moved out," croaked a gravelly smoker's voice.

Startled, Lila whipped around. There stood an old woman, barely five-feet tall, wearing a tattered Chinese embroidered robe and mukluks. "When?" Lila asked.

The old gal shrugged indifferently. "Who knows? Maybe a few days ago." She gave a wave of her hand, pawing the air. "Go ahead, see for yourself—it's unlocked." She stuffed her hands deep into her pockets and leaned back against the wall.

Lila tried the doorknob and tentatively pushed the door open. The woman was right—the room was empty. "Where'd she go?" Lila asked.

"Who knows? Russia, I'm thinking."

Lila gave the old docent a nod and headed through, shutting the door between them. Exhaling a deep breath, she began cautiously looking around. The place reeked of garlic and looked like it hadn't been repainted in decades. Looked like renovations for the next tenant had yet to be started, which made her wonder whether Marina had given proper notice—maybe, she thought darkly, she'd had to leave in a hurry. Moving methodically through the apartment, Lila checked every closet, every cabinet, every nook and cranny, using her booted foot to comb through the bedroom's freshly vacuumed carpet, looking for anything that might shed some light on who, exactly, Marina Resnick was.

"Nothing, right?" the old smoker said, standing in the open doorway.
Lila started at the intrusion.

"Back to Russia, like I said." Pawing the air one last time, the woman
turned and left.

Crossing the living room's parquet floor, Lila stood at the mullioned
windows and tried to visualize exactly what had transpired that night.
Down below, street-side, North Dearborn was jammed with cars.
Watching a yellow cab stop to pick up a fare, Lila suddenly had an idea:
maybe the wee hours of the morning might offer a fresh perspective on
Wolf's fall.

She pulled out her phone and sent Mark a text:

*Hey, something's come up so I'll be working late, didn't want you
to worry. I'll catch up with you tomorrow.*

She chose a spot on the carpet in the bedroom where she could see
into the living room, set an alarm for 02:55 AM, laid her phone next to
her so she'd be sure to hear it go off, and then, after clicking *Do not
disturb* and fluffing up her coat to use as a pillow, she settled in, closed
her eyes, and began her breathing exercise.

Lila woke before her alarm and rose groggily. Stifling a yawn, she stumbled to the bedroom window and pressed her face against the glass.
Outside, the familiar streets of Chicago stretched on, looking oddly naked
without the gridlocked cars. Frowning, she went to the living room
window and looked southward toward the university campus, checking to
see if any landmarks from the campus were even visible from her
sixteenth-floor perch.

Bleary-eyed and suddenly wishing she was lying naked in bed with
Mark instead of standing there in a cold, empty apartment, she chastised
herself for being an idiot. What'd she been hoping to find?

All she knew was that she was achy from her stint on the floor and
dehydrated. She glanced over to the kitchen and realized she hadn't

checked the refrigerator. Hoping for a bottle of water, a beer, or a juice box, *anything* other than tap water, she threw open the door. Nothing—completely empty, and the freezer too. She sighed and swung it shut, noticing marks in the white where clearly there'd once been magnets. She knew from experience that items posted on a refrigerator door could be very telling of a person's life—photos, phone numbers, reminders, and the like. She peered into the narrow gaps on either side of the fridge in case any such artifacts might have been inadvertently left behind and, when she couldn't see anything, used her cell phone's flashlight function to illuminate the space. Nothing. She bent down and peered underneath and there, among the thick layer of dust, was something flat—a business card perhaps. Unable to reach it with her finger, Lila turned to her coat and dug into a pocket for a pen. Sticking the pen under the fridge, she carefully nudged the card forward. Finally, she grasped it and pulled it out into the light.

The name on the business card read *Dr. Gail M. Ross.*

Suddenly, a brilliant flash of blue-white light caught her eye. Lila wasn't sure if it had been inside her head or outside. For some reason, *particle accelerator* was the first thought that sprang to her mind. She dropped the card and the phone and ran to the window, pushing her face against the glass. There it was again: a blue-tinted flash followed by a sequence of unusual fireworks that looked like some kind of filigree scrollwork light show, brilliant white lines looping around each other before fading. The trails of explosive curlicues accelerated toward her until a tsunami of phosphorescent lights broke against the building.

Lila staggered back, her mind reeling, awash with images and colors and fleeting secrets. When the lights quieted and stilled, she straightened, feeling vaguely dislocated—both inside and outside her body—both subject and object. Two realities existing at once.

She shivered, her heart pounding as she sucked in a breath. And there he was—Wolf Holzinger stood silently, partially concealed by the shadows across the room. Instantly, Lila's mind switched modes, from linear to universal, and she somehow grasped that she was no longer seeing things from her own perspective—rather, she was behind Marina's eyes.

Instead of lingering in the shadows or dangling from a TV cable outside the window, Wolf stepped through the constantly moving filigree scrollwork that hung in the air between them, his hands outstretched, reaching for her face. He was saying something, but his voice was distorted—she couldn't make out the words.

Then, feeling his ghostlike thumbs press hard against her temples, something else shifted—it was as if a dormant self-defense program inside her brain suddenly activated. Lila felt her body seize up and a booming, unearthly *scream* split suddenly from somewhere deep within her mind. Another *flash* consumed the room, arcing lights washing over the peeling walls.

Her scream struck Wolf with the blunt force of an explosive blast, throwing his body across the room. Lila stood frozen, watching, horrified, as Wolf flew—*too slow*, she thought—not into the wall, but *through* it, as if the entire building were made of mist. He hovered there for a long moment, frantically checking his body, astonished that he could feel anything physical at all. Then, his body began to jitter. He bounced up and down and back and forth as if struggling to find a state in which to exist. Lila watched his saucer-wide eyes, his trembling flesh, the phasing of his body in and out of the wall. A glint of light caught her attention, a vertical sliver around which space seemed to bend. Slowly, without knowing why, she raised her arm, and another preternatural expulsion of energy tore from her, arcing toward the point. Wolf tried to lunge into the blast's path, but it swept him aside, pushing him at last beyond the wall. There was an awful silence—she pictured him falling, and heard the distant *thud*.

As quickly as it began, the light storm ended, and darkness returned to the room. Lila let out an explosive gasp and crumpled to the floor. Between ragged breaths, she ran her thumbs over her fingers and palms, checking to see if she'd suffered a stroke, and touched her lips, fearful that she might be drooling.

No paralysis, no drool. Nothing.

A loud *Bang! Bang! Bang!* on the door interrupted her heavy breathing. She stared at the door, terrified, trying not to make a sound.

"Lila?!?"

Was that ... Mark?!

The door slammed open, and it *was* Mark, frantic and pale and wide-eyed. *"Lila!"*

He rushed to her side, took her into his arms, and held her to him. She attempted an explanation but no words came out, only unintelligible groans.

"You're all right," he assured her, hugging her, lightly stroking the back of her head. "Quiet now. You're all right—everything's okay."

Finally, her body tightened. *"How?"* she managed, "how do you know?" Grunting, she pushed him away. "How did you know I was here?" She felt for her phone in her pocket, then looked toward the kitchen—it lay face-down on the floor. She glared back at him. "Are you fucking tracking my *phone?!*" When he hesitated, she stood up and lurched back a step.

Mark got on his feet and held his arms out. "Lila ..."

The more he approached, the more she backed up. "What ... who ..." She held her palm up. "Who the *fuck* are you?!"

"Lila ..." He took a step back. "I'm here to help you."

"Help me? *Help me?*"

He stuttered for a long moment, his struggle, Lila thought, betraying his guilt. "To protect you. To watch over you."

She backed further away. "What are you saying ..." Her eyes darted from him to the door to the window. "Are you saying ... you were *assigned* to me?!" She looked at him, aghast. "By *whom?!*"

"Lila ..." He approached cautiously, hands raised, even as she continued to retreat. "This whole case, everything you've been going through ... it all runs way, way deeper than you realize."

"No shit!" She said, pointing her finger accusingly. "Who assigned you to shadow me?"

He scanned the room before answering. "Military Intelligence. In cooperation with the CIA. And the NSA."

She took another step back toward the wall, shaking her head. *Again with the ... fucking ... CIA!* You're with Hans, aren't you?" she said shivering, trying to hold back the tears threatening to burst free.

"No."

She rounded on him. *"Gus?"*

"Yes," he admitted with unsettling calm.

She let out another involuntary gasp. "That fucking bastard ... He's been pulling the strings all along, hasn't he?"

"Actually, no, he hasn't."

"Then who is Hans? What's his connection?" she demanded sharply.

He glanced around the room again, as if suspecting someone to step out of the shadows. "Look, Lila, can we go talk somewhere else ... ?"

"Answer my question!"

He put his hands up and took a long, deep breath. "Hans is part of a rogue international organization," he said, his voice barely above a whisper, "a super-secret and very powerful *cabal* ... made up of bankers and industrialists ... scientists ... ex-military and ex-intelligence from around the world."

She stared at him. It all sounded vaguely familiar.

He continued almost nervously, "Their technology and resources match or surpass almost any intelligence agency in the world, but they don't answer to any nation or government. And that's why they are of grave concern ... to people like us."

That's right ... Charlie-O talked about this! And Lila had thought the wacky woman had just been going off on a tangent. She glared at Mark, still cautious, trying to process everything he was implying. She had heard so much, and so much of it was so contradictory, so plain *weird*, that she didn't know what—or who—to believe. And there were still so many open questions. She felt drained, exhausted.

"Then ..." She gestured around the room, her voice shaking. "What is all of this? What's been happening to me?"

Mark approached again slowly, hands still raised. "I will explain. If you'll give me a chance. Just ... not here." He stopped, waiting for her response, his lips bending into what looked like a careful, compassionate smile when she didn't back up.

She stared back at him for a long moment, trying to work out who this man was, to assess his true intentions. Then, all at once, she began to weep. It started slow, with a catch in her throat and a steady throbbing in her temples, but quickly turned into a torrent of hot tears. Despite everything, there was a part of her—a vulnerable, hopeful part, she realized bitterly—that sensed or wanted to sense something more; that his feelings for her were not fake. He opened his arms, imploring her to come to him. She looked at him through her streaming tears, wondering if she could or should ever trust him again. She stumbled a little, the evening catching up with her, and, slowly, allowed herself to collapse into his arms. He held her with what seemed like genuine compassion and, after a while, placed a timid kiss on the top of her head. They left the apartment in silence.

Stepping out onto North Dearborn, Lila stopped, wriggled free from Mark's embrace, and slowly pushed away from him. "If you're still working for the military," she said, frowning, "then what was all that about interviewing for an AI job?"

"Well, truth be told," Mark said, "he wasn't interviewing *me*; I was interviewing *him*."

She looked surprised. Just how much more was there that she didn't know about this man? Behind them, a metallic blue high-performance BMW M5 with Y-spoke wheels prowled from the shadows. Lila tensed, recoiling, ready to bolt. "What is this?"

Mark gently took her arm. "It's all right. Friends of mine."

"Oh, really?" She reluctantly allowed him to lead her to the car. He opened the backseat door but she stood there, glaring at him. "Seriously? Why the hell should I trust you?"

"Hello, Lila," a woman's voice said from inside. Sitting in the front seat was the same couple she'd spotted on the road to Ann Arbor.

"Lila, meet Betty and Barney." Mark gestured inside and made an imploring face. "They're fellow operatives. And yes, they are the good guys."

"Betty and Barney? *Seriously?*"

"Ha!" the man responded with a chuckle. "We wanted Fred and Wilma but they were already taken."

Lila sighed, fighting down her swelling frustration, and slid into the back seat. First, she'd get some answers—anger could wait.

"Barney" made sure the windows were securely closed and started driving.

"You've been trailing me," Lila said. It wasn't a question.

"Keeping an eye on you," Mark clarified.

"Oh yeah? Then what happened in Ann Arbor?"

"Yeah, we're really sorry about that," said "Betty" with a look of regret that seemed genuine enough. "That one slipped by us."

"If it's any consolation," Mark added, "they *did* save your brother's life."

"*What?*" Lila stared at him. "What's Ulli got to do with this?" She looked at the couple, who were both nodding like dashboard bobble-heads. "So that—that mattress delivery ... wasn't just a warning shot?"

Betty shook her head grimly.

"At least you know he and his family are safe and the one responsible is in custody," Mark assured.

Lila ignored him. "How did—"

Abruptly, she lifted her hands and sank back into her seat. "You know what, I don't wanna know."

"Lila ..." Mark began cautiously. "We'd like you to tell us what you experienced up in that apartment."

She glared at him angrily. "Don't you know? I mean—your arrival was timed awfully ... *conveniently.*"

"Tell us what you saw."

"I thought you were supposed to be explaining things to *me*."

"We will, just ... please, indulge us."

She started at him for a moment, then quietly said, "I saw Wolf

Holzinger." The memory affected her to a surprising degree. "Except, it wasn't me—it seemed like I was seeing things through Marina's eyes. He was just ... there, and he started walking toward me, saying 'There's something in your head—let me help.' And then he put his hands around my head." She paused with a faraway look.

"And then what happened?"

"I ... I *screamed*."

"You screamed?" Mark glanced briefly at the couple.

"But it wasn't a normal scream, it was ... something else."

"Okay," Barney said.

She continued to relate the experience, feeling like she was trying to describe a dream that didn't make any sense. Once she got to the part where Wolf fell to his death, a pall fell over the car.

"So what was the deal? How did Wolf get into Marina's apartment?" she pressed.

Mark turned away and looked out the window briefly. "Are you familiar with the concept of astral projection?" he said, not looking at her.

"I've heard of it, sure."

"Well, it's kinda like that, but ..." he shrugged, "with a lot more math involved."

She squinted, remembering what a nerd he was at his core. It was almost comforting to feel like he was the Mark she used to know rather than the liar he had become. "Okay then. The more important question is, why?"

They seemed hesitant to field that one. "It's actually super complicated, Lila," Barney finally responded.

"Okay, I'll ask another way: Who was Marina Resnick? Was she a spy or something?"

Betty answered, "She was a spy all right, but she didn't know it."

"Excuse me if my line of questioning is a little rough, but ... *what?!*"

Mark took over again. "Marina Resnick was a product of experimentation in remote sensing. Over a number of years she was surreptitiously conditioned through drugs and other means. The sub-subconscious part of her brain—all that untapped processing power—was, well, 'reformatted' to become a data collection and storage module. And when you unlock the potential of the brain like that, it's capable of picking up an enormous volume of information clairvoyantly, parsing it, and archiving it until it can be downloaded by handlers."

"So that sounds pretty much like bullshit to me. You're telling me that's why she hung out in the greenhouse? Because of its proximity to the Army research lab?"

"Very likely, yes." Mark said.

"She wasn't even aware that she was compelled to be there," Betty added.

"So she was an asset of Russian intelligence."

"Oh, no," Betty corrected, "the Kremlin had nothing to do with it."

"Then who?"

"Remember the cabal I mentioned in the apartment?" Mark said. "That's who."

"Hans's people."

"Yes."

Lila shook her head. It was too much to take in. "You keep talking about Marina in the past tense. What happened to her?"

"We don't know. She disappeared under our noses—without a trace."

"So what exactly happened to Wolf? If he was 'astral projecting' then how did he end up dead on the sidewalk?"

"That's what we can't figure out. He was not supposed to literally materialize in that space—we don't even know how to do that. How that all came about is the big mystery in all this."

"And what about Louis Breem?"

The mention of that name seemed to strike a chord in Mark. "He was a good man too. Losing both those guys in the same night was a blow."

"So the same thing happened to him?"

"No. We strongly suspect his fall was self-inflicted."

"Suicide? Why?"

Mark took a breath. "The secrets that he harbored ... he pledged to protect with his life. He could have found himself in a situation where those secrets could be compromised."

She stared at him for a long moment. *"Fuuuuuuck."* She lowered her head into her hand, trying to wrap her brain around it all. "Why," she said at last, lifting her head, "was I able to see Marina's experience? Why was I able to see Sofia's murder?"

Betty and Mark watched her, expressionless.

"Why did Hans insist on—"

And then she remembered Gail Ross's business card—the "therapist" both she and Marina had shared. She let out a horrified gasp. *"They did the same thing to me!"* She put her hand over her gaping mouth. *"Why?! How?!"*

Mark leaned toward her, but then she lashed out, catching him across the face. *"Don't touch me!"* she growled, *"who are you? Don't you dare touch me!"*

Mark pulled back as Lila flung herself back into her own seat and tried to steady her breath. "Who are these people? What are they called?"

"They don't actually have a name," Mark said quietly.

"What do you mean they don't have a name?!"

Barney looked at her through the rearview. "They have a common motto—a little 'code' they use among themselves. *'Le plus fort'*—'the fittest.' So they are informally referred to as 'LPF.'"

LPF—why did that sound familiar? Images shuffled through her mind, and then it hit her: the tail markings on the model plane on Jim Savage's desk.

How could she have been so stupid? How could she have let herself be manipulated so egregiously? "Take me back to my car," she said quietly.

"Lila, I think it's a better idea if—"

"Don't argue, *do it!*"

Mark nodded at Barney. The car turned.

When they arrived at the rented SUV, Lila jumped out. Mark leaned out the window. "Lila."

She stopped and looked at him.

"I want you to know ... even though our relationship was based on false pretenses, my feelings for you are genuine. They always have been. I know this is a ... pretty serious bump"— he laughed sadly—"but ... I do want to make things right. I'm here for you. I'm serious."

She stared at him blankly. "Goodbye, Mark," she said, and slammed the door.

32

February 17, 2018

Law Offices of Savage, Lutz, Finnegan & Foehl
Chicago, Illinois

IT WAS SIX AM, AND THE EARLY MORNING LIGHT SHONE THROUGH
the wall of windows behind Jim Savage's desk. Lila was sprawled in her
boss's chair, fiddling idly with the solid-pewter model of the Convair CV-
540 turboprop plane that she'd lifted from its mahogany stand. She had
just given one of the propellers a spin when Savage came through the
door.

"Lila!" He crossed toward his desk, his black leather catalog case
rolling behind him. "Making yourself comfortable?"

She held up the model plane and glared at him. "Care to explain
this?"

He looked at her curiously from across the desk. "You know perfectly
well what that is." He grinned. "It's the majesty of Alaska, it's freedom,
it's clarity of mind and the exultant peace of the soul."

"Not this," she said, shaking the plane's fuselage. *"This."* Her forefinger came to rest on the tail, specifically on the underscored *LPF* written in slanted script.

He dipped his head and put his rolling briefcase aside before calmly moving toward her. With a slight nod, as if seeking her permission, he carefully took the model plane from her hands and returned it to its stand. "Let's you and I take a walk, Lila," he said.

She hesitated at first, resentful, in no the mood to take orders of any sort from anyone, least of all from one of her betrayers, but she suspected he probably had a good reason for wanting to change their venue. Secret groups, lies, betrayals—such things needed to be discussed away from the office. So she got up and followed him, determined to keep her anger at bay until she knew exactly what had been going on behind her back for all these years.

They walked silently through the office and crossed to the elevators where Savage turned back to her in silence, flashed a grin, and pressed the down arrow.

"So, where are we going?" Lila asked.

Savage blinked both eyes twice and slightly shook his head. Lila got the message. She ignored the security camera and stared straight ahead as they descended, the familiar flutter in her throat, usually assuaged by his calm demeanor, kicked into high gear. The doors opened to reveal the half-lit basement.

The "catacombs." Years upon years of old files were stored there; the staff only went down into the dimly lit pharaonic space when it was absolutely necessary. Savage guided her over to a utility room that housed the building's mechanical systems, the droning hum providing adequate privacy.

He leaned against a small filing cabinet. "Can I ask where this question comes from?"

"No," she replied dismissively, waving her hand. "No, you cannot."

He gave a slight nod and took a deep breath. "I want you to know, kid, right upfront, that I am *not* a member of that organization."

"Funny, your good friend Hans Holzinger sure is," she spat.

He gave a small, almost apologetic nod.

"Exactly how are you involved?"

He seemed to choose his words carefully. "*Peripherally*. In return for being let in on some of what's going on, I sometimes do ... *favors* ... for Hans and various members of his group."

She stared at him, clearly annoyed. "Like *what?*"

"Like ... giving you a job, for one."

"*What?*" Lila lashed out at the chain-link cage beside her. "So it was all part of the plan? Our little tryst?"

"Yes, Lila, all part of the plan. All part of the *deal*."

"*Deal?*" She took a step forward, staring him directly in the eye. "With whom?"

He squared his shoulders, almost as if anticipating the blow to come. "Your father."

Lila froze, her mouth gaping open.

"I shouldn't be talking about any of this," he said, "but you deserve to know."

"Why?" She swiped at her eyes, pushing the hot tears away. "*Why?*"

"Several members of the organization knew your dad, Dr. Piper—the military guys and some of the bankers. They were going to approach him to join, but his failing health became an issue. He was in some serious legal and financial jeopardy, as you recall, and they offered to help—*quid pro quo*."

"Quid pro quo."

He nodded. "They needed a subject that fit a certain profile. And it just so happened ... well, that subject was you, kid. Bear in mind that your father agreed to it because he thought it would ultimately be beneficial for you; he was impressed with your heroic heart, he told me. Something about you saving your little brother's life. Then, later, with the drugs, the running wild ... he was worried sick about you, Lila. I guess, in his mind, his earlier ambitions gave way to hope that this might be a way to help you dig out from under all that, get you emotionally stable, secure a future for you ..."

She put her hand up so quickly that she nearly smacked him in his face. "Nice of you to try to redeem my father, Jim, but there's no defense for selling out your own flesh and blood."

Again, Savage nodded. "Part of the deal was that they agreed *not* to activate this ... this *thing* they put in your head ... not unless it was absolutely necessary. So, when Wolf died and the Russian gal 'blew her fuse,' so to speak, they needed to find out what the hell was going on. It became essential."

"So what you're saying is you've had me go around 'sensing' things by remote, gathering a bunch of extraneous data in my head? Christ! And I wonder why I have all these mental fucking problems! *That's* the reason for putting me on this case?"

"In a nutshell, yes."

"So that's why Hans called off the investigation—not because Gus was put away, but because the contents of my head had already been *downloaded* at the shrink's office? And *that's* what he wanted?"

Another nod.

She stood there a moment, the hum of the machines the only sound.

"Who's the devil who struck the deal with my father?"

He shook his head, almost apologetic. "You're not going to like what I'm about to say."

"Try me."

He took a deep breath. "Len Seidman."

"Oh my God!" she whispered. The so-called friend, lawyer, and fiduciary who had teamed up with her father all those years ago to freeze her out of the family business; it had all been part of a huge scheme, way bigger than she had imagined. "Oh my God! Is there anyone who *wasn't* conspiring against me?? I'm gonna kill him ... I'm gonna track him down and strangle him with my bare hands!"

"Lila, come on. I don't think you're capable of that."

She whipped around and shot him a burning look. "Does Ulli know?" she growled.

"No. Your brother knows nothing of the organization or any of this. He's been purposely kept in the dark."

She let her breath out through her nose. That was probably a smart move on their part, she thought, relieved for this one small reprieve at least—that Ulli and his family were not in danger. *But why me?* And then all the things she had done in the past came rushing forward: all the ways she had lashed out against her parents and their problems and their indifference toward her. She would show them. She would show everyone that she was in charge of her own life. She would toy with whatever strangers she wanted, have empty sex with them, and take their money. She was the one in control. She would buy drugs and get high, and—

But she'd never been in control at all.

It occurred to her that they likely had hired Maurice in Lawndale to lace the drugs he sold her with whatever the fuck they'd used to "condition" her brain. She'd been a puppet—blind, *stupid*.

She paced back and forth, her hand on her forehead, trying to assimilate everything. "Help me sort this out, Jim," she said at last. "The LPF created two remote-sensing assets in Chicago. While they had me on 'standby,' they used Marina Resnick to gather information on whatever the military and government intelligence agencies were up to on campus."

"Something like that," Savage responded.

"Meanwhile, CIA is busy trying to figure out what LPF is up to."

"Yes, what they're *doing,* what they *possess,* and what they *know.*"

"So CIA and LPF are at odds." She was thinking about her long conversation with Mark and his friends. "How does CIA know so much about *me* then?"

Savage looked at her knowingly. "Maybe they were tipped off."

She looked into his eyes, searching for a glimmer of the friend she thought she'd had, but saw nothing but a look of profound discomfort. "You absolute sonofabitch! You're playing both sides!"

He remained silent.

She couldn't help but grin. "*Why?*"

"Because, to be perfectly honest, this is a situation where I don't know who can claim the higher moral ground."

"*Morality?* That's what this is about?"

Savage nodded earnestly. "Absolutely that's what it's about. Both sides are out to protect our society, our civilization, our way of life, with whatever resources they have. And from what I understand, LPF's resources are *vast*. But they don't answer to anyone—not a nation-state, a UN council, military, *nothing*. No one to provide checks and balances, no one to rein them in if necessary." He swallowed. "There are certain pros and cons to that. On the one hand, they're not subject to the vagaries of an inconsistent political climate, to the whims and biases of national leaders, to uncertain budgetary numbers. And, in that context, they've operated extremely well."

"Operated in what way?"

"Preventing certain ... *catastrophes* ... from happening."

"Like what? Nuclear war?"

"Among other things."

"What about Nine-Eleven?"

"Nine-Eleven, monstrous as it was—close to three thousand people killed—was small potatoes next to some of the doomsday events LPF have stopped."

She frowned, but said nothing.

"Now, CIA," Jim said, "for all its missteps and occasional moral failings ... is at least accountable to a government that is in turn accountable to its people. And that's important. When you concentrate a huge degree of unregulated power into just a few hands—as LPF has done—corruption inevitably follows. So, if I can help keep an eye on them without interfering in the good they do, then that's the role I intend to play."

"*Are* they corrupt?"

He paused. "I'm not in a position to make that judgment at this time."

"Do they *know* you're a double-agent?"

"CIA most certainly does. Hans ... no. And please, let's just keep it that way."

She let out a little snort. "I doubt I'll be talking to him again." She stopped abruptly. "Unless ... unless he wants to 'activate' me again."

Savage looked at her with somewhat sad and regretful eyes. "I can't guarantee he—or they—won't do that."

"Well, I damn sure can."

He looked at her inquisitively.

"Now that I know what's been happening to me ... now that I know what's inside of me ... I intend to control it myself. No one else is going to control me."

"I don't know if that's possible, Lila."

"I'll make it possible, if it's the last damn thing I do!" A sudden feeling of unfamiliar confidence welled up from somewhere deep within her. All her previous bravado, however real or imagined, could not compare to this feeling of possibility—it reminded her of the awakening she'd experienced when she'd jumped into the deep end those many years ago.

Spinning on her heel, Lila marched back to the elevator.

Savage watched her go, unmoving.

"By the way," she threw back over her shoulder, "you and me—we're done."

33

February 17, 2018

Stone Mental Health Center
Chicago, Illinois

LILA RAPPED LIGHTLY ON THE DOORJAMB AS SHE STRODE INTO DR. Ross's office. "Thanks for seeing me on such short notice," she said, going directly to the seat facing the desk.

"Happy to do it," Gail said, frowning slightly as Lila plopped down in the chair. "Just ... glad we had an opening. How have you been feeling?"

"What can I say? It's been a roller coaster," Lila replied, speaking more rapidly than usual. "But, you know, I think I've really learned a lot about myself these last few days."

"Hey, that's really good to hear!" Gail smiled, carefully scrutinizing Lila. "In what way?"

"Oh, you know ... that in spite of all the shit life throws at you ... you can still be in charge of ... you, y'know?"

"Well that's what it's all about. Sounds like you've maybe you've made a breakthrough, of sorts."

"Yeah." Lila leaned forward in her chair, looked idly around the office, then said, "Breakthrough. Definitely. So ..." she faced Gail directly, "what say you tell me about the fucking *LPF*?"

Gail slowly leaned back in her chair, a pained look on her face, as if, deep down, she'd known this day would inevitably come. After staring at Lila in silence for a moment, she calmly placed her pen in her notebook, set it aside, and stepped out from behind her desk. Catching herself, she opened a side drawer and started fiddling with something inside.

Lila shot up from her seat. "What the hell are you doing?"

Gail put a finger to her lips. Scowling, Lila sat back down purposefully.

After a moment, Gail quietly slid the desk drawer shut and crossed the room to shut her office door. "Tell me what you already know," she said, returning to her desk, her voice eerily calm.

"Oh no you don't!" Lila snapped. "This time *I'm* asking the questions!"

Gail cocked her head to one side. "My office, my rules. You want answers, you tell me what you know, and we can go from there."

Frustrated, Lila hesitated, contemplating where to begin. "You want to know what I know? Well, for starters, I know 'LPF' isn't a real name. Apparently, the organization has no name, because, well, makes sense— why would they? Not like you people are advertising your services."

"What else?"

"I know it's a rogue operation that doesn't answer to anyone and, apparently, it's pretty well funded. I know it was formed in part by operatives who abdicated from CIA and other black bag agencies who brought a lot of their science and technology with them."

Gail stared at her, stone-faced.

Lila stared back. "That's it. That's what I know. Now it's your turn. Are you a full member? Or just an associate?"

"Full member."

Something dropped like a stone in Lila's gut. She'd suspected, of course, but to hear it out loud ... "Like Hans Holzinger, I suppose?"

"Yes."

"And Len Seidman?"

"Yes."

Lila nodded in disgust. When she looked up again, she squinted as if to bore a hole in her duplicitous friend and then hit her with the question they'd been circling since she'd arrived. "Okay, so how about you tell me this—What the *fuck* did you do to me?"

Gail took a long, deep breath. "We actually tried to *help* you, Lila. We used some cutting-edge tech that's been in development for decades to enhance the natural capacity of your brain, to utilize neural connections that were latent but unrealized deep within your cerebellum. It's increased your potential, I think you know that; it's made you a sharper, more intuitive—"

"I'll tell you what I know: I know that what you've done to me was done without my knowledge or consent. So why not just … *ask?* Why the hidden agenda? Why force all this on me without my buy-in? I thought we were friends!"

"We actually tried that at first. Not with you, of course, but with a number of your predecessors. In all our experiments, we found that the conscious mind had a way of interfering with the process. Assumptions, second-guessing, disruptive intent … all these tended to 'poison the well.' We found out early on that we needed subjects with zero awareness of the process in order for it to carry on unimpeded and achieve optimum results."

"All to serve your own corrupt purposes."

"All to serve the greatest possible good."

"Oh, please. Cut the crap. You put Marina Resnick out there to spy on the Army and CIA. You wanted to see what they were doing with that particle accelerator because you couldn't *stand* the fact that they had something that *you didn't!*"

Gail's finger came up unconsciously and lightly touched her lips. "It's … *complicated.*"

"Yeah, it usually is."

"Look, you have to understand something, Lila. There are a number of serious existential threats to our civilization, threats to our entire species, coming from so many different directions it's hard to—"

"As you've said, I've grown sharper and more intuitive, not more gullible. I'm afraid you're going to have to give me an example."

"I can't get into specifics. But I can tell you about our motto, 'Survival of the fittest.' The *fittest*—that's you and me, Lila, the evolutionary pinnacle that is the human race right now. There are those of us who are determined, no matter what the cost, to *remain* the fittest. We are determined to *survive*. But in order to ensure that survival, we need to know what we're dealing with—see over the horizon, if you will. I can tell you this—what our friends in the government have been dabbling with, it could potentially pose the most serious existential threat of them all."

"Bullshit."

"You'll believe what you will—that, I cannot control. But, on one very important level, at least, I'm glad we're having this conversation. Finally."

Lila leaned back and rested her head on the back of the chair. She closed her eyes and pressed her fingers lightly to her temples.

Gail's voice continued: "Because there's something I've been waiting to discuss with you for a long time."

Lila didn't look up. "And what's that, Gail?"

"The process you've gone through ... it's only the first phase of the program."

Lila's eyes blinked open. "What do you mean *program?*"

"The next step is to break down the barriers between the conscious and unconscious mind; to integrate the whole brain, frontal lobe to brain stem. That can only be done once the unconscious conditioning process is firmly entrenched—only then can we allow conscious thought, conscious intent, to enter the picture." Gail leaned forward, her eyes sparkling. "And that phase can only be embarked upon by the candidate voluntarily."

"Wow! A choice! How magnanimous of you."

"Look, I know you're feeling violated, Lila, but hear me out." She leaned forward a little more, white teeth glinting like knives. "Once you have full access to the entire potential of your brain, what you'd be capable of is ... practically unimaginable. You'd be smarter and think faster than any computer out there; you'd develop highly enhanced perception well beyond remote sensing. We're talking telepathy, perhaps telekinesis ... maybe even precognition."

Lila leaned forward, mirroring the woman she had trusted her brain with for years. "So exactly how many people have done this?"

"Actually ... you would be ... the *first* to take this step."

She fell back against the chair. What kind of screwball offer was this? To be the progenitor of a new, more highly evolved species? "You know, Gail"—out came an involuntary chuckle—"sounds a lot like the deal ol' Mephistopheles had for Faust."

Gail rolled her eyes. "Come now, Lila. A familiar story. Demons we create to bring us together. They scare us to help us cope with what we dread the most." She gave a dry laugh. "Look, nobody's asking you to sell your soul to the devil, Lila—your power would come with certain ... *responsibilities*. Besides, we live in the modern era. We no longer live under the thrall of medieval superstition. We believe that those who are so gifted will emphasize the value and agency of human beings, both individually and collectively; that they will honor and elevate duty to the common good while exercising tremendous restraint."

"Well, I guess you're just *waaay* more optimistic than I am."

"It's the demons we don't recognize that concern me—the ones that live in plain sight. Institutions with no accountability, playing with powers that can destroy the planet ... No. The gifted have to be properly prepared; they must be of a certain *kind*. A uniquely *gifted* person. You were chosen because you had the combination of qualities that we were looking for."

"As determined how? By Len 'Slimebag' Seidman feeling me up in a hotel bar?"

"I know what you think of Seidman, and that's understandable. I'm not saying that I agree with his less-than-perfect methods, but his purposes were ultimately benevolent."

Lila shook her head. "This is unbelievable bullshit."

"I know, it's a lot to take in. I'm ... *sympathetic* is what I'm saying."

"First of all, I am not interested in your sympathy, Gail. But I am listening. So, what's the upshot? Why are you guys intent on creating these super-brain people? What exactly is the plan?"

Gail glanced at her office door, then leaned closer still. "Eventually, the members of the organization are going to die off. And, to be frank, we're not confident we can replace them with a new generation who share their, as you call it, *optimism*. So, in case our operations wind down and we dissolve, we want to leave behind a legacy: a small cadre of enhanced individuals, posted around the globe, extremely perceptive, extremely conscientious, extremely well-suited to address the challenges our society is likely to face in the future. They'd operate well under the radar, avoiding mainstream attention."

"Furtive guardians of humanity."

"You could say that."

What Gail was saying was hard to believe—and harder still to evaluate. There was optimism, she knew, and then there was sheer naivety. "You want *me* to be ... part of humanity's—what—*salvation?*"

Gail nodded earnestly. "Yes, Lila, we do. But we can't compel you; you have to *choose* to be."

Lila sat back, staring at Gail. She was overwhelmed on the one hand, and yet ... captivated on the other.

"Of course, there will be a series of procedures—we'll use a modified TMS, a certain amount of chemical and gene treatment, and a comprehensive course of deep psychological training."

Lila nodded absently.

"You'll meet other members of the organization and we will introduce you to a much, much larger world than the one you're accustomed to." Gail smiled, seeming genuinely excited. "I think you'll find it ... *exhilarating!*"

Lila hadn't stopped nodding. She looked to the side, suddenly perplexed.

"So ... what do you say?" Gail prodded. "Shall we get started?"

Lila turned back to Gail, a sad smile on her face. "I don't know if I ever told you, but there was something Sofia told me that first tipped me off to the idea that something was off regarding her alleged romantic involvement with Wolf."

"No, I don't think you did."

"She recited a quote from a Djuna Barnes book she'd read in high school. It seemed odd to me at the time—how something you'd read in high school could come close to summing up the essence of the life you live as an adult. Now I don't think so."

"No?"

"No. I read something of Joyce's in school. One character, something Daedalus, said, 'You behold in me ... a horrible example of free thought.'"

"Grim displeasure?"

"Free thought. Totally, completely, absolutely *free*. Which is to say, I lack the smallest scintilla of anything even approaching the kind of Faustian ambition one would need to go along with the fucked-up plan you just described." Lila shook her head. "Let me tell you something ... You're never putting that machine on me again."

Gail's excited smile vanished.

Lila stood up. "And no one is going to get inside my head, in any manner, to *any* degree, ever, *ever* again. And that is my final answer." She walked to the door.

"Lila."

Gail was perched on the edge of her chair, seemingly caught between sitting and standing. "You realize, don't you, that without regular TMS therapy, the data you've already gathered will overload, back up, and possibly lead to psychosis and other severe psychological difficulties?"

Lila glared at her through squinted eyes. "I'll cope. I always have." She turned away.

Gail rose. "*Lila!*"

Once again, Lila stopped.

"We'll be watching you."

34

February 17, 2018

Milwaukee County Jail
Milwaukee, Wisconsin

Lila stood at the Milwaukee County lock-up's Inmate Visitation desk, tapping her fingers nervously on the counter. She checked the wall clock above the head of the officer scanning the computer behind the desk. "Well?" she finally asked.

"He's not here," the corrections officer said with a shrug.

"What do you mean, 'not here?' I know he's here."

"He's been released."

"Released?"

He stared blankly up at her, shrugged once, and turned back to his computer screen. Lila had a quick flash of something like a memory, and thought of the CIA swooping in and silently extricating him right out from under everyone's noses. She let out a snort and shook her head. "Figures," she said quietly.

"What'd you say your name is? *Piper?*"

"Yes. Lila Piper."

"Okay, so he's left something for you."

"For me?" She leaned in the opening in the partition, trying to get a glimpse of the computer screen.

"Yeah, a package." He reached into his desk and pulled out a manila envelope. He pushed it over the desktop along with a release form attached to a clipboard.

Lila signed for the envelope, hurried past the security scanner, and slipped out the door. When the cold air hit her face, she stopped and tore the envelope open. A tattered copy of Gibran's *The Prophet* slid out. Shaking her head, Lila flipped open the book. A fresh inscription waited for her on the book's front page.

Lila,
The last few lines in the book are yours.
Some things you just can't stop.
—Gus

She flipped to the last page in the book.

Only Almitra was silent, gazing after the ship until it had vanished into the mist. And when all the people were dispersed she still stood alone upon the sea-wall, remembering in her heart his saying:

A little while, a moment of rest upon the wind, and another woman shall bear me.

SECRETS HIDDEN IN UNKNOWN ZONES BELOW THE SURFACE

35

October 31, 2017

Holzinger's Lakeview Dairy
Kewaunee, Wisconsin

HANS HAD BEEN ASLEEP FOR ALMOST FOUR HOURS WHEN HIS CELL phone began vibrating, shaking him awake. He rolled slowly onto his side, groped around in the dark, and squinted down at the unread message alert.

He tapped the screen.

Toolshed, the message said.

Casting a furtive glance back at his wife asleep in bed beside him, Hans eased himself into a sitting position. *Okay.*

Ten minutes later, he strode into the small, unlit office in the heart of the dairy's metal-frame equipment shop. His visitor was sitting at the worn Steelcase desk, his face hidden in shadows. Hans pulled out a chair, twirled it backward, and sat down, crossing his arms on the slatted chair-back.

"Sorry about your son," the man said, his gravelly voice seeming to hang in the air.

Hans nodded curtly. "Do we know how it happened?"

"We do not. The packet's been downloaded from our asset and the experts are parsing through the data now."

"How long will that take?"

"A while. Two, three months perhaps."

"I don't know if I can sit around that long. I know who's responsible, down to the person."

"No you don't, Hans, and this is no time for personal grudges. Why don't you take a vacation? Take that lovely wife of yours on a cruise."

"A *cruise?!*"

"We'll contact you when we have something."

Hans paused a moment. "How is the asset?"

"She's fine ... personally speaking. We don't know if we can ever use her again though. Something ... either glitched-out terribly, or something foreign got inside of her. We don't know yet."

"Can she be trusted?"

"Fortunately, our experts were able to implant false memories. The other side managed to concoct a very tidy cover story, so we made it match that. Seems to be holding."

"If that façade ever breaks down, she will have to be taken out of the picture."

"We're on top of that."

Hans was silent for a moment then said, "There is another local asset, you know."

"Of course. But let's sit that one out for the time being."

Hans looked out over the equipment yard and shook his head. "The human soul can be re-tempered only in blood. It is 'the manure of the plant we call genius.' Mankind is a tree *und*, as with a tree, 'the skillful gardener directs the pruning less towards lush vegetation than towards the fructification of the tree; he wants fruit, not wood or leaves.'" He turned to back to face his visitor, "That's Joseph de Maistre preparing the ground for the French Revolution. You see how little we've changed."

"We both know the lightning strike of awesome and terrible violence that is coming"—he leaned forward on his elbows until his heavily lined and pockmarked face appeared, greased like a commando's, eyes nothing more than dark patches beneath heavy brows—"wielded by the posers and preening politicians we have to contend with today, women and men who have somehow managed to slime their way to the top and now find themselves in positions of unimaginable power ..." His hard, stubborn face shifted, seeming to crumple for a moment. "Believe me when I tell you, we are facing an existential threat that will spare nothing that lives but we have to move incrementally."

Hans let go of the chair-back and took a deep breath.

"Hans." His visitor leaned back, his face once again hidden in the shadows. "I strongly encourage you to take that cruise."

October 29, 2017

Army Research Lab
Chicago, Illinois

WOLF HELD THE DOOR AND GUS PASSED HIM WITH A NOD. AHEAD was the accelerator building, the greenhouse glinting above in the blue Chicago moonlight. Wolf had just undergone the final preparation for the operation he was about to embark upon, but he still had questions. It was almost two o'clock in the morning and time was slipping away.

"All I'm saying is, there's not a quantum computer in the world with the processing power necessary," Wolf said, falling in step with Gus. He stopped at the sight of Louis Breem's Hummer pulling into the parking lot and waved when Louis climbed out, wearing the same puffy black jacket and black watch cap as he was wearing.

Louis smirked as the two greeted each other with bumped fists. "Sup man? You lookin' fly tonight."

"Louis," Gus said, coming forward.

"Gus, my man!" Again, the fist bump. "Ready for this?"

Gus cocked his head and strode across the freshly plowed and salted street, the two others following. "Let's get a move on," he said over his shoulder.

When they stepped into the cone of yellow light from the single bare bulb burning above the building's side entrance, Gus turned and regarded them seriously. "As you're aware, all your training and all briefings have been conducted on a strict need-to-know basis. But now that we're about to 'light the candle,' it's been determined that we should share with both of you what's inside this building."

"The particle accelerator?" Louis snorted. "Come on, they have tours running through here!"

"Not where we're going," Gus responded. "What you are about to learn and what you are about to witness are to remain within these walls at all costs. This knowledge is to be protected with your lives. Are we understood?"

"Understood," Louis and Wolf responded simultaneously.

"Good," Gus said. "Follow me."

As soon as they were inside, the three of them slipped out of their coats. Wolf took off his gloves and knit cap and stuffed them into his coat pocket, then flashed his badge at the security guard. The guard led them down the hall toward a pair of double doors guarded by two Marines clutching M27 rifles.

Again, the badges came out to be checked and double-checked before each man leaned into the retina scanner.

With the scan complete, the Marines stepped aside and the door opened to reveal several empty glassed-in office cubicles and a small bullpen in the center of the room. Upon each desk stood an old legacy-looking computer workstation—relics from a forgotten age, Wolf thought. The sign hanging over the bullpen read:

Don't feed the operators!

"Elevator will take you down to the cyclotron," the sergeant said, pointing to a set of reinforced steel doors at the back of the room.

Gus hit the button. Once they'd filed in and the doors had slid shut behind them, Louis broke the silence in hushed tones.

"So is our player the one you've been reconning one floor up from you?

"One and the same," Wolf replied softly.

"What exactly are you going to do to her?"

"Just scramble her programming a little—try to block her ability to see inside our buildings from her greenhouse perch."

Louis snickered. "Strange world we live in."

When the elevator opened, they were greeted by a tall man with dark hair graying at the temples. Gus shook his hand and turned, a stony smile on his face. "Wolf Holzinger, Louis Breem ... this is Dr. Mark Morgan. He's running the show down here."

"Gentlemen," Mark said with a curt nod. "Welcome."

Gus placed a hand on each of his men's shoulders and looked directly into their eyes. "Remember your confidentiality oath. And *all* its covenants."

A sober nod from the two operatives.

Mark gestured to the side. "This way."

The underground chamber was where the real activity was taking place, Wolf saw—he wondered what the ancient bullpen they'd passed through was for. The scientists and technicians eyed them as they passed, obviously mystified by the strangers now in their midst.

Then, they saw it—a huge titanium cube taking up most of the floor that wasn't already occupied by whiteboards or computer workstations or the cyclotron's 1940s-era aluminum coil cover, which looked like a couple of stacked rectilinear rings fashioned out of sheet metal air-conditioning ducts. It seemed something of a miracle that the place had ever worked in the first place, Wolf thought, and that it was still standing now was, by his measure, unbelievable.

The titanium cube in the center of the room, far from archaic, appeared otherworldly, as if it had been designed by aliens and bolted to the floor with four outsized industrial shock absorbers. Next to it were a pair of chairs that looked like they'd been torn from a dentist's office and, between them, a kind of supercharged TMS machine rigged up with two identical headsets studded with wire leads braided into a thick connector cord.

"This is the *Abyss Box*," Mark said, gesturing to the cube, "taking its name from its sister aquarium in Brest, France, which was built to house *hadal* fauna. Hadal, of course, refers to 'Hades,' the Greek mythological underworld, which gave rise to the scientific term for the deepest region in the water column, lying deep within the oceanic trenches—the *Hadopelagic*.

"The Abyss Box contains forty-four gallons of water pressurized to 15,000 PSI, equivalent to a very cozy one thousand atmospheres. Snug as a bug."

"What's in it that requires so much pressure?" Wolf asked.

"And I don't even *want* to know how you got this thing in here!" Louis quipped.

Gus leaned in. "They found her down in the Challenger Deep, the lowest point on the surface of the Earth."

Wolf and Louis glanced at each other—"*Her?*" they both blurted.

"Pacific Ocean, several hundred klicks southwest of Guam. Just shy of seven miles straight down," Mark added. "Nothing down there but sea cucumbers, giant amoebas, shrimp-critters, and bits of the ever-ubiquitous plastic trash you find floating everywhere in the ocean these days."

Peering through the three-inch glass portal centered on the face of the cube, Wolf asked, "This regular glass?"

"Borosilicate. The small diameter is due to the enormous water pressure it has to withstand." Mark cracked a self-conscious smile. "Where was I?"

"Plastic trash floating around," Louis put in.

"Oh, yeah. In 1990, something anomalous was going on in the oceans around the world. Migratory patterns suddenly changing, beaching deaths all over, just ... really strange behaviors. My predecessor was deployed on a super-secret research sub at the time and, when his investigation determined that the anomalies seemed to have their epicenter in the Challenger Deep, they went to have a look. And that's when they found her."

Wolf pushed up against Louis, both men trying to peer beyond the three-inch portal.

"Go ahead," Mark gestured. "She won't bite."

Louis retreated, allowing Wolf to press his face up to the glass. What he saw floating in the forty-four gallons of highly pressurized water was, by his reckoning, some kind of gelatinous, bioluminescent dandelion, resembling something like a spider with one hundred translucent legs. "I have no idea what I'm seeing," he said at last.

"Let me get in there," Louis said, nudging Wolf aside. He held perfectly still, evidently mesmerized by the sight of the creature's writhing legs, their glowing tips painting polygons briefly in the dark.

"We call her 'Inez,'" Mark explained.

"*Inez?*" Wolf smirked.

"Stands for 'Interdimensional Nexus Entity.'" Louis and Wolf stared at him, waiting. "The 'z' comes from the z-beam that initially brought her to our attention."

"Wait—*interdimensional?*" Louis interjected. "You mean like ... from some other universe?"

"Another universe, another dimension," Gus replied. "There are certain touchpoints around the Earth where the borderlines between realities get a bit ... *fuzzy.* The Challenger Deep is one of them." Gus went to look through the portal himself. "We don't know if she got 'lost' or if she came here intentionally. We're not even sure we can consider her a living being—she could just as easily be a biomechanical probe of some kind."

"Yet when we found her," Mark expounded, "we got clear indications that she was sentient—or connected to some sentience—and that she wanted to communicate. So we turned to Gus here and the CIA to help us recruit a couple of telepaths from *your* program."

Wolf glanced at Louis with a slight grin. "Anyone we know?"

Gus shook his head slightly. "Don't ask."

"As she learned about us humans," Mark said, stepping forward, "she came to realize that our attempts to understand and define our world—our science, our quantum physics, the whole shebang—were sorely lacking. So she offered to lend a hand."

"And she's not lacking hands ..." Louis remarked. "How's she helping?"

"And does it have something to do with all this equipment hooked up to her tank?" Wolf added, pointing to the two tanning bed-esque recliners nearby.

Mark pointed at Inez. "See all those patterns running up and down her body?" Wolf and Louis nudged one another, trying to see through the small glass simultaneously. "It's her way of processing information."

"The polygons ..." Louis uttered. "How many shapes can she generate?"

"That's a good question," Mark said. He crossed to the nearest whiteboard, where he picked up a black felt-tip marker.

$$factorial$$
$$x! = \prod_{k=1}^{x} k = 1 \cdot 2 \cdot 3 \cdot 4 \cdots x$$

"What you're asking is how many distinct shapes, or polygons, can you create over X number of nodes—in our case, the tips of Inez's tentacles or legs ..." Mark began.

Louis stared at the whiteboard for a long moment. "Yep," he said, nodding studiously, "that looks like it all checks out."

Mark couldn't help but grin. "Thanks, Professor. As I'm sure you know, to calculate the number of permutations you use so-called 'factorials.' Easy example: a factorial of five is—"

$$1 \times 2 \times 3 \times 4 \times 5 = 120$$

"Getting back to our mysterious friend here, we can calculate the number of all permutations—patterns she can generate—as—"

x! (where x! is factorial of x, and x = number of legs)

"Why it's such a good question is that it's particularly relevant to our mission tonight. We need to parse a massive amount of data to do what we're about to do. First, some terms: there are one billion *gigabytes* in an *exabyte*, right? And one thousand exabytes in a *zettabyte*—that's a one followed by twenty-one zeroes. One of our cloud computing companies recently estimated that there were 1.8 zettabytes of data in the world as of 2011. That's everything that's ever been written, photographed, stored on video or on computer going back to the beginning of recorded history. Looking at the color shifts our friend here is displaying, we can easily get to that number of permutations—distinct polygons—with just twenty legs."

$$(20! = approx.\ 2\ E{+}18)$$

"In other words, a two followed by eighteen zeros. But, remember, we're not dealing with twenty legs—this thing has a hundred legs, and with a hundred legs you get to—"

$$(100! = approx.\ 9E{+}157)$$

"Numbers like that are hard to imagine. You could easily fit all the information about the entire universe into such memory."

"I get it," Louis cut in. "That solves the riddle of the processing power needed for these missions. You're about to measure the information that describes the energy of Wolf's body, his mind, his thoughts, his memories. I get that. But here's the other elephant in the room"—he turned toward Inez—"no offense." He nodded at Mark. "Why the particle accelerator?"

"We're going to create an artificial singularity," Gus answered, "which will be amplified and sustained with Inez's help. That's how we're going to 'project' Wolf into Mysh's apartment. We've got to get into her head. She's a remote-sensing asset, that much we know, but is she part of the fentanyl conspiracy? Is she stealing secrets for some other, even more nefarious reason? We need to find out what she knows and wipe the slate clean."

"An overly simplified description of what will be going on," Mark qualified. "We'll actually be playing with the quantum properties of causality." He turned back to the whiteboard and put the pen down. "This is where things start to get a little arcane."

Wolf let out a snort. "A *little* arcane?"

"If we think about you and Louis as *geometric objects* in *spacetime*, we know that these objects must obey the laws of *causality, thermodynamics,* and *information theory.* We are more than a sequence of all the events—past, present, and future—that we experience. We are each the complete *worldline* that joins the points of our birth and death. The *geometric object,* the Wolf or the Louis in between those two points, we call a 'causal diamond.' See, when you get right down to it, we're not moving through the events of our life; the events themselves are *tenseless.* Our future isn't merely predetermined—*it already exists.*"

Wolf turned to Louis and swiftly passed his hand several inches above his own head.

Louis grinned. "Exactly, man."

"However," Mark said, undeterred, "the moment we map and store your information, we create a totally new 'prior-free' causal diamond and, depending on the time variable we choose, we can slice it up however we want—which gives you your moment. And that, my friends, opens infinite possibilities where practically any future can be obtained merely by selecting a suitable time slicing. So, with our deep-sea savant in there standing in for our big-iron data processor, we can project you, holographically, anywhere we want."

Wolf chuckled. "*Mind-blowing!* All I can say."

"Let me ask you something," Louis said with a squint Gus's way. "So we're on a 'need-to-know' basis—right?"

"That's right."

"So why bring both of us here? Why"—he gestured toward the tank —"am I here? I get it with the Wolfman, he's your holographic man on the mission. But me?" He shook his head. "Why am I here again?"

Gus looked at Mark, who glanced through the portal and then back to the two operatives. "Inez wanted to meet you." Their eyes went wide as Mark broke into a wide smile. "After all, the three of you are going to be working together!"

Louis scrolled through his phone while Wolf was strapped into his chair and wired into the modified TMS machine. "Louis," Mark said, tightening the straps around Wolf's arms, "go ahead and take a seat on the second bed."

"Change your mind? I'm going too?"

"No, not tonight. You're here an observer, for training purposes only."

Louis sat down on the bed and took out his phone while Mark finished with Wolf. He recoiled suddenly, squinting at the screen. "What the *fuck?*"

Gus shot him an admonishing glance. "Problem?"

"Nothin'. It's ... *nothin'*. I got it."

"Not good enough, Louis," Gus said, scrutinizing his subordinate's every blink and twitch. "Let's go—out with it."

Reluctantly, Louis held up the phone. Gus took it and read the text:

You drug-dealing piece of shit. We're done. Don't bother coming home.

Gus frowned and shook his head. "Which part of 'keep your activities secret from your neighbors and especially from your wife' did you not understand?"

Louis slumped, avoiding his gaze.

Gus looked back at Mark, then at Wolf. "Fact is," he said to no one in particular, the gears turning, "we don't *really* need you here." He handed the phone back. "Go on. Take care of this."

"But —"

"Just ... make it right, Louis."

Louis got to his feet. "I'll let myself out."

"Get it done."

Meanwhile, Mark was adjusting the skullcap on Wolf's head, fine-tuning the leads that sprouted from it like a gorgon's snakes.

"You've done tests on this thing, right?" Wolf asked.

"Once or twice," Mark replied.

"On humans?"

"You're the first."

Wolf chuckled. "I guess this is what the Apollo astronauts felt like."

"You *are* blazing a trail, Wolf. Hold still." Mark's tone turned apologetic as he reached around the skullcap. "Too bad no one will ever know! There."

He helped Wolf straighten and shift back in the recliner, then crouched beside him.

"Okay, Wolf. You'll appear in Ms. Resnick's apartment as a conscious hologram. You'll experience everything as if you were there—it'll be rather like playing an immersive virtual reality video game. You'll be *here* physically, but you'll be able to interact remotely through your projection. The reason we're doing this holographically is that the telepathic energy you will impart will be exponentially more concentrated and more powerful than it would be through physical contact. That's important—it'll let you target the areas of Resnick's unconscious mind that we need to reach. Just ... remember your training."

Wolf settled in and gave a thumbs-up.

Mark went to his computer console and made a few quick entries. He nodded to the rest of his team, who were hunched over console screens, and, as the noise of the machines rose, watched Wolf slip into a state of self-hypnosis. At once, Inez began to glow—gently at first, then a brilliant white cascading like the Northern Lights. Glancing to Gus, Mark said, "It's working."

Gus watched Wolf's still body, wondering what the young man was experiencing and how it felt. Seconds stretched into tense minutes ... then a shockwave tore through the lab.

A dazzling flash of white light hurled Gus backward, his head snapping back against the floor. He rolled, seeing Mark fall, and scrambled unsteadily to his feet. *"What the hell just happened?"*

Mark was already up, eyes darting across a console screen. "I don't know," he managed, "some kind of ... feedback."

Gus looked over at Wolf and watched with growing concern as his body began to glow. It was as if the contours of his body were blurring ... they shifted out of focus, and Wolf began to quiver gently.

"Morgan!" Gus shouted, "what the fuck is happening?"

Wolf's body was convulsing now, whipping back and forth in the recliner, eyes wide and blank and awful. His arm rose slowly, jerking savagely, veins bulging ... and then Wolf Holzinger was gone.

The machines whined as they shut down and the lights from the tank faded into darkness. Gasps filled the room, followed by an eerie silence as the observers realized that Wolf was no longer there.

Mark stood, frozen to the spot.

Gus stared at the empty recliner, the gears in his head whirring, the totality of the situation sinking in. Abruptly, he turned and bolted for the elevator.

3 7

October 29, 2017

Angela Breem's Apartment Building
Lawndale, Illinois

"Angela? Angela!" Louis rapped on the door, trying not to make too much noise—it was three o'clock in the morning, after all, and he didn't want to rouse the neighbors. She was in there, he knew—just ignoring him.

"What up, homes?" the hulking man said, approaching with a cigarette in his hand.

Louis acknowledged him listlessly. "Maurice."

Maurice leaned against the wall and took another puff. "Domestic problems?" He stepped over to toss his cigarette out the breezeway. "Had an interesting conversation with your old lady. Told her about your little side hustle."

"What!?" Louis glared at him.

"C'mon," Maurice said, jerking his chin toward the next apartment door. "Somebody wants to see you."

"What are you talking about?!"

Maurice opened the vacant apartment and jerked his head again, ushering Louis in.

"Hello, Louis," came an unfamiliar woman's voice.

Louis did a double take, dividing his attention between Maurice, who was stood behind him, blocking the door, and the stranger in the white pantsuit and red turtleneck seated on the window sill directly across the otherwise empty room. "Who the hell are you?" he said.

"My name is Dr. Ross. Call me Gail. Most of my patients do."

"I don't need a doctor."

"Maybe not, but you do have some information that I'm interested in."

"Yeah? What kind of information?"

"You've been spending a lot of time on the University of Chicago campus of late." She got up from her seat on the window sill and slowly walked toward him. "I'd like you to tell me what's going on over there."

Louis glanced back at Maurice and shrugged. "I don't know what you're talking about."

"Your wife, Angela, is lovely."

"Whatever the hell this is, you keep my wife out of it."

"Maurice told me how surprised she was to hear about your unfortunate shenanigans with Gus Ambrosia."

He shrugged, squinting at the woman. "Who is that?"

She stepped up to him and peered into his eyes. "You're good, Louis! Fairly convincing." She motioned to someone in the kitchen. The man unfolded a side table and placed a weird-looking device and a headset on top. He returned briefly to the kitchen, reemerging moments later with a chair.

"What is all this? Who are you?"

"Okay, let's try this again ..." She glanced at the set-up, then at Louis. "We know you just came from the university—you were trailed, Louis. We know your friends are firing up the particle accelerator tonight. We simply need you to tell us why."

"I don't know what the hell you're talking about. And who the hell is this 'we?'"

"For now," she said, "you are talking to me. So, tell me ... how are Gus Ambrosia and the CIA involved?"

Louis glanced back at Maurice and shrugged before staring into Gail's face and grinning broadly. "I don't know what the *fuck* you talkin' about!"

Gail dropped her head. "Louis, Louis, Louis ..." She looked back up at him. "I can tell you're not an ordinary operative." She sighed. "Under different circumstances, I would treat you much more benignly, but alas, time is scarce." She nodded at Maurice. "Sorry about this."

Immediately, Louis felt a jolt in his back. His whole body seized and he hit the ground, his muscles locked. Dr. Ross kneeled quickly beside him, a syringe in her hand, and injected something into his neck.

"Getting high on your own supply, Louis," Dr. Ross said nonchalantly, "that was a big mistake. Because it allows me to do this." She looked to her associate, who opened the folding chair. Maurice and Dr. Ross propped Louis into the chair, and she reached for the headset while her associate bent over the machine, turning dials and pressing buttons.

Barely conscious, Louis slurred his words: "Whaddaya mean?"

Gail carefully fit the headset on his lolling head. "The drugs you've been dabbling with were spiked with a virus, courtesy of our mutual friend here—" She nodded at Maurice. "This virus was bioengineered to deliver certain genetic material directly into a set of very specific neurons that will make them produce two kinds of proteins. One absorbs light when the neuron fires, while the other binds to nanoparticles that can be stimulated by a magnetic field. Hence the headset you're now wearing." Once the headset was secure, Gail turned to the controller. "We can decipher what you've seen, what you've heard, what's been done around you —in essence, you've become a book we can read. All we have to do is turn the pages."

"Not going ta," Louis protested groggily. The clicks grew louder. Within thirty seconds, the sense of invasion shocked Louis out of his lethargy. *"Nooo!"* he screamed, whipping his head back and forth.

A moment later, a brilliant blue-white flash of light filled the room, a sudden shockwave knocking Maurice and the doctor to the floor. Louis fell, pawing at his head until the set came loose.

"What was *that?*" Dr. Ross said, scrambling toward the controller.

Louis was breathing heavily, crouched face-down on the floor.

"You see *that?!*" Maurice shouted, pointing at Louis.

Louis lifted his glowing hand. He turned it back and forth, regarding the alien luminosity with wonder. He stumbled to his feet and swayed toward the window, his body pulsing with light. "Not stealing my brain!" he slurred.

Dr. Ross reached out, trying to grab at his arm. "Louis, we can fix this! Whatever this is, we can correct it! Let me help you. We need to get you to my office. I have better equipment ..."

"*No!*" Louis continued backing up, pointing at her accusingly. "Get the fuck away from me!" He stepped up to the window, his hands on the sill.

"Louis," Gail said.

"Sorry Angela ..."

Louis turned, opened the window, and stepped onto the sill. Without a second glance, he jumped.

"*Louis!*" Dr. Ross dashed to the window, Maurice right behind her. They both leaned out and watched his body fall eight floors, stopping abruptly as it hit the spiked iron fencing that encircled the building. He twitched once, then was still.

"*Fuck ... me ...*" Maurice managed.

Dr. Ross turned from the window, her hand pressed over her mouth. She stood there a moment, an anguished look on her face, and then a sense of urgency took over. "Pack it up, now!" she barked.

"Where are we going?" Maurice asked.

"Uptown. I have a very strong feeling we've got another subject to contend with."

October 29, 2017

1100 North Dearborn Apartments
Chicago, Illinois

GUS ARRIVED AT THE 1100 NORTH DEARBORN APARTMENTS, slowing to a crawl as he inched past the fire truck and ambulance in front of the building, their flashing lights intermittently illuminating the rolling ground fog of exhaust. Emerging, he turned onto West Maple and parked next to a small mob gawking at something laying on the ground.

He jumped out of the car and muscled his way through the circle of gawkers to catch sight of Wolf's body sprawled face-up in a frozen pool of blood. Keeping his emotions in check, he retrieved his phone from his coat pocket and sent a text to Detective Bobby Krzyskowski.

EMERGENCY. 1100 NORTH DEARBORN.
Get over here ASAP, need you on this case.

By the time Krzyskowski got there, twenty minutes later, Wolf's body had been placed in the coroner's wagon. Two techs from the crime lab were busy taking a series of measurements from various reference points around the building to the still-widening pool of blood that had yet to be mopped up.

Gus spotted Krzyskowski approach and stepped away from the crowd. He pulled up his collar against the cold, stuffed his hands into his pockets, and greeted the younger man with a silent nod.

"What's the story?" Krzyskowski asked, the Chicago wind carrying the vapor trail of his breath over his shoulder.

"Wolf Holzinger," Gus replied. He waited while the detective fished out his notebook and wrote down the name. "He was ... rappelling down the side of the building to get into his girlfriend's apartment."

Krzyskowski furrowed his brows. "I don't see any climbing ropes," he said. "Does he have a girlfriend here?"

"He does," Gus replied. "Name's Sofia Alejandro Castellanos. As for the ropes, *that* I leave that to you."

Krzyskowski nodded somberly, put away his notebook, and turned to look up at the roof. "Suppose he could have improvised. Maybe he used TV cables."

Gus followed his gaze. "Plausible." He nodded absently. "And they snapped due to the cold."

"Okay," Krzyskowski said. "Guess I better get up there before somebody else beats me to it."

"I'll speak to the girlfriend—she's staying at her cousin's a few blocks away."

Krzyskowski turned to leave and then stopped. "One more thing."

Gus waited expectantly.

"Don't be alarmed, but on the way over I got another call."

"Go on."

"There's been another fall-from-height across town."

"Where, exactly?"

"Down in the Lawndale district."

"Unfortunately," Gus said grimly, "I think you'll need to be on that one too."

January 21, 2018

Central Park West
New York, New York

"WHAT DO YOU MEAN NO CONCLUSION? IT'S BEEN THREE MONTHS!"

Hans shook his head, staring up at the gray New York sky. Ahead of him, his wife headed toward the Museum of Natural History. The cruise had been an exhausting exercise in self-restraint, having received word that another member of the organization was ready to talk to him about the one thing foremost on his mind. While Sabine toured the Museum of Natural History, Hans made his too long awaited rendezvous in the Strawberry Fields section of Central Park.

"We need to gather more information," the contact said. "From a different perspective."

"A different perspective?"

"To put together a more complete picture of what happened. The information we have is a little too ... subjective. We need to engage our other asset in Chicago."

Hans wasn't surprised. He nodded a little before saying, *"Ja-ja,* I know exactly what to do."

January 26, 2018

Army Research Lab
Chicago, Illinois

"You must watch over her. Protect her. Guide her."

Months into his intense study of Inez, Mark realized that the telepathic intermediary he'd been working with so closely was no longer needed. He had received one subtle thought, and then another before he realized that she was communicating directly with him.

"Why me?" he thought back to her.

"She will be attracted to you."

An intriguing and flattering notion, he felt. "How will I know her?"

An image appeared in his head—but it wasn't just visual. Her personality, her aura, the fascinating complexity of her character seemed to emanate from her.

"She is special. She is important. She will be crucial to the future of your species."

EPILOGUE

March 19, 2018

Grand Saline Beach
St. Barthélemy Island, French West Indies

IT WAS ALMOST SUNSET WHEN LILA HIT THE BEACH AT ST. BARTHS. She'd flown in from Chicago on American stopping for a short layover in San Juan. She had come alone. Seeing the ocean gleam in the late light, the heaviness—the soul-crushing depression—that had been coiled around her shoulders since childhood gradually, finally, began to lift. She could almost see it effervesce.

She dropped her towel on the sand, kicked off her sandals, and headed for the water. The splashing surf made her feel strangely giddy. Surprised by the water's warmth, by the gentle give of sand beneath her feet, she watched the delicate lacework of seafoam encircle her bare legs. Beyond, the red disc of the sun was just starting to dip below a great pile of billowing clouds.

Exhaling for what felt like the first time, she waded deeper into the water until the lapping surf came up to her chest. Sucking in a deep breath, she pulled her goggles down over her eyes and pressed them snugly into place before diving beneath the waves, using a fluttering kick and a wide-sweeping breaststroke to go deep. Like a child new to swimming, she felt an inexpressible freedom, as if she was flying.

She was a full twelve feet down when she spotted the giant sea turtle gliding below. She watched the impassive reptile until it disappeared among the coral and stone dotting the seabed like the mountains of the moon. With daylight fading and the underwater realm rapidly losing color, the sight of something faintly aglow among the shadowy rocks brought her to a halt.

Suspended for a few seconds, her hands slowly undulating at her side, she finally recognized the object. It was the spider—glowing, multi-hued, ever-shifting. Strangely, she was no longer agitated by the sight; she felt only ... the benevolence of *familiarity*, she supposed, familiarity and the kind of profound peace that brought a wide, welcoming smile to her face. Her hatred was gone, replaced by a totally unexpected acceptance. She watched its light intensifying until it was the only source of color beneath the surface. For an instant, the creature appeared like a burning bush engulfed with flames of gold and yellow and white. A flood of old encounters, struggles, nightmares ... all flashed in her mind and then, as quickly as they'd come, vanished. Only the memory of her little brother languishing at the bottom of the pool persisted.

Why should she be anything other than appreciative of the recollection? Why should she feel anything other than profound thanks?

She looked down at the thing once more; she was not herself somehow. Her thoughts seemed new—how had she never noticed, quantified even, the relationship between her so-called "visual space" and the space of the physical objects she could see? And from this, a terrible idea surfaced—that all her life was a mere distillation. She nodded to herself as she rose to the surface. A subjective counterpart, an interpretation. A shadow.

She blew a breath and took another before ducking once again beneath the waves.

This time, she noticed the geometry of the water molecules—one oxygen, two hydrogen. She could visualize its pyramidal shape, half ghostlike—the phantom bits unbonded electron pairs. She could perceive the precise wave measurements of the subtle currents around her, the temperature gradations, the water pressure, and yet such intellection did not in any way interfere with the grandeur of the moment. It was as if her mind had room for it all, the analytical and the experiential—as if the barrier between her surface thoughts and the rest of her brain was breaking down on its own, without any help from any machine and with none of the psychosis that Dr. Ross had predicted. Inexplicably, she began to comprehend the underlying mechanism of consciousness itself; she began to understand that the water column was so much more than her country's stealthiest asset, as it was once described to her ... that it was *conscious*—it was a living, breathing, conscious *being*.

Again, she surfaced and, this time, drifted with a small wavelet toward the shore. Her slim powder-blue bathing suit shed rivulets of water as she emerged from the surf.

She grabbed her towel and watched the sky darken. Her perceptions, her intelligence, her thoughts—all of it took on an enhanced, almost mystical, relevance. She thought of the difference between *explicate* and *implicate* order—one, the space-time order we normally perceive; the other, an enfolded holograph-like order where the true reality of the multiverse exists—where, if you can perceive it and master it, literally anything is possible.

As a stand of tiki-torches cast dancing light over the handful of beach-goers passing by and as other trappings of the explicate order transpired in her periphery, someone's boombox blasting island music, Lila stood and once again faced the sunset. Sensing the movement of Earth beneath her feet and of the sun through the galaxy and the galaxy through the cosmos, she saw the unseen implicate order opening before her. Her mouth curled into a smile. She felt empowered, released from captivity.

More than that—omnipotent. Omniscient. She felt ... like a god.

No! she admonished herself, pressing her feet into the shifting sand. *Only this, and no more.* On one side were arrayed the multiple govern-ments of the world threatening one another with mutually assured destruction; on the other were the LPFs of the world trying to pre-empt their governments' first-strike strategies with equally insane strategies of their own. In between, all living things hung in the balance. *No, the earth will rise up*, she pledged with steely resolve, looking out across the ocean, *the sea will rise up, and the entire chain of life mysteriously interconnected throughout this infinitely foaming multiverse will rise up, and I will be its instrument.*

No, I can do this ... this I can do. I can do this.

THANK YOU

Thank you for reading *The Water Column*. If you enjoyed it, please take a moment to leave a review on Amazon, Barnes and Noble, Goodreads, or your preferred online retailer.

Reviews are the best way to show your support for an author and to help new readers discover their books.

For more books by Aran Jane, please visit:

www.aranjane.com

ACKNOWLEDGMENTS

I am indebted to Sandy Stone for his keen judgments regarding story development, and to my editor, Frederick Johnson, with Standout Books, for his sharp eye and priceless sense of humor. Thanks to Alex Hemus and his entire team at Standout Books for their excellent work and thorough professionalism. Thanks also to Bill Callejas for the benefits of his comments in reading early drafts of the work; to my daughter, Dr. Autumn Roque, for her insights into clinical psychology; to Dr. Filip Ponulak, for his thoughts on permutations; to Greg Stearns, for his remarks involving chain of command; to my dear friend and fellow bibliophile, Pamela Marnell, for her kind words and eagerness to share a good read whenever she finds one; to my daughter, Dana Malstaff, and her Boss-Mom cadre of readers for their early reviews and for Dana's ongoing marketing genius. And finally, my deepest gratitude is reserved for my lovely wife, Sheri, who is my first reader, my principal editor, and my muse. Her love illuminates every word of this work, just as it lights every day of our life together.

ABOUT THE AUTHOR

Aran Jane was born in Camp Pendleton, California, attended college at Indiana University-Purdue University Indianapolis, and now lives with his wife, Sheri, in Carlsbad, California.

CPSIA information can be obtained
at www.ICGtesting.com
Printed in the USA
LVHW030722170220
647168LV00001B/9